A LONDON AFFAIR

Book 4: The Hotel Baron Series

MARY OLDHAM

Kindle: ISBN: 979-8-9907139-0-1
Ebook: ISBN: 979-8-9907139-1-8
Print: ISBN: 979-8-9907139-2-5

Any references to historical events, real people, or real places are used fictitiously. Names, characters, and places are products of the author's imagination.

Story Editor: Sue Grimshaw, Edits by Sue
Cover Art: Lynn Andreozzi
Interior Book Design: Teri Barnett/Indie Book Designer
Author Photo: Tanith Yates

Printed in United States of America
By-Creek-Ity Publishing
Portland, Oregon

www.maryoldham.com

To my brother John, Would it have killed you to bring home a Mitch for your little sister?

And

To Leslie, thank you for the fabulous opening line.

CONTENTS

FORWARD

Dear Readers,

This book is a bit different for friends who have enjoyed The Hotel Baron Series. It is a prequel. We finally have the love story of Rebecca Stark and Mitchell Wilder, who are very much together in the other books, but nobody, including this author, knew how they got together until I wrote it. I liked to think of Rebecca as a quiet force, happy and in love with Mitch. But next to her brother, father, and cousins, the man she chose would need to measure up in a big way. And I wanted her to be spicy and savvy in her own right.

This story takes place before Alex and Daisy's adventures in Paris. At this point, Adam hadn't met his true love, Laura, because he was still with his first love, Melinda. Similarly, Laura hadn't yet left her horrible husband, Leland. Maria Medici is nowhere in this book because our favorite characters didn't know she existed...Yet. Garrison Stark is alive and a bit dense. It saddens me not to see my friends Daisy, Laura, and Maria, but we get the gift of seeing Victoria happily married to Garrison. We get to see Alex as a doofus playboy. And, for the heck of it, Cousin Spencer always visits when needed.

Most intriguingly, we finally uncover the reason behind one of our heroines' pregnancies in *A Roman Affair* after years of having only one child.

This book was originally titled *A Night at the Rosemont*. It was a Golden Heart Finalist with the *Romance Writers of America* and took first place the same year in the *RWA Chicago Fire and Ice Contest.*

A line editor I completely respect has read it three times in the last two years and has had issues with it three times, as illustrated by the 1,500 track changes she added after the last read three months ago. After each read, I rewrote vast parts of this story. This version has a new front and middle but almost the same end. In a concession to her, I've toned down the swearing and increased the intimacy. My favorite note at the end of a relatively chaste love scene: *"You can do better than that."* Swearing is easier to write than a love scene any day...

I did vast amounts of research for this book. I went to London for a week to refamiliarize myself with one of my favorite cities. I did a bit of a deep dive on the following subjects: London, London taxis, Claridges Hotel, Hyde Park, The London Ritz, Heathrow Airport, Virgin and Delta Airlines, Windsor Castle, the U.S. State Department, the Defense Base Act, the Longshore and Harbor Workers' Compensation Act, foreign kidnappings, visa/passport issues for visiting Middle Eastern countries, Farsi, Middle Eastern food, foreign military contractors, and security training with the U.S. Department of Homeland Security. And finally, Yachats, Oregon, is a small beachside community I've been going to for over forty-five years. It is where I go to reset, which is why it becomes important to Rebecca. This story is a work of fiction, so I pushed the envelope, and stretched the truth where I wanted to.

This story is now one of my favorite stories right up there with *A Summer Affair*, my first Golden Heart Finalist book, also titled *Laura Takes a Lover.*

Enjoy!

Much Love, MO

CHAPTER ONE

Six Years Ago

"Go ahead, underestimate me, Mitch. That will be fun," Rebecca Stark said to her brother Alex's closest friend in her best sultry voice. She picked up the dice from the coffee table to roll them during their spirited game of Monopoly.

"You know, Alex," Mitch said, his eyes never leaving Rebecca's face. "I think she might be the scariest of all the Starks. Watch out."

Alex and Rebecca's family owned a large hotel empire. Ironically, they were playing a game that involved properties and hotels. Things were getting interesting in life and the game.

The fourth player was their cousin Spencer, who was from Texas. He went to Wharton with Alex and Mitch and was too laid back to know he was the designated sacrificial lamb. That little news item had been determined before they even opened the Monopoly box. Sometimes, Rebecca felt bad about starting the game by knowing Spencer was a pawn, just not today.

Mitch owned Rebecca's favorite properties on the board: Boardwalk and Park Place. Each dark blue property had a red grand hotel sitting proudly on them, and Mitch sat back and watched Rebecca, a spider about to pounce on her fly. While Alex was flashy, Mitch was quiet and contemplative. Strategic. The man matched Rebecca in competitive spirit, and she loved it. Heck, she'd cared about him since her brother had first brought him home four years ago. But lately, her crush had turned a bit more serious.

Despite the fact she was now eighteen, Mitch had never looked at her as anything other than Alex's little sister.

"If I roll an eight or ten, I'll be staying at my own place tonight," she said, looking at Mitch. Her properties might be the cheapest land on the board, but she owned them and had developed them to the game's limits.

"A six will put you on Boardwalk, and it is the most common dice combination," Mitch said as he watched her, and she felt it, his eyes taking in every little detail, which made her want to blush. Correct that. She was blushing.

Her brother and Mitch were each twenty-four, getting their master's degrees in management, and about to graduate from Wharton Business School in Philadelphia. They lived together in an apartment near campus. But the Stark family home was much closer to New York City, which meant endless access to parties, nightclubs, and women, not to mention laundry service and good food.

"I'm feeling like you need to take a walk on the Boardwalk. Stay at my lovely hotel," Mitch teased her, his mouth forming an easy smile. "I'll give you a complimentary cocktail and massage. Heck, I'll even waive the valet parking fee."

"You wish," she said back to him, purposefully not looking at him. He could massage her any time he wanted. Really, if he snapped his fingers, she'd gladly be naked for him. He just didn't know it.

Spencer chuckled; she suspected that he knew about her infatuation with Mitch...damn it. He might look all mellow and did not have the killer gene of a Stark because he was from their mother's side, a Whitlow, but he was more devious than he looked. His country bumpkin was actually city slick.

"Come on, sell Pacific to me. I'll give you $600 for it," Alex ordered with a little whine in his voice as he looked longingly at the green property just down from Mitch's monopoly.

Was he underestimating her intelligence again? She would take him down with only the anger a little sister could manage and execute.

Rebecca stopped jiggling the dice in her hand and looked at him as if he'd grown a third head. "Let me explain the rules to you since you seem to have forgotten. First, this is my turn. You are not supposed to conduct your business on my turn. Remember that, because the next time you do it, I'm going to fine you $500."

"You can't do that," he protested.

"Really? Vote of the players. All in favor of fining Alex for trying to conduct business when it isn't his turn, please raise your hand."

Mitch and Spencer raised their hands, and Mitch actually winked at her.

"We have a majority. The fine is in play. Next time you do it, $500 to Free Parking in the center of the board," she said. "Second, if you want my land, the price is $3,000, and I want free rent on the green properties for the remainder of the game. Third, that is my final and best offer."

Spencer whistled. Mitch shook his head and said to Alex, "Damn, if I were your dad, I'd groom her to run the business. She is ruthless. Got to say, I kind of like it."

Spencer nodded with a chuckle. He held up his hands to Rebecca, and said, "Respect."

Alex ignored his cousin and Mitch. "Okay, you give me no choice. Your offer is ridiculous, so I will bury you, big sister." She was his younger sister, but the nickname had been a joke between them because she always acted older.

"You and what army, bro?" She dropped the dice and didn't even look at them as her green eyes bore into her brother's of the same color.

"Ten and doubles puts her on Baltic. How the hell does she do that?" Mitch asked. "I had the massage table ready and a lovely beverage waiting."

"I'd say the dice are loaded, but we are using the ones that I brought back from my recent trip to Vegas," Spencer said.

"Aw, thanks, Mitch, but I'm staying at my own place tonight. Feel free to come over and deliver the cocktails," she said sweetly.

Alex rolled the dice next and landed on Boardwalk.

"Ah, damn it. How much?" he asked Mitch.

"$2,000 or one of your green properties."

"One of the greens and free rent next time I land on Park Place or Boardwalk."

Mitch looked agitated, held out his hand, and then said, "Fine."

Alex handed over one of his green properties, and Rebecca shook her head. They were going to gang up on her. She knew it. Now she, Alex, and Mitch had one of the green properties each.

Turning to Spencer, she said, "Battle lines are being drawn in a way that is unpleasant to me. I'll give you free rent on any of my properties for the rest of the game if you do the same with yours. I need to stockpile money for my next move."

"Deal," he said, and they shook on it.

"Hey," Mitch said. "Wait a minute, maybe I want to partner with you, Bex, and we take down Alex and Spencer. Don't be hasty. Listen to my offer."

He'd never called her a pet name before, and she liked it. This moment would be burned into her mind forever. *Bex*. It was cute. And it had come so easily she had to wonder if he'd come up with it earlier.

"Hmmm...intriguing. Okay, I'll listen to your offer, and you had better get creative with it."

Mitch smiled, his dimples showing. "Partner with me, and

I'll take you to your choice of restaurants in New York for lunch next Saturday. You name it, and we will go. Or I will take you to Neiman's and buy you the perfume of your choice. I know you like perfume."

Alex put down his money and held up his hand.

"What the hell is going on here?" Alex asked. "You can't seduce my little sister with food and perfume outside of the game. Who says she'd enjoy your company? I don't like this."

"I thought we had a deal, Rebecca," Spencer added. "What is going on here? Are you showing a weakness to Mitch's feminine charms?"

"I'm like a brother to Bex. She can trust me," Mitch said, and Rebecca immediately felt deflated. He wasn't a brother to her. No how, no way. It was like he was challenging her. Well, she was up for it. She was already picking out her outfit in her mind for next Saturday.

"Sorry, Spencer, Mitch is taking me to lunch next Saturday in Manhattan. He made me a better offer. Do you want to up the ante?" Say no. Spencer and Alex looked offended. Rebecca was elated as she laughed and shook Mitch's hand.

An hour later, Alex threw down what remained of his cash, all $5s and $1s. "You are both assholes," he said, which made Rebecca and Mitch smile.

A figure appeared in the doorway, Victoria Stark. Hands on hips, the matriarch of the Stark family spoke in a tone that would freeze water. "And here I was, just to announce that it is twenty minutes until dinner, and I'm greeted with vulgarity by my own son. That's it. This 'to the death Monopoly' with hard feelings has got to end. There is a reason it has been banned by the royal family."

"Mom, we are just blowing off some steam," Alex complained. "We aren't the royal family." It was a well-known fact the British Royal Family was forbidden from playing Monopoly.

5

"He's blowing off steam because he is a sore loser," Rebecca added. "Mitch and I won."

"Unfairly," Alex protested. "Mom, he enticed Rebecca to be his partner, and they teamed up against us. He bribed her with lunch in New York City next Saturday."

Victoria smiled and looked at Mitch. "Smart. Good for you, Mitch. You two have fun. Where are you going?"

"I was thinking it would be fun to act like tourists and go to Katz Deli," Rebecca said.

"I'd have held out for Tavern on the Green, but hold that in reserve for next time," Victoria said with a wink. Her mother was a troublemaker.

Rebecca smiled and said, "So noted."

"Wait until I have my new job secured, then I'll take you to Tavern if I stay in New York," Mitch said, looking at Rebecca, who had to hide her sadness. These fun weekends at her parents' house were about to end because graduation was but three weeks away for Alex and Mitch.

"You two," Victoria said with a shake of her head and left the parlor.

"Hey," Alex called, "What's for dinner?"

His mother reappeared, smiled at her son, and said, "Crow."

CHAPTER TWO

Mitch

"What is your problem?" Mitch asked as he slipped into his jeans and a black cashmere sweater the next Saturday morning not wanting to look at Alex. He was in his modest bedroom of the two-bedroom apartment he shared with Alex.

"I don't like one damn thing about this," Alex said from the doorway to Mitch's bedroom.

"I'm having lunch with a friend who I've known for years," Mitch said. "What is wrong with you?"

"You know. I don't like one of my best friends bullshitting me. And that is what you are doing. You've always had a thing for my sister. I saw it the first time you met her. Do you remember what you said when you saw her walking in the garden when she was like fourteen?"

"Yeah. I asked, who is that?" Mitch said with a little smile as he remembered the exact moment he'd laid eyes on Rebecca Stark for the first time. She was just Alex's kid sister, but the promise of a bright future when she grew up was all there. She'd been wearing a green sweater that matched her amazing emerald eyes and a long navy pleated skirt. Later, he found out it was a private school uniform. He was always nice to her, though in a few years, it might get interesting, but in the moment, she was just a kid. He had treated her like a kid sister, careful and protective. Well, she wasn't a kid any longer. She was eighteen...and legal.

"She is my sister," Alex said. "I wouldn't mess with yours if you had one."

Mitch was an only child, and now he was an orphan, which was a punch in the gut. He'd always thought his parents would be there. As he'd gotten older, he hoped his mom would always be there and his father could go to hell.

"Your sister is eighteen now, and I would think I'm the lesser of many evils."

"You admit you like her?"

"Relax. I passed the background check at Donovan Security. I have a start date. I'll be going to London right after we graduate in a little over two weeks, and then I'll be out of your hair."

"Come on. That isn't what I meant. You are my best friend. I'll miss you a helluvalot."

"Good, I'm glad you will. I'll miss you, too. But hey, there is a Stark International Hotel in London. Come for a visit. We will cruise some pubs, look for British women."

Alex and Rebecca's parents were letting Mitch crash at the corporate suite at the Stark International Hotel in London for a month until he found a place of his own.

He was still vacillating about Rebecca. His Bex was still off-limits to him. He didn't want to mess up the relationship he had with the Stark family. They had taken him in and treated him like a son after his mother died. He was especially close to Victoria, whom he considered to be a second mother. He was the only one who could get away with calling her Vic. Taking Bex to lunch was playing with fire, but he couldn't stop himself.

"Don't hurt my sister," Alex warned. "She's just a kid, and I think she had a crush on you. Actually, she *has* a crush on you."

The news was music to Mitch's ears, but he didn't want Alex to know how much the information affected him. He had suspected as much, but no one had ever discussed it with him. His crush on Bex was legendary, at least in his mind, but he was not in a position to do anything about it. Alex's strong opposition made him mad.

"Did you ever think that might be okay?" Mitch asked.

"No, I don't think of my sister that way. And to know that you do does not make me feel good. Just how long has this been going on?"

"There is no 'this.' She's a woman, a beautiful woman. She has dated and will continue to date. I hate to tell you this, but eventually, she might sleep with one of them."

"Thanks a lot for that. Well, it isn't like she can go into a bar and order a drink. She is a kid. Leave her alone," Alex warned. "She's a freshman at NYU for shit's sake."

"Do you not think I'm good enough for her?" Now that he had said it, the thought of her with another guy really bothered him. And what did Alex have against him?

"I never said that," Alex said. "But you are my friend. I don't want you having carnal thoughts or knowledge of my little sister. And just so we are clear, you aren't snowing anyone with this little bet that turned into a date. I'm onto you. I know what you are trying to do. You found a way to have a date with my sister."

"Oh, for crap's sake, it is only lunch. I think this is our business, not yours."

"Now you are just trying to piss me off. 'Our business, not yours.' I don't like the Bex cutie nickname bullshit. Stop it."

"Too late. She likes it."

"Don't do this."

"Listen, Alex," Mitch said, facing his friend for the first time in the conversation. "I'm not going to ghost her because the thought of my having lunch with her upsets you. Bex and I have been friends for years."

"Look, tell her you met someone else. Let her have a chance

to meet someone her own age," Alex said in his parting words. "You are about to move to London. Make it a clean break...for her sake. I don't want her pining for a relationship that will never be."

"Is that what you object to? The age difference? I'm six years older. So what? Why am I asking you? This is a ridiculous conversation."

"I give up." Alex turned and left not only the doorway but the apartment, slamming the door behind him. Mitch had purposely antagonized him, but he was left wondering why Alex found him so objectionable. Was it just that Rebecca was his sister, or was it something else? He didn't have a sister, so he couldn't relate on that end. He didn't come from a monied background, not like the Starks. Heck, his parents were dead, but he would make something of himself because that was just who he was. He would show them all just how successful he could be.

He glanced at his watch. In three hours, he'd be with Rebecca.

Mitch caught a train for the two-hour ride to New York City. He arrived with an hour to spare and made his way to the Katz Deli. By the time he got there, he was a half hour early, but to his surprise, Rebecca was waiting with an anxious look on her face. Maybe Alex was correct to worry. She was gorgeous.

When she saw him, her face softened. She smiled, and then he watched as color kissed her cheeks. She was blushing. He loved it when she blushed. He had first noticed that when she was younger. It was a tell that she might have a little crush on him. He closed the distance and pulled her into a hug. It took her off guard, and then she melted into him. He liked it. Uh-oh.

Did it last too long? Yes. He needed to be careful. He didn't want to change the dynamic of their relationship. Some of Alex's words had sunk in on the train ride.

"You're early," she said.

"So are you," he said. There was tension where there had not been tension in the past.

"I've been looking forward to this all week," she said.

"Me too," he said. Okay, that was a bit of a declaration. He had to watch it. This thing could get out of hand quickly. He had a job waiting for him in London.

They were early enough they didn't have to wait long for a table. They had Reuben sandwiches for two, which included pickles, fries, and coleslaw.

Once the orders were placed, they sat across from each other, and for the first time in several years, they didn't seem to have anything to say to one another. Truly, he had a lot to say, but he wasn't sure it was the time or the place.

"Is it true?" she asked.

"What...exactly?" he asked.

"Alex told me that you have interviewed for a position in London, and they were just waiting on the background report. Did you get the job? Are you really going to move?" she asked as a look of pain crossed her face. Mitch saw it. He knew she had more feelings for him than he had originally realized. It made him happy, but he had to tread carefully.

"Yeah, it is looking good. It is a security company that would be a great experience for me. They need a new VP of Operations. At least, I think that will be my title. I don't look forward to moving to London, but I need to make the most of the opportunities that come my way. I have to put my education to use and start paying my student loans. My mother's life insurance didn't cover grad school. But as for the job, I passed the background check." What he didn't say is that he didn't come from a family that was loaded with opportunities. He wasn't angry about it. It was just a fact.

"Did you talk to my father? I'm sure he could find something for you at Stark International. That way, you wouldn't have to move. They love you. They...especially Mom...isn't going to be happy about the London move. What will we do without you on the weekends?"

Mitch shook his head. "Your father is a kind man. I have no doubt he'd find something for me. But I need to get experience. Then, when the right position opens up at Stark, I'll apply for it. Hopefully, I'll get it on my own merit, not because of who I know. It's important to me to work my way up."

"I'm going to miss you, and I don't know how I feel about that," Rebecca said, and then, to his great surprise, a tear leaked from her eye.

"Bex, honey, don't do that. I have to take this opportunity," he said. "You've got four years of college ahead, maybe more if you get a master's degree. I want you to enjoy every moment. Don't think about me."

"I bet within a few months of living there, you'll meet someone and forget your time with us...with me. And if I was twenty-four instead of eighteen and had my college degree, you might consider me a woman and not a girl. I'm sorry. I don't even know if you like me, but I like you, and maybe it is stupid." Mitch could tell by how flustered she was that disclosing this was costing her something, and it was embarrassing her.

"I've tried to forget you," she said, "but I can't. It's a crush, a stupid crush. I know it, and I feel like an idiot."

He wished at that moment that he wasn't going to London. She was adorable, and he didn't think she should feel like an idiot or feel embarrassed. He was touched. He reached across the table and grabbed her hand. "You are not an idiot, and I've never felt more flattered. We have a connection, Bex. I feel it, too, but the timing...We are at two different places in our lives. Who knows what will happen? Maybe someday we will meet again, and it will be different."

"Sure," she said. "And my brother has no doubt told you every embarrassing and horrible thing there is to know about me. He probably threatened you, too."

"He worries about you," Mitch said. "He's a good brother to you and friend to me."

"I didn't ask to feel like this. I'd like to punch Alex, just because."

Mitch really didn't know what to say. He wished he was drinking something stronger than Coca-Cola.

"Okay, new subject. Tell me about school. Do you realize I don't even know what you want to do when you graduate?"

"In four or six years, if I go for my masters," she said. "Nice segue."

"Time passes quickly. Before you know it, you will have a degree or two under your belt. Do you want to work in the family business?"

Ignoring him, she said, "I have an idea, something I've been thinking about for a long time. You won't like it."

"Okay, I'm listening," he said.

"I can't believe I'm going to tell you this."

"If anything, we are friends," he said. "You can tell me. I'm not going to tell anyone."

"My brother, my parents, they can never know. I know you are best friends with my brother. Can you keep a secret—a secret from him?"

He did seem to ponder this, and that made her happy. If he had answered too quickly, she would not have believed his answer.

"Yes, I can keep your secret," he answered, and she felt like they were the only two people in the deli. All the other conversations seemed to dim. They were possibly the only two people in the world.

"You care about me," she said.

"Of course, Rebecca. Are you in some kind of trouble?" he asked.

"I need you to do something for me."

"What?" he asked, as his other hand covered the hand he held.

"I want you to be my first," she said, meeting his eyes.

"Your first what?" he asked, then the answer dawned on him as he took a sharp intake of breath. She saw the moment he understood what she was asking. A lightbulb not only went off in his head. He jerked with the realization.

It was unnecessary, but she clarified it anyway. "Mitchell, I want you to be my first lover. I want you to take my virginity."

CHAPTER THREE

Rebecca

Mitch gulped for air like a fish out of water. Maybe she shouldn't have said a word. Through all her internal dialogue, it had seemed like a good idea, but now she was feeling like maybe this was a bad idea.

Mitch was her friend, and she cared about him deeply, but also, she knew he'd be careful with her and make this experience as pleasurable as possible. She'd heard him talking to Alex when they didn't know she was listening, and those two seemed to have been around the block a time or two when it came to women.

"Rebecca, you can't mean that. You cannot be serious. I'm about to leave the country. It isn't something you just do. You want your first time to be special."

"I've thought a lot about this, so hear me out," she said.

"Do you know what your brother, hell, your father would do to me?" Mitch asked. "I think your mother might kill me too. She looks like she could be ruthless. She might like me now, but that would change if she ever found out. I'd be dead."

He didn't say no.

"They will never find out. Look, you are about to move to another country and exit my life. I want something to share with you that I haven't shared with anyone else. I want it to be special with you."

"You are special to me," he argued as he squeezed her hand. "You are my Bex. I'm honored, really, but I think you are rushing into this."

"No, listen to me. Sex is this big thing. I know that. No one ends up with the first person they make love with. I want it to be someone I care for, who cares for me. I want it to be special. No strings. Heck, in a few weeks, I know you'll be on another continent."

"This conversation is crazy. I'm so uncomfortable," Mitch said. "I don't know what to say."

"Well, deal with it because it is about to get worse. I've thought a lot about this. It is one of the most logical, well thought out things I've ever done. I don't want to lose my virginity to some random date because I'm in the mood or drunk and want to have sex. I want to enjoy it with someone I really care about. I've had offers and up until now, I've turned them down because I want it to be with someone special. I want it to be you."

"Me?" he asked. "I—"

"This is the largest favor I've ever asked of anyone." Rebecca met his eyes and tried to let them plead her case.

"No kidding. And making love with you isn't really a favor. It is kind of mutually beneficial. What happens afterward?" he asked.

"We have a memory that we share and we'll never discuss with anyone else."

"What if you get pregnant?" he asked.

"I've been on the pill for two months," she said. She could see that he was conflicted.

"For this? You've been thinking about this for two months?" Mitch asked.

"Yes. I've thought this through. I just wasn't sure how it would come together. And if you are worried, you can wear a condom, but for my first time, I think that could hurt more, so I really wish you wouldn't. I know that you've slept with a few women, so I know you know what you're doing."

"Bex, of course, I know what the hell to do..."

"Well, I've just been paying attention to your conversations with my brother—"

"What? Well great! Rebecca, think this through. Think of what you are asking me to do."

"I'm quite aware. I'm asking you to be my first. You know, some men would consider it an honor. Shit, I could go to a party tonight and sleep with someone to get it over with, but it wouldn't mean anything to them or me, and it probably would be horrible."

He looked at the ceiling, then back at her. "Please, please don't do that. I know what you are asking," he said. "I'm just... damn it, I don't know what to do."

"Then what is holding you back?" she asked.

"If Alex ever—"

"He won't know unless you tell him because I certainly won't. It isn't like I'll ever ask anyone else to do this for me. It is you, Mitch. You are the only one."

"I'm worried. We like each other. If we have sex, that doesn't go away, it will get more intense. It might hurt you. And I'm leaving in a couple of weeks."

How was the sandwich at Katz Deli? Rebecca didn't know. She couldn't eat and neither, it appeared, could Mitch. It wasn't like he had turned her down, but there was a new tension between them as they left the restaurant behind and walked aimlessly on the sidewalk into the warm spring air.

"Now what?" he asked as he walked beside her.

Rebecca reached into her pocket and pulled out a key card for the Marriott Marquis at Times Square. "Can we at least go look at the room?"

"Holy shit. You got a room? When did you decide this?" he asked.

"Last Sunday, after Monopoly, Alex told me about your job in London. I called and made a reservation that night."

"That…that is the catalyst for you losing your virginity? A game of Monopoly and news of my job in London?"

"I think you worry too much. I want to experience this first time with someone I really care about. If I like it, and you aren't here, there are other males on campus."

"No, don't talk like that. I can't think about it," he said, looking pained.

"In a couple of weeks, you'll graduate and fly to London. I don't have a lot of time. And this was our first opportunity to be alone."

"Bex—"

"I love it when you call me Bex. Where did you come up with that?"

"You're not making it easy to do the right thing."

"Do you want my first time to be with some random beau hunk who then tells everyone about popping my cherry?"

"No, do not do anything stupid. I think I'd have to fly home from London to kill him and ask your brother to help me hide his body."

"Breath mint?" she asked as she popped an Altoid in her mouth.

He took a mint and looked at her. She smiled, leaned up on her tiptoes, and quickly kissed him. It was better than she thought it would be.

"Aw to hell with it," he said with a resigned sigh, grabbed her by the forearms and pulled her to him. Then he kissed her in the way she had always dreamed he would.

At the end of the kiss, they looked at each other, and then Mitch held up his arm and hailed a taxi.

He opened the back door, indicated for Rebecca to get in, and then said to the driver, "Marriott Marquis. Times Square."

His words sent a little thrill through her whole body. How in the world had she pulled this off?

Mitch

Mitch held onto Rebecca's hand as if his life depended on it as they rode through traffic. He had wanted to kiss her for years. Now, she'd put him in a no-win situation. He couldn't let her do something reckless with a stranger, but what they were doing was reckless on a whole other level.

They rode in silence until he turned to her and said, "Why today?"

"As my father always says, make hay while the sun is shining. It is a beautiful day. Memorable. At least I know I'll never forget today."

"For the next few hours, I need you not to mention your family, especially your brother or father, okay?"

"Okay. Thank you," she said and kissed his cheek. He smiled a little and quickly kissed her on the lips. Damn, she was a good kisser, and he had to be honest, he wanted her. The thought of her curvy body being about to be his to explore was a little too much to think about.

They'd come this far, so he said something that had been on his mind for years. "I love your green eyes. They are more emerald than green grass."

"I love your dimples," she said, and he leaned close and kissed her again.

Where they were going and what they were about to do was such a mistake. Yet he couldn't stop himself. Rebecca Stark wanted him to make love to her, to be her first lover. He had a feeling that although she said it had to be him if he didn't step up, she would find someone else. Some bumbling freshmen or sophomore wouldn't appreciate what kind of gift she was bestowing upon him. It would be some inebriated stupid boy, and it wouldn't be good for her, for his sweet Rebecca. Mitch knew he would be gentle. He would make it good for her. He couldn't stand the thought of someone else touching her. How would he leave her?

He had to, and when he looked back, he would smile and remember this with sweetness. Or it might be the biggest mistake of his life.

If Alex knew, he'd kill him. He just hoped that afterward, tomorrow, next week, his best friend wouldn't figure it out. This would be the hardest, darkest secret he would ever keep, but he would do it for Rebecca. Maybe what they were about to do would get her off his mind.

Not bloody likely.

And someday, maybe their paths would cross again. And then it would be game on.

CHAPTER FOUR

Five and a Half Years Later
Mitch / Christmas

I f Mitch could give his boss's daughter a nickname, it would be Sugarplum. But he would never give her a nickname because she would hate it and him for giving her one. One thing he knew, she had a bad temper. So, he called her Lily. She called him Mitchell, and that was the end of the story. He had been dating Lily for six months, and she hadn't changed. She had a sweet personality and appeared to be everything she was: sweet, kind, and always optimistic. He loved her—well, the thought of her—with growing affection. Was he madly, passionately in love with her? No, but that didn't make for long-lasting success in relationships. Passions that burned hot, burned out. He knew from experience. His thoughts flashed to Rebecca and shook his head. Lily was a nice, safe bet. If he wanted a stable life with a good job, happy kids one day, and loads of financial security, all he had to do was pop the question.

Well, tonight, he was going to propose. He'd bought her a big ring from Tiffany's after her father had been dropping hints, and Mitch had picked them up. Lucien Donovan wanted to see his daughter married. Okay, he got it.

If he could further describe her, describe their relationship, he would call her chaste. She had an older sister who had been anything but. Gemma, the sister who had renamed herself

Topaz, now lived in an Ashram in Norfolk with her common-law husband, a man named Dublin Ireland. Dublin's greatest claim to fame was that in his thirty-six years on this planet, he had never had his hair cut. He wore the web of dreadlocks like Carmen Miranda used to wear her fruit bowl on her head. And his beard was past his waist. Sometimes, he let his older kids braid it and put fun beads on the braids. Mitch wondered how often the man washed his hair or his beard. He thought it was probably something he didn't want to know the answer to.

They had three children, all of whom Topaz had birthed naturally in a Birthing Yurt at the Ashram. They had names like Passionflower, Drumbeat, and Mitch's personal favorite, Sapling. Topaz and Dublin didn't believe in Christmas or money for that matter, so Topaz had decided her well-to-do Mums and Daddy were as close to poison as possible. Topaz and her family had only visited once in the last three years. Rumor had it Topaz was pregnant again, but there was no way to tell for sure until she sent sketches of the baby done by Dublin, who was actually becoming quite the artist in his own mind.

Lily had equated her personal freedom—her difference from her only sibling—to her ability to stick to her personal morals. Therefore, she kept herself what she called tidy and chaste, virginal, at least, she said, until she got married. Mitch respected this antiquated stance, but it had done little to curb his normal appetites. The normal sexual appetites of a thirty-year-old man. He was beyond frustrated. His need to move this thing along might not have him rationally looking at the facts, such as whether he really wanted to spend his whole life with Lily. Would the chaste, almost cold body language suddenly go away if she were married? Did he think Lily would scream in ecstasy or tell him exactly what she wanted in bed? Well, it would be his personal challenge to get her to that point.

Lily's family had encouraged their relationship, practically serving Lily to Mitch on a silver platter with a "Do Not Touch

Until Married" warning sign, punishable by death. If he just did the right things at the right time, things would go very well for him. Lucien Donovan had talked about him being the successor to the business he now worked in, Donovan Security.

Would he want to propose if Donovan Security wasn't on the table? Sure, he would. He was lonely, and Lily was a pretty woman.

Mitch didn't have a family in London or anywhere else in the world, for that matter. The closest thing he had were the Starks, and they were in the United States. He'd been an orphan since he was eighteen. His mother had died of cancer, and his father had been long dead and not part of their lives for years before that. It was just him. At least he'd proven himself and become a highly paid employee of Donovan Security.

He'd kept photos of his family, but there was little else had that held any sentimental value from his past. People probably wouldn't understand. He knew for sure that if his mother was still alive, he wouldn't have Lily in his life. So tonight, he was going to do it. He was going to propose. Once he'd made this decision, he thought the stress and trepidation would leave him, but it hadn't. Instead, he felt a little sick.

Rebecca

Rebecca watched her mother from the sidelines. Their New York home was decorated immaculately for Christmas, with a large tree and lots of poinsettias, which had been lit with twinkle lights. The whole of the house was effortlessly elegant and meant for the holidays. It was very unlike the new, modern space on the top floor of a Portland, Oregon, hotel that her parents now called home.

No, the New York house was the scene for the happiest of holiday tales. Rebecca felt comfortable in fancier clothes and more makeup, including her red lipstick, which her live-in boyfriend really wasn't that fond of and liked to tell her it made her look a little cheap. She thought his conclusions were a bit unfair, but she was used to his criticism. He didn't seem to mind when she left lipstick prints on his skin, the Tool.

This was the first time she had brought someone home to meet the family, and during a holiday, nonetheless. Her mother was speaking to Rebecca's live-in boyfriend, Kenneth, now, but there was something wrong with her face. She was trying to smile, but the smile wasn't quite making it to her eyes. This wasn't good, for Rebecca knew it was an indicator that her mother didn't like Kenneth.

Her mother politely ended the conversation and went into the kitchen, and Rebecca followed. She leaned against the kitchen door as her mother gave last minute instructions to the staff who came in at Christmas to cook a meal so Victoria could spend time with her guests. When Victoria turned, she seemed surprised to find Rebecca standing there.

"Darling, you startled me," she said as she fondled her pearls.

"I just wanted to chat with you if you have a minute," Rebecca said.

"Of course. Privately?" Victoria asked.

"Yes," Rebecca said.

"I know just the place."

Silently, Rebecca followed her mother through a labyrinth of halls until they were in her father's private study, far away from the other revelers.

Victoria turned to her daughter and said, "What's up?"

"I watched you with Ken. You don't like him."

"He's a very nice boy. He just isn't for you."

"Why would you say that? We are number one and two in our class at Wharton. We understand each other. We live together. He's gorgeous, and we are practically engaged."

Victoria shook her head, "That would be a mistake. He's too

conservative, almost a bit of a prude, and you are too edgy for someone so strait-laced. You've got no passion with Kenneth. I worry you'll get bored. I want you with someone who makes your heart race. I want you to be so crazy in love that you can barely think when in their presence."

"Gee, thanks, Mom. By all means, tell me everything that is on your mind," Rebecca encouraged as she folded her arms and tried not to say more.

"I'm your mother. I will tell you how I see it. You are fabulous, my darling daughter. You deserve the best. I just don't think that is Kenneth."

"Maybe my heart sings when I'm with Kenneth."

"Sure," Victoria said, with a tone that showed she didn't believe her daughter.

"Why are you doing this?" Rebecca asked. Kenneth was from a good family. He was good-looking. He knew how to make her happy in the sack. Was he the best she'd ever had...no, but he got the job done.

"I'm worried. I think he will be fine with your accomplishments as long as his are more valued. They might not be as important, but he will want you to know your place."

"Are you saying he thinks he is smarter than I am?" Rebecca asked.

"Yes. He might not come out and say it, but when you start making more money than he does, I predict problems."

"Ken wouldn't care. He wants me to be successful."

"Sure. Why don't you ask him? Ask him if it is all right if you make more than he does," Victoria said.

"Okay, I will. But why do I think there is more? Why do I feel you and Dad just don't like him? I've seen you warm up to other men, but not this one."

"Are you talking about one sweet boy that was like a son to us?"

"Unbelievable," Rebecca said and rolled her eyes.

"And I believe you had feelings for him, too," Victoria said. Her mother had known about her crush since it began.

"Well, if you haven't noticed, he is in London. Heck, he hasn't come here for Christmas in nearly six years. Mitch isn't coming back. He has moved on."

"Maybe he's just had his head buried in the sand. Maybe you should walk by him and let him know what he is missing."

Rebecca shook her head. She didn't want to think of Mitch. Before she could say anything, they heard running footsteps, and then her brother Alex burst into the room where they were talking.

"Guess what?" he asked, a smile on his face.

"What?" Victoria asked, holding out her arms.

"Mitch is getting married. And guess who is going to be the best man?"

Rebecca didn't give a damn. She just wanted to cry.

CHAPTER FIVE

Mitchell, London, England
June, Present Day

"Earth to Mitch," Lucien Donovan said as he stood in front of his senior vice president and future son-in-law's desk. Mitch was looking at the photos of the MBA graduates from Wharton in his alumni magazine. His eyes had fallen on one raven-haired beauty by the name of Rebecca Alexandra Stark, who had an undergraduate degree in computer science and a master's in finance. Alex had said she was graduating in their last phone call, yet seeing her now, the woman she had become, he could not tear his eyes away. She was gorgeous, and he thought she'd been gorgeous at eighteen. What he didn't know, and her brother would never say, was that she had gotten prettier with time.

Mitch remembered the afternoon she'd asked him to be her first lover. He would never forget the look on her face, the depth of her eyes. She haunted him.

He was proud of her. She had graduated second in her class, missed first by a nose. He bet that really pissed her off. She was competitive like that, a trait he had always loved, especially when she bested her brother. He and Alex had not been in the top five of their class, so Rebecca's placement probably pissed Alex off too. Good.

"I'm sorry," Mitch said as he shook his head, put the magazine down, and looked at the president of his company. He needed to get a grip. His time with Rebecca Stark had come and gone years ago, and whose fault was that? His. One hundred percent. It was the biggest mistake of his life and one that he thought of every day.

"Oh please, don't let me interrupt. You have a lot on your mind, least of all being that three months from now, you will be marrying my daughter."

"Yes, sir. Well, I'm not too worried about the wedding. I think Lily and her mother are taking care of all the details. I just have to show up in the cutaway and say, 'I do.' She is letting me plan the honeymoon, but we have yet to agree on a location." Lily had shot down every one of his ideas, although Iceland intrigued her, which, ironically, was not a surprise.

Lucien smiled. "Yes, women are like that. They love things like weddings with all the little details. How many flower girls? Should we serve halibut or salmon? Should she have a white runner down the church aisle? I believe *yes* to that. The fact she has kept herself intact for all these years is a testament to her faith and belief in marriage. And I know you will take care of her. I know you will be a decent husband to her in that regard."

Mitch had to keep himself from wincing. *Intact.* What an ugly word. Their lack of physical affection had always been a sore spot for him, but Lily was bound and determined not to have sex until they were married. It had been hard, but he respected her wishes. His thoughts drifted to Rebecca again. She looked at her virginity as an obstacle that needed to be cleared for her future. She wanted to experience passion, and he had made sure she did.

Lily looked at her virginity as a prize to be savored. Where did he fall on this strange scale? Somewhere in the middle. Would the marriage be happening so quickly if they were having sex? Truth: probably not. Her father had hand-selected him to be his little girl's husband. Once it had started, there was no way to stop it. It was a runaway train, and stupidly, he'd settled in for the ride of his life. It was too late to get off. He was sure the old man had him checked out. Not just the initial background check when he'd been hired at Donovan Security, but something much more detailed.

"Her dress is almost ready for her first fitting," Lucien said, "but I'm not crazy about the look. A little too modern if you ask me, lots of skin viewed through scant lace."

"As long as Lily likes it, that is all that matters," Mitch said.

"You're right. She has so few opinions. It is good to support her when she does." Was he kidding? When Lily had an opinion, look out. She had vetoed Fiji, Hawaii, the Maldives, and even the Caribbean. Mitch was a little brokenhearted, as he'd always pictured that his honeymoon would be someplace warm enough that clothing wouldn't be necessary, and they would drink lots of pretty colored drinks with fruit hanging off the rim of his glass.

Mitch wasn't going to touch any of the slightly sexist comments his future father-in-law was making with a ten-foot pole. He had spent a lot of time trying to free Lily from her own outdated, traditional thoughts. He'd tried to make her understand that despite her father, she could be a smart, career woman in her own right. She loved her charitable work, which he encouraged. Maybe she didn't want to run Donovan Security one day, but there were a lot of other things she could do. She didn't really hear or want to hear what he was saying. Lily seemed content to want to marry him and have babies, just as her father had ingrained in her from an early age. She would be just like her mother, whom she called Mums. What had Mitch learned? You can't change people. Possibly it was a cultural difference between the British and Americans, but he didn't think so.

Mitch loved her. What was not to love? She was sweet and kind and had a very nice smile. But she lived to please him as long as it pleased her, which he wasn't so crazy about. Okay, so they didn't have a passionate love. Those burned out quickly, right? Sure. They weren't meant for the long haul, so it was good that it was so docile.

Sweet. Kind. Nice. These were not the words he ever thought he would use to describe his future wife, but the bottom line was—and he'd finally given himself permission to admit it—he was lonely. He'd spent possibly one too many winters in London, and Lily had been a convenient companion and always available. They got along most of the time. They were mellow together, or as they liked to say in the United Kingdom, they got along like peas and carrots.

And on some things—things where she thought *men knew best*—she deferred to him sometimes a little too much in his opinion. He wondered what her real opinions were. Because occasionally, like with the honeymoon, she showed a stubborn streak. It bothered him that she was going from her father's house to his. He had voiced this concern to her, but she said she wouldn't have it any other way. The thought of living on her own terrified her. She was a people pleaser. He just wished he'd known how insecure she was before it was too late. Now, it *was* too late. He'd made his bed and would lie in it. And at the moment, he was lying in it alone.

Now, if he walked away, it would not only shatter Lily, but it would also be career suicide. Lucien had hand picked him in business and for his daughter. Lucien had told him several times that he was being groomed to run the company one day. Mitch thought it was short-sighted that the man hadn't brought Lily in at the time he had hired Mitch. She might be capable of running the business, or she might fail, but Lucien would never know because he never gave his daughter a chance.

Garrison Stark, however, gave his daughter every opportunity he could. Rebecca would be capable of doing anything her brother could do. She was a force. Mitch always loved the way she was. She didn't ask for permission. She'd rather beg for forgiveness. Alex better watch out. His sister had been released from Wharton and would give him a run for his money.

"Say, I wanted to run something by you," Lucien said.

"Shoot," Mitch said, coming back to the present.

"As you know, we need another associate for cyber security."

"Badly," Mitch said.

"I thought since we have enjoyed such success getting you from the United States, we should look there for another potential associate. Maybe even place them in our New York office but have them be a bit of a hybrid worker so they can assist us in London too."

Donovan Security protected assets. If you had a contract in a foreign country and needed a little extra security, Donovan had you covered. Armored cars, yes. People with guns, yes. Computer firewalls, yes. Basic security services, yes. Advanced security services, oh yeah. If you had it and wanted to keep it, Donovan Security would make it so.

Donovan Security London worked predominantly in Europe and the Middle East. Donovan Security New York helped Donovan Security London when any of their clients were on United States soil or with things like computer networks. Mitch handled seven clients—the largest, biggest clients who needed to know that help was but a phone call away.

Lucien didn't announce anything until it was well underway. Mitch wasn't stupid enough to think his input was really wanted or needed. Lucien had probably already extended an offer to some guy from Harvard or Yale. He wouldn't think of a woman. He was too sexist for that.

"Where are you on the progress of this idea?" Mitch asked.

"I have made an offer to someone from the United States."

Bingo. Mitch stopped himself from nodding.

"Who?" Mitch asked.

"Well, you see, I know her dad."

Her. This was interesting in itself, but Mitch felt the little pangs of unease start with his spine and spread to all his extremities. Lucien had only ever talked of one person they knew in common. *Her.* It couldn't be.

Lucien and Garrison Stark had gone to school together. Garrison didn't care much for Lucien, as he said the man was an egotist and power monger. He was right.

"Her?" Mitch asked, hoping it was someone else but knowing that it wasn't.

"Well, yes. You know I don't tend to hire women, but she is a bit exceptional."

Mitch knew that Rebecca was quite exceptional. And he had no doubt that was exactly who the man was talking about. Surely, she would want to work in her father's company.

"You are hiring Rebecca Stark," Mitch said flatly.

"You know her?" Lucien had a little sparkle in his eye. Lucien knew that Rebecca and Mitch had 'known' each other. Was this a test? Or should Mitch wonder about whether this was yet *another* test?

"Yes," Mitch said, "But I haven't seen her in years. Her brother is my best friend."

Five years, eleven months, and twenty-three days since they'd last made love, since he'd held his Bex in his arms and then made the biggest mistake of his life by walking away from her. What had he been thinking? He wondered if she had ever told her parents. They were still speaking to him and inviting him to visit, so he had to assume she hadn't. Alex had never challenged him on their stolen afternoon or the other stolen times that followed in the two weeks before he left for London, which he was grateful for. Mitch had made excuses at the time. Heck, he'd lied, but Alex had been distracted with his own activities, which had been a blessing.

All Mitch knew was that visiting the Starks had become much more complicated in the years that followed. He never went there in the summer or on holidays when he knew she'd be there. No, he went on off weekends when he happened to be in New York. Now that the Starks had decided to relocate the company headquarters to Portland, Oregon, it was much less convenient to visit them. About once a year, Garrison and Victoria would show up in London to see him under the guise of checking on their hotel. He missed them terribly. And from what Alex said, they missed him, especially Victoria, who still sent him his favorite cookies at Christmas along with a hand-knit sweater she'd made or a perfectly picked gift she wanted him to have. It was not unusual to arrive home to a care package from Victoria containing food or books, things she knew he'd like.

When his own parents died, well, his father had left his mother, never to be heard from again until the police showed up and told them his body had been found floating in the Hudson River. Then his mother died from cancer and Mitch suspected a broken heart. The Starks had adopted him as their own. He'd lost his family as an adult at eighteen, then met Alex's family when he was twenty, and for the last ten years, he had been close to Garrison and Victoria. Yet, he couldn't be around Rebecca. It was a mess. And it was getting worse because they had mentioned it to him, and he had played dumb. He had yet to introduce Garrison and Victoria to Lily, but he made sure they would be able to attend his wedding.

"Rebecca is flying in tomorrow for a final interview. I interviewed her last week when I was in New York and pretty much decided she was the right fit for the position, but I'd like to have another look. Besides, she is very nice to look at." He whistled as if Rebecca was a piece of meat or horse flesh he wanted to ride.

Stay away from her, old goat. Old *married* goat.

"Tomorrow? I've got a pretty busy day—"

"This is a priority. I want you to sit in on the interview. Then we will take her to lunch and see how much she drinks. Yanks are always opposed to drinks with lunch, or they drink like fish. If she behaves herself, I'll offer her the job. There is the background check, but that is just a formality."

Mitch's heart beat faster than it should. How many times had he thought about Rebecca and wondered if he should reach out to her? Well, almost every day for the past six years. He always rationalized not calling her with the idea that if she wanted, she knew where to find him. She had always driven every decision that involved them. Why should their future be any different than their past? It was passive aggressive, but it was too late now. He had chosen his path.

That night, he took Lily to Borough Market, and they had dinner at Fish! for fish and chips. Not surprisingly, she had one hundred and one different things to share with him about the wedding. As he ate his traditional halibut fish and chips with a glass of buttery chardonnay, he tried to act interested when she asked if he preferred lemon cake or lemon cake with elderflower essence. He despised elderflower but had no idea what he had said to her.

She decided for him. Elderflower it was.

He took her back to his flat for a nightcap, which she didn't mind because she wanted to tell him how she would be redoing the space once they were married. They had decided to live in his flat for a year or two until they decided to have children. She wanted three. Mitch had thought better than to contradict her about his ideas to have two. She might change her mind after childbirth, he hoped.

She wanted to redo the living room in sage-colored fabric and lots of chintz, like a proper English country home. Only theirs was a modern flat with a view of the Thames. To his surprise, she pulled a tape measure from her expensive handbag and took measurements for ten minutes. Somewhere in the conversation, he heard *Laura Ashley*. He didn't like Laura Ashley with all her pastels and flowers, but Lily was going to start ordering fabric tomorrow. It would look so much better once she had made improvements. He thought it looked pretty good now.

He would not admit it, but seeing Rebecca's photo earlier that day and knowing she was coming tomorrow—heck, was traveling in the air tonight—he needed Lily to blow his mind this evening. He needed to remind himself how much he cared for his fiancé. He needed to remember what had prompted him to propose at Christmas. He remembered thinking she was sexy in her own way, like an adult dressing much younger than she should. It was new for him, but he had done a lot to find it appealing. Finally, when she was done with the measuring, she sat next to him on the couch. He built a small fire in his tiny living room fireplace to ward off the end-of-spring chill. After a few minutes, he placed his glass of Amaretto on his coffee table and took the glass she held tightly out of her hands.

"What are you doing?" she complained. "I'm not finished."

"I thought maybe we could make out on the couch," he said and leaned close to kiss her. She allowed him to kiss her three times, but when his hand moved to cup her breast through the fabric of her floral dress—which was no doubt Laura Ashley—she quickly removed it.

"You know Mitch, all you think about is sex," she said. "I'm getting a little tired of having to be the one who puts on the brakes all the time. I'm not in heat, and you are not a wild animal, so stop trying to hump me."

"If you are tired of always being the passion police, then don't. Try letting go and see if you like it. We are going to get married," he said. "There is a lot we can do that doesn't involve sex. It might involve getting you out of that dress, but I assure you, you will still be a virgin when we are through."

She stood and looked down at him. "I'd be semi-virgin, for sure. I don't know how many times I have to say no to you. We are not going to treat our bodies that way outside of marriage. I made a promise to my family, to my faith, and to myself. Sometimes I think I'm a test for you as well. I cannot believe you think I don't respect myself or that I would compromise my values."

"I respect you more than you know. If I didn't, I'd do the ungentlemanly thing of plying you with alcohol, lay out a blanket, and make love to you in front of the fire. You'd have one hell of an orgasm because I'd make sure you did. I'm not doing anything like that because I'm a gentleman. I respect you, and I listen. I just want to be close to you. Don't you have any desire to be closer to me?"

"This is a ridiculous conversation. Let me speak directly so that you will hear me. I don't need sex until we are married. Now, take me home. Hopefully, when I get there, Daddy and Mums will already be in bed. I don't need them looking at me and seeing my shame that my fiancé has his little needs and thinks of me as a vessel to fulfill him. I really don't want to tell them that all you can talk about is sex."

"This might come as a surprise to you, but any other woman would already be living with me," he shot back. "We would be making love on a regular basis. It would be a way for us to express our love for each other. You know, by making love."

"So now you are trying to guilt me into sex? My own fiancé? Is that how our marriage is going to be? You are going to demand your husbandly rights? I have to put up with you letting me service your needs?"

Mitch couldn't believe this conversation. Lily was getting more skittish the closer they got to the wedding date. Shouldn't it be going the other way? "I seriously hope not. I don't want it to be a one-sided experience. I hope it will be something you really like and want to do a lot."

This was a no-win conversation. He always thought Lily might be a latent tigress in the sack. He just needed to show her the way. Now he was starting to think she wouldn't like sex or making love with him or anybody else for that matter. It was a scary prospect. A sexless, non-physical marriage. He wanted his partner to enjoy the physical aspect of their marriage.

His mind wandered back to Rebecca, for good reason. She was the most sexual being he'd ever met. She liked him enough to ask him to be her first. But that was a long time ago, and this is now. And he was scared. What was in store for him with Lily and their marriage?

A traditionally chaste kiss at Lily's father and mother's door in Belgravia called an end to a disastrous evening. Then a cab ride home left Mitch with one thought: It was now only hours until he saw Rebecca.

He remembered every little detail of their last time together.

How many men had come after him?

Was there someone special in her life?

Why hadn't Alex called to tell him that Rebecca was interviewing with their company?

When he got to his flat after dropping Lily off, he did a quick calculation in his head and picked up his cellphone. He dialed Alex's cell from memory.

"Hey, it's Mitch. Can you talk?" he asked as Alex answered on the second ring.

"Good timing. How is London?" Alex asked.

"Rainy and cold, like every other damn day."

"I hope you start to like it a bit more. It is about to be your forever homeland."

"Yeah, we will see," Mitch said. He still had delusions of running from the altar and heading back to the New York office of Donovan Security. "Is your sister interviewing with my company?"

"So you heard?"

"Why is it a big secret?"

"I don't know. I do as I'm told," Alex said, "Why don't you

tell me? Everyone is being quiet. The old man is pissed that she doesn't want to work in the family business. She's second in her class, and there is a part of me that wondered if Dad would make her my boss, but she has other plans. It is quite the mess."

"Why do I feel like I'm in the middle of some brain teaser?"

"Okay, because you are my best friend, I'll tell you this even if it costs me something. Rebecca is cagey anytime I talk about you. When I asked her if she was going to call you when she was in London, she got all weird and then admitted that she was interviewing with Donovan Security, and I wasn't to tell you because she didn't want special treatment. I think that is bullshit. I'll ask you again. What happened between the two of you before you left for London? Nothing has ever been the same. You won't visit when she is home, and neither of you will talk about it."

"Nothing happened," Mitch lied. He kept their secret. Ever since he'd left the States, it felt like part of him was missing. He tried to chalk it up to being homesick. But Mitch knew the truth. He was Rebecca-sick.

"See?" Alex said, and Mitch knew that he didn't believe a word he said. "That is the kind of evasion I'm talking about. Are you still marrying the boss's daughter?"

"Yes," Mitch said with no enthusiasm. For the first time, he really acknowledged that he was hoping something would prevent that from happening.

"Try to sound a little more excited," Alex said. "Lily is pretty from the photos you've shared."

"I'm just trying to understand everything with Rebecca. Let's stay on the subject."

"Your little Bex is single, by the way. She broke up with her boyfriend, Ken, about two weeks ago. He said something about her being second in her class, and it made her angry, so she told him to stick it and moved out of their apartment. Dad was upset because he was sure she would marry him, and it would justify the last two years of them living in sin. Mom thought he 'didn't bring out Rebecca's passion,' whatever the hell that means, so she was happy about the breakup. Becca does everything to the beat of her own drum."

Mitch did know what the hell "bringing out Rebecca's passion" meant.

He had to swallow his jealousy. He wondered what kind of a lover Ken had been to Rebecca. He wanted to punch him, but at least she was single.

He had no right to be jealous. He was getting married to Lily in three months. He loved Lily. Everyone was right. They'd be great, and they'd have a great life. Boring, but great. That was unfair of him. Their life would be perfect. He liked perfect, so what was his problem? It was just that sometimes, coloring in the lines wasn't as fun as coloring outside.

"I'm sorry she had a bad breakup," Mitch offered. "She doesn't deserve that, and he sounds like a jerk. I trust Vic's opinion."

"My sister is fine. She has this way about her. She gets what she wants."

Mitch knew this to be true.

"Well, you can ask her about it tomorrow. I think she will be in your office at ten in the morning."

Rebecca

She had turned down Lucien Donovan's offer to have her stay at Claridge's or the Savoy. It was actually a bit insulting. No, she was staying at her family's hotel. In light of the fact that Lucien knew her father, she was pretty surprised he would suggest a competitor. She arrived the afternoon before the big interview.

It was a long day of travel, but she had a nice flight and even managed to sleep somewhere over Canada. Now, she was in the

VIP suite at her family hotel. The room service menu was uninspired, but she found something to order. It tasted as bland as she feared. Or was she just stressed about her final interview tomorrow?

One thought was on a continuous loop in her mind: What would it be like to see Mitch after all these years? A quieter voice in her head wondered if she still had a crush. The fact he was her first lover made him special, but it didn't make him the love of her life.

When Lucian Donovan approached her to discuss career opportunities, she was initially skeptical, but then she thought of the benefits. She had planned to work for her father, but then she remembered how Mitch had decided to take his own career path that had nothing to do with his connections to her family. She had come to admire him for it, getting a little real-world experience. When she told her family she might want to work for another company for a few years before tucking into the family business, they were initially surprised, a little angry, and then finally supportive. She knew she could thank her mother for cajoling her father. Her brother was another story.

Alex had been the one to catch up with her while she was packing the night before. He had appeared in the family bedroom she was staying in between graduation and her first job. "Hey, why are you doing this?"

"What exactly am I doing?" she asked, looking at the different clothing on her bed. "I thought I was packing. What do you think I'm doing?"

"Dad could use you in about six different positions as of yesterday. You are kind of slapping him in the face. Interviewing across the pond?"

"Oh please. Don't sound so dramatic. He did just fine for the last couple of years that I was at Wharton. I want to experience another business before joining the family firm. Weren't you listening when I explained it at dinner a few nights ago?"

"Why Donovan Security?"

"Why not? I love cyber security. I have a degree in computer science, and that is what they are hiring me to work on. Who knows, I might even bring this knowledge back to Stark International. Wouldn't that be cool?"

His next words threw her off her center. "Is this about Mitch? Does he get a finder's fee or something?"

She dropped the skirt she was carefully folding. "Lucien Donovan approached me. I don't even know if Mitch knows about it."

"You could have said no," Alex said. "You've had a few very interesting offers. Dad thinks Lucien Donovan is a dick."

"This work intrigues me," she said. "Global cyber security. Sounds ominous. That would be a good foundation for a lot of other things."

"Mitch is what intrigues you. And haven't I mentioned that he is engaged? Why are you doing this?"

She knew Mitch was engaged. Did she want to get a look at the other woman? Yes. Was this a good way to go about it? Not at all.

"I'm worried about you. You are sounding a little paranoid," she said. "I haven't even seen Mitch in six years. He's an old friend, and it is good for him to get married. I hope she is a nice girl."

"I'm going to ask you again: What happened before he left for London?"

She momentarily remembered the feel of Mitch when he held her close, and there was nothing between them but their skin. She'd never known such passion as what he'd brought out of her when they'd made love.

"Alex, what did or didn't happen is none of your business. It doesn't concern you. I think you are kind of obsessed. Maybe you should look into that. Get some help."

"Is that supposed to make me feel better? Something

happened, and it changed our friendship. I can't attribute it to anything else. It has to do with you and Mitch. He never comes here when you are here. He takes great pains to never see you."

This was not new information for her. It hurt a little, the ways Mitch avoided her.

"Give it a rest. It is none of your business," she said and resumed folding the skirt.

"Fine, I'll just think the worst. He met you for lunch in New York and seduced you."

"Maybe I seduced him," Rebecca said with a laugh, hoping to shock Alex enough that she would throw him off the trail.

"Why would you say that?" Alex asked. "Is that what happened? Did you get carnal with my best friend?"

They got carnal at every possible opportunity, for two wonderful weeks of her life. He'd done things to her no other man had ever done.

"Please. You are so crude."

"Answer the question."

Rebecca tossed her skirt to the side, folding it, but it was proving too difficult. "Because I was in love with him, and everyone told me it was just a crush. It wasn't. So maybe I made him an offer that he couldn't refuse. Maybe I seduced him and used guilt as a motivator. Or maybe we had a nice lunch, and that was it."

"Please, please tell me you didn't seduce my best friend."

"Alex, we are both adults. How much further do you want to push this? Because if I tell you something, it can't be unsaid. You might never look at me in the same way."

Her words seemed to register. "Stop. I don't want to know."

"No, you don't. Mitch is one of your best friends, and nothing that happened with us should change that."

"Just answer one question for me."

The second skirt she was trying to fold ended up in a heap in her luggage. "What?"

"You didn't have sex with Mitch, did you?"

"Did you pay any attention to the conversation we just had? You don't listen. Go away," she said and made a shooing motion with her hand.

Rebecca dressed in her favorite red suit for her interview in London. With her raven hair, which she wore up in a twist, and makeup to accentuate her green eyes, she looked not only professional but fashionable and very sharp.

She accessorized with a faux black patent crocodile bag and matching shoes. Thankfully, the concierge made a hotel car and driver available to her. She was namedropping, and on the day she was about to see her ex-lover, she didn't care that it was something she would never do when her mind was completely clear. She called down to the concierge ten minutes before she wanted to go to her Donovan interview. The car was waiting when she emerged from the front of the hotel. The driver was standing next to an open door of a midnight blue Mercedes. Well, at least she'd be going in style.

Arriving ten minutes early for her ten o'clock interview, she sat quietly in the well-appointed lobby of Donovan Security, and people watched. All the furniture was deep espresso leather as were the walls and the carpet. When a blonde in a pink Chanel suit—smelling of bubble gum and cotton candy swirled in carnations—arrived shortly after Rebecca sat down, Rebecca took notice. The woman carried a dark pink quilted Christian Dior bag that perfectly coordinated with her shoes. She walked up to the receptionist, who greeted her by calling her "Miss Donovan" and asked her who she wanted to see.

"Mitch, if he's available. If not, then Daddy," she replied.

Rebecca immediately pegged the other woman as Lily, Mitch's fiancé. She had a big diamond on her engagement ring finger. Nice job, Mitch. Wasn't Lily the lucky woman?

Rebecca tried to block out her memories of Mitch.

Lily had to be close to Rebecca's age, but the similarities

ended there. Where Rebecca was dark, this woman was light. Did it surprise her that Mitch would be so attracted to a blue-eyed blonde after her? Maybe her dark hair and green eyes had never been his type. That was a disappointing thought.

Lily's figure was slight, whereas Rebecca's was full and curvy. Rebecca had big breasts and lush hips, which she never apologized for because she looked like a woman, not a boy. She had never wanted it any other way, but maybe Mitch hadn't liked those elements of her body. Maybe he liked a more athletic figure. A boy's figure? Poor Mitch. He was a breast man six years ago, and she would be surprised if that had changed. Well, Lily didn't appear to have much to offer in that department.

"Miss Donovan, you can go back. Mr. Wilder is waiting for you in his office."

The longing, the sadness, and the jealousy cut Rebecca to the quick. What she would give to have Mr. Wilder waiting for her. She only hoped Lily Donovan knew how lucky she was. She doubted it.

Rebecca flashed to a memory of Mitch's face leaning down to give her a sweet kiss as they were joined in that soft bed at the Marriott, with its stiff white sheets. They had been a couple of kids, but it hadn't taken long for Mitch to find out what she liked and vice versa.

As long as she lived, she'd never forget the feel of Mitch inside of her or the tenderness he showed her the first time they made love. The lovers who had come after Mitch had not measured up. But she had tried to turn them into what she needed to no avail. Why hadn't she tried harder? How many times had she almost jumped on a plane to London? Well, why hadn't she? She was finally in London, but now it was too late. She was an idiot. But it was a two-way street, and he had tried his best to avoid her. She couldn't forget that. He obviously regretted their time together. But she didn't, and she never would.

A few more minutes passed, and Rebecca was feeling worse and worse as she reflected on Mitch and what he'd done to never be in the same room with her. It hurt her feelings.

"Miss Stark? They are ready for you now," the receptionist announced in a clipped London accent.

Rebecca stood and followed the woman who'd gotten out from behind the desk. A grim-looking Miss Donovan passed them on her way out and said goodbye to the receptionist. Miss Donovan had a short meeting with Mitch, and it looked like it hadn't gone well. Too bad. Barely time to kiss, Rebecca thought as she followed the receptionist into a conference room occupied by Lucien Donovan and Mitchell Wilder. He was better looking, if that was possible. Now thirty, but he had some gray at his temples. Not a lot, but enough that she noticed. It made him more distinguished. He'd grown into his features, and damn, it worked.

Blindly, she shook hands with Lucien, but Mitch stood, walked around the long, shiny table, and pulled her into his arms. She tried not to lean into the hug he offered. Of all the hugs and arms that had been around her for the last six years, nothing felt as good, as reassuring, as blindly intoxicating as this moment with this man. But she had to keep it professional for both their sakes.

Was it her imagination, or did he sigh into her ear as he held her? It didn't matter. The hug lasted at least two beats too long.

By way of explanation to Lucien Donovan, Mitch said, "We spent a lot of time together when I was her brother's roommate in college. I practically lived at the Starks' home."

She said the most intelligent thing that came to her mind, "We used to gang up on my brother and decimate him at Monopoly. Actually, I think you both came home to do laundry and have Mom cook for you."

"Vic used to iron my jeans. She is a sweetheart. Those were

45

fun times," Mitch said. "The Starks were some of my best memories from that time of life."

Was she a good memory too? She hoped so.

"We had a blast," she said, and she grabbed one of the chairs for support so as not to allow her emotions to overwhelm her.

"Allow me," Mitch said and pushed the leather chair toward the table after she sat. Then he walked around the table to his vacated chair and sat down.

The blush on her cheeks was there. She could feel it. Her face probably matched her suit. Mitch always had that effect on her.

She focused on Lucien Donovan, but it wasn't easy. She felt Mitch's eyes on her, and she wondered what he was thinking. Had he dodged a bullet or missed a wonderful life? She knew which camp she was in. Life had really let her down on this one.

Lucien asked her a series of questions, while Mitch merely appeared to listen but did not engage. Every time she stole a glance his way, he smiled at her, his dimples standing out in approval. Lucien discussed the certifications she'd need and how there would be an extensive background check. It was daunting, but she liked a challenge.

Finally, Lucien said, "Well, what do you think? Pending the background check comes back clean...Would you like to join our family?"

CHAPTER SIX

Mitch

Rebecca was stunning. He'd heard the term "stops traffic." Rebecca not only stopped traffic, but he also bet she caused accidents. Because he was sure having a problem even walking or thinking now that he'd seen her again. His company didn't encourage social media, and he didn't participate. He wondered if he should have broken the rules to follow her on all her social platforms.

Was she that beautiful six years ago?

If she was, he hadn't fully appreciated it. Shame on him. He'd really messed up the last years of his life.

Holy shit. Donovan was hiring her for New York. Mitch was screwed. His world was imploding. He hadn't even taken his marriage vows yet, and all he could think about was touching Rebecca in any way that he could. She was in a red suit, and he knew every inch of the body under the fabric. He'd held her, kissed every inch of her. Hell, he'd been her first lover. He hated anyone who had come after him. Why had he ever let her go?

Guilt. A gut punch.

Remember Lily.

He had a fiancé. Her name was Lily. She was pretty. She adored him. Well, at the moment, she was mad at him because she thought he didn't respect her values or morals. Hadn't she said that in his office but twenty minutes ago? She was cotton candy, pure and sweet, but Rebecca was fine-aged whiskey. He was so screwed.

They went to some Gordon Ramsey restaurant no one could get reservations to. Lucien knew Gordon, so a call was made, and a table was found. They rode in Lucien's black BMW, driving way too fast down the crowded London streets. Rebecca rode in the front, Mitch in the back, where he could look to his heart's content at the back of Rebecca's head, specifically the complex, inky color of her hair, which was both blue-black and like nothing else he had ever seen. She had some crystal butterfly clip holding it in place. It took sheer willpower not to reach up and pull that butterfly away so that her hair would fall in deep cascades down her back. He knew how the silky locks felt. He'd run his fingers through them at every opportunity. Some things hadn't changed. Her hair still smelled like sunflowers, just like it had six years ago. It was dark, but it smelled like bright sunshine.

They parked with the valet. Mitch followed behind and watched Rebecca as she moved each leg up the steps to the hotel. She had nice gams, which hadn't changed. He knew from personal experience that she had muscles. Hell, when she'd put her legs on his shoulders when they'd been making love, he felt how firm they were. It looked like nothing had changed.

She was wearing crocodile print high heels with sheer black stockings—at least, he could picture them being—with garters. She liked fancy lingerie. Under that suit, she probably had black lace panties and a matching bra. He wished he knew for sure. He wished he could reach a hand inside that suit and touch her breast. She used to like that. He'd once been able to do it freely, but he no longer had permission.

He had to look at the floor. He had to look at anything but her. He looked at the pretty floor bouquets. Then he counted blossoms. Too many to count. Then he pictured running one of those soft blossoms along her skin. How she'd react and tremble. Hadn't they done that with a piece of ice once? Damn it! Getting an uncomfortable erection while having lunch with his old lover and his future father-in-law wasn't a prudent idea.

They sat, and he could smell her perfume. Damn, she always liked perfume. He liked smelling it on his skin after they made love.

What did he eat? He didn't know. Lucien ordered something, and Mitch said a creative, "Ditto." Like an idiot! He hoped it wasn't something horrible. It arrived and didn't have any flavor. It probably did, but he was too distracted to taste it.

Rebecca had a salad that she picked at. She would be starting in the New York office in two weeks. Mitch would be her London advisor, but she would have a New York boss as well. Great; he hated sharing with New York, especially Bruce Jones, who was a single mesomorph. Forget that she was who she was. Mitch wasn't good at sharing. There would be a lot of training before she was ready to be client-facing, but they had all done it. It would suck, but she was up for it.

They dropped Rebecca back at her hotel, and Mitch moved up to the front seat next to Lucien at Lucien's request.

"I think she will be good," Lucien said as they pulled away.

Mitch agreed. "I think she will be fabulous. She's a very smart woman. She's a wonderful hire, Lucien."

"I'm going to say something, and I want an honest answer."

"All right," Mitch said, feeling the trap before it had been sprung.

"Did you two ever date?" Lucien said.

"What?" Mitch asked, taken by surprise.

"Come on, Mitch. I've known you for six years. At lunch, you both looked shell-shocked, and then you both tried to avoid looking at each other. Anyway, I'd never have hired her if she was going to work in the London office. I love my daughter too much. And I've never seen anyone who could fluster you, well, until today."

This was a problem.

"We dated briefly, but it was a long time ago. Really nothing. We were just kids."

"I can't blame you. She's a beautiful woman, but you are spoken for, not that I need to remind you, which I hope she knows."

"Lucien, please. Yes, she knows. Her brother is going to be my best man. Her parents are coming to the wedding," Mitch said. "I'm well aware that I am spoken for." But in truth, he wasn't sure who he was saying it for—himself or Donovan.

They were stopped at a light, and all the cabs and pedestrians crowded around them. It was one of the reasons why Mitch hated driving in London. He couldn't get used to the frenzy.

"Well, there is still something there. I could see it. Just make sure it is dealt with before you marry my daughter, or we are going to have a big problem, okay?"

"It will not be a problem, sir," Mitch admitted reluctantly. But even as he said the words, he knew he had a big problem.

Rebecca

She sat on the edge of the bed in her family suite at the Stark Hotel and swallowed hard. She had not only seen Mitch, but she'd also hugged him. It felt better than anything had felt in years. Why had she denied herself for so long? Well, it was too late. What in the hell was she going to do?

Maybe taking this job wasn't a good idea. She'd be in New York, and he'd be in London, but their paths would cross. The reminder of him, even from such a distance, would be hard.

Why hadn't she ever felt this way about another man?

The phone on her nightstand started ringing. Her whole body tensed. A distraction was what she needed. She quickly made the time change in her mind. She had told her parents that she would call them later that night, so they wouldn't be calling. Not yet, anyway.

Picking up the phone, she answered, "Hello, this is Rebecca Stark."

"This is Mitch. I was wondering if we could have a drink in your hotel lobby."

It was hard to speak, but she managed. "Sure. That would be good, I think."

"Good."

"What time?"

"I'm here now. Do you have a few minutes?"

Her heart skipped a beat. He was here. As in, he was in the lobby, less than two minutes away.

"I'll be down shortly." She took a deep breath and counted to five after she hung up. Why were they being so formal with each other?

He hadn't wasted much time. They had only dropped her off an hour and a half ago.

Rebecca went into the pretty marble bath and checked her makeup. She touched up her lipstick, added a little perfume to her wrists, and made sure everything else looked good. She powdered her cheeks to get rid of any lingering shine and to make sure it helped to cover any blush. Too late. She was already blushing.

The ride in the elevator down to the lobby seemed longer than usual. This was a bad idea. Such a bad idea.

Mitch was easy to find. First, it was a little early for the cock-tail hour, even in the hotel bar, Windsor. And second, he was watching for her when she walked in.

He stood when she arrived and helped her into her chair.

"It's good to see you," she said. "I've wondered about you for years."

"I didn't like the way things ended. I should have called you and invited you to London. I know it would have freaked out Alex and your parents, but we have unfinished business."

"Well, you didn't call, and neither did I. Though, I have to admit, I really, really hoped you would," she said. "You should have."

"I'm obviously an idiot," he said.

"No argument there. And you are an idiot who is getting married to the wrong woman," she said as the waiter arrived and took her order for a gin and tonic. Mitch indicated that he'd like a refill.

"You might be right. Life has a wicked sense of humor," Mitch said.

"What is that supposed to mean?" Rebecca asked.

"I blew it, Bex. But you will be in New York, and I need you to be there. I just don't think I could be around you and be married to someone else."

"What if I was in London?" she asked, wondering if he was thinking the same thing she was. "Use your words, Mitch."

"I've seen you for two hours today, and it is like no time has passed. It is wrong, but I cannot deny that I still have feelings for you. If only we could go back in time."

She nodded. "Oh, I'm sure you will get over it." She was being flip, and she still wanted him. But he had to say it. That is why she hadn't called him. She needed him to come to her.

"Stop it, Rebecca."

"What? People who don't have feelings don't make love like we did," she said. "Do you want me to say it?"

"I'll say it. It wasn't a crush. Not for either one of us," he said softly and took a long draw on the beverage the waiter placed before him.

"And now you're engaged."

"I am. Lucien Donovan's daughter Lily. She is a very sweet person."

"Gee, isn't that nice? She is sweet. When is the wedding?"

she asked sarcastically. She didn't like this side of her personality. It was bitchy and jealous, but damn it, long dead feelings were resurfacing.

"September 26th. Your brother is part of the wedding party. I made sure your parents were free to be there. You'll get an invitation in August. Please don't come. I don't need the distraction of you."

"Congratulations. I'll send a gift with Mom and Dad," she said. "I think I saw her, your bride, in the lobby of Donovan Security. Pretty, blonde, in a pink suit. Smelled like sweet candy."

"Rebecca, I'm very glad you will be in New York. We need someone like you there. If I had to see you every day...I just don't know."

"Don't you? What a ridiculous thing to say to me! If you have such strong feelings for me, isn't that a sign that you maybe shouldn't be getting married to sweet Lily? I mean, thinking about making love to another woman while, you're, well, you know...that isn't good."

"It's a mess. Yesterday, I was content. It was maybe boring, like vanilla, but now I'm a mess. I'm thinking about things I should not be thinking about."

"All because of me, your Bex. Do you want me to apologize for your feelings? Should I apologize for the passion we feel for each other?" she asked sarcastically.

"No, I want to do the right thing. You need to go back to New York as soon as possible. And I need time to think."

"Or what? I've cast a spell on you, and you cannot control yourself. You'll throw me on the nearest flat surface and make passionate love to me." She was being cruel, and she knew it. But it was the most honest conversation she might have ever had with Mitch. Marrying Lily was going to ruin his life and hers, too.

"Don't tempt me, Bex. I'm strongly attracted to you, but I

don't know if it is real or if it would endure, so I need to distance myself from it. This, this thing between us needs to be nipped in the bud. I will not cheat on my fiancé."

Rebecca stood, she didn't need to hang around and hear how she was like some disease to Mitch, something to recover from because she was scared, she might do something really desperate, like cry over him. If he couldn't admit that he loved her, she had to get away from him.

"Where are you going?" he asked, with a sadness in his voice she hadn't heard before.

"I'm removing temptation from your presence so you can think and make order out of the chaos of your life. I wouldn't want you to toss me on the table and start ripping my clothes off. Making love in public has never been my style."

"No, no...don't go," he said, standing quickly. "Please, Rebecca..."

She didn't think, she didn't rationalize, but she did grab the lapels of his suit jacket and used surprise to her advantage.

She pulled him toward her, and when he was close, she kissed him. Not the kiss of a lovesick teenager or that of unrequited love. She kissed him like the lovesick woman that she was. She kissed him for all it was worth. And then he surprised her by kissing her back. His hands rested on her hips, then they wrapped around her body, and he pulled her flush to him as his lips moved in perfect harmony with her own.

The kiss lasted a long time. Too long. The chatter around them stopped as the two lovers found each other again. When he pulled back from her, his warm eyes met hers in surprise. They had kissed a lot six years ago, but this one kiss was more powerful than anything they had ever shared.

"Wow," he said.

"I'm sorry," she said as his hands loosened their hold on her. "I know I shouldn't have done that."

"I'm not sorry," he said, his hands running along her curves. "Which is why we have a problem."

She pulled a tissue from her pocket and touched it gently to his lips, removing the red lipstick she had left there, but when she was about to stick the tissue in her pocket, he took it from her and put it in his pocket.

"I guess I'll talk to you from my office in New York," she said.

"I can't wait. There will be a weekly video sales call on Zoom. I'll see you then."

"What day is it on?"

He had to think before answering. "Tues...um...Wednesday. I'm not thinking very clearly at the moment. I'm sorry. The idea of taking you upstairs and making love with you is dominating my brain and other parts of my anatomy. I feel like six years just disappeared."

"It hasn't. A lot has changed. And you know me. I don't poach. See you in a couple of weeks," she said as she stepped away, turned her back, and didn't look back as she walked out of the Windsor bar.

She walked to the elevator and punched the button. Glancing over her shoulder, she saw Mitch standing at the entrance of the Windsor bar. One finger wag, one acknowledgment was all it would take. He would join her. They would go to the suite, and in about five minutes, they'd be making love.

She stepped into the open elevator, met his gaze across the lobby, and shook her head as the doors closed.

CHAPTER SEVEN

Rebecca, one week later, New York

E very day since she'd seen Mitch in London had been bad. She had cried on the flight home like the little girl she no longer was. He was about to make the biggest mistake of his life, and she didn't know what to do. She still had feelings for him, and if that kiss was any indication, it wasn't one-sided. And then what he'd said to her—well, that was a whole other animal that she spent a lot of time thinking about, usually at 3 a.m. She looked around her new home and tried again for distraction. It wasn't easy.

"In case I didn't say it earlier, I really appreciate your help, Mom. I can't believe how fast you pulled all of this together," Rebecca said to her mother as she folded some of the red towels and placed them next to a pile of emerald towels her mother had already washed. It was amazing all the things that now adorned her new atrium apartment in New York City. Yes, she would have been able to afford an apartment in NYC, but her parents insisted that they help her, and they had, which upgraded her living situation incredibly. She had a cool loft on the top floor of the building that had atrium-curved windows. And the windows covered one entire wall. The space was amazing and urban, stylish, and fun. If a space could be sexy, it was sexy, especially with her mother's decorating, which was a little surprising.

"I love this. It is like decorating a wonderful dollhouse,

which just happens to be my daughter's, the second in her class at Wharton and a brand-new executive."

"Well, who knows if they will keep me? I have to prove myself. And the certifications and training, they never stop."

"You'll pass those easily. If they are too stupid to recognize your talent, your father will find a place for you. Heck, he'll snap you up. He is still a little hurt you chose not to work for him from the get-go, but I think he now understands it. And he is very proud, but then he has always been proud of you. He's never liked Lucien Donovan, so there is that too."

"Thank you, Mom, but I really want to prove myself...I think I understand why he doesn't like Donovan. The man is kind of slick. Hey, what are these?" Rebecca opened a bag from Ralph Lauren and pulled out some very non-traditional sheets. "I thought you only bought white sheets. Was there a mistake? These are red...and very, very nice."

Rebecca's father met her mother when Victoria was called in to handle a remodel on one of the Stark Hotels. After all this time, she knew the hotel business as well as her husband.

"Well, hotel sheets must be white so we can bleach the hell out of them, but I wanted something special and kind of pretty for my daughter."

Rebecca had a flashback memory to stiff white sheets when she had made love with Mitch for the first time. She had worried that she might bleed and have other injuries from losing her virginity, but it had been sheet burn on her side that had hurt the most. She had wondered at the time if the sheets were made of fiberglass.

Her mother proceeded to pull out several red damask shams and coordinating silk pillows. They were all red or patterns of red, green, and other colors that looked wonderful together, but they were elegant. Much more elegant than she'd have bought for herself or felt she deserved.

"They are gorgeous," Rebecca said, wondering if her bedroom suddenly looked a little like a bordello.

"You aren't a powder-puff pink girl. You were always my jewel-tone girl. I mean, look at your eyes, for goodness' sake. You were meant for diamonds, emeralds, rubies, and sapphires. So, I went with that theme."

"I like what you are saying, and you aren't wrong. I like the jewel tones," Rebecca said, glancing at her closet that contained twelve new suits, thanks to a shopping spree with her mother. All of her suits were emerald, ruby, sapphire, white, or black. They hadn't tried on any pastels. Nor had she wanted to—especially after seeing Lily Donovan.

Rebecca had turned the decorating completely over to her mother, and she was glad she had. Would she have decorated as boldly? No. Her mother had taken Rebecca's college Ikea tastes and turned them into sexy sophistication.

Victoria, standing on a short ladder, asked for the drill.

"Mom, how did you learn to do this? You know, using power tools and stuff."

"I don't know. I just picked it up along the way. It impresses the hell out of your father. Seeing a fashionable woman who is at ease with power tools. I think it is a bit of an aphrodisiac. Okay, hand me that bracket."

Rebecca did as she was told and tried not to grimace. She knew her parents had a rough patch when she was a small child, but it hadn't lasted long, and now they were very happy. She had not asked what happened because, frankly, she didn't want to know. And she saw the way her father looked at her mother as if the sun rose and set with her. He not only loved her mother, but he also adored her. He was always touching her. Rebecca wanted a love like that.

The curtain rod was next, and then she was handing up some heavy ruby silk damask drapes with an edge of gold tassels on the opposite wall of the atrium windows. She didn't know where her mother had found half of this stuff.

"I can't believe you threw this together in a matter of days."

"Darling, before I married your father, it is what I did all the time. Days? Really? I did this actually in a day. I did have a car waiting with a driver who carried my packages, but aside from that, it all came together very easily."

Her doorbell rang, and Victoria said, "I think that is Williams Sonoma with your kitchen."

"Mom, Williams Sonoma? That had to cost a fortune."

"Darling, your daddy and I are loaded, so let me have my fun."

Rebecca thought her eyes would bulge from all the deep green, dark blue, and bright red enamel Le Creuset cookware, then the designer China and silver was unpacked and loaded into her new dishwasher.

Once the helpful delivery men left, Rebecca said, "I hope this doesn't come as a surprise, Mom, but I don't cook."

"Oh, you never know, you might meet someone who does," Victoria said.

"Maybe I'll have to take cooking classes on my days off. If I have any days off."

Over DoorDash-delivered Caesar salads from Dean & DeLuca and glasses of wine, Victoria said, "You haven't said much about our hotel in London. How was your room? Did they treat you well? They better have."

Rebecca left the maid a twenty-pound note on the end of her bed for her two nights in London. Heck, she hadn't even seen the maid. After her drink with Mitch, she'd called the airline and moved up her flight. She left early the next morning.

"The hotel might need some attention. The room looked a little dated, but it was okay. The room service menu was a little plain."

"It is slated for a remodel in a year or two. I just don't know if the manager will survive. Alex can't stand Benjamin Renwick, and I don't think I'm much of a fan either."

"Thankfully I didn't see him. I think he is a jerk."

"I think it might be unanimous. No one in the family likes him. By the way, how did my sweet Mitch look?"

The bomb had been dropped. The salad churned in her stomach. She wanted to run, but she had a feeling her mother would chase her. Time to look cool.

"I forgot how much you liked him. He looked fine. He's getting married in September."

Her mother smiled, the crooked smile she reserved for the inept, and looked at Rebecca. "I know. I've heard the rumor. Well, we will see."

"What do you mean by that?" Rebecca asked.

"Did he get a look at you?"

"Of course. He interviewed me. We talked for two hours with Lucien Donovan. I told you all this when I was in London when they made me the job offer."

"Yes, I see," Victoria said with a smile. "Mitch is so handsome now. We dropped in when we were in London last year. I thought about it later. He is kind of dashing, like a young Pierce Brosnan."

Rebecca knew when her mother was toying with her, and she wasn't in the mood. She set down her fork and said, "What are you trying to say, Mother? And by the way, Pierce is Irish and about seventy. Mitch is still American, and he is only thirty."

Her mother smiled. "I can't help it. He is a young Pierce. Oh, Rebecca, I know it isn't easy. Neither one of you fooled any of us back then, six years ago. I always predicted that we were all just waiting for the other shoe to drop. But it hasn't quite yet. I shouldn't have said a word. You weren't ready to hear it. We will talk again soon. I'm here for you, darling."

"What? What did you want to tell me?" Rebecca asked, getting angry.

"You two have been in love with each other since he started coming home with Alex. I was a little worried about it at the time because you were too young, but there was a way you looked at each other. I worried a little. Your father wanted to sit you down and talk to you and Mitch, but thankfully, he didn't need to."

Rebecca held her arms up in frustration, feeling that her mind had just been blown, and said, "He is getting married in September to a woman who wears pink Chanel and perfume that smells like candy. Do you hear me?"

"Darling, that wedding isn't going to happen. He's in love with you." Rebecca agreed, but she couldn't say anything.

"And I love him," Rebecca said in a small voice.

"I know. It isn't over yet."

"He had six years to do something about it, and he didn't. How in love with me can he be? I'll tell you. He isn't. Every time he came to the United States since, he has avoided me."

"He is overwhelmed. He's probably thinking of how to get himself out of this mess."

"*Mom*, please…stop!"

"Oh, stop being so dramatic. You are an adult now. It isn't like when you were eighteen and had that fling with him before he went to London."

Rebecca felt her cheeks redden.

"How…do you know any of this?" Rebecca was embarrassed and wanted the floor to open up and swallow her whole. But why did she feel the need to ask the question? Now would have been her time to shut up.

"Madge Cunningham, my bridge partner at the time, was the concierge of the Marriott Marquis at Times Square. I remember telling you at least six months earlier, but you ignored me, ever the rebellious teenager. Anyway, she recognized you as you walked through the lobby with Mitch.

"Poor Mitch, he had such a rough life," her mother continued. "A boy without a father in his teens, and then he lost his mother. I'm glad your father and I could be there for him. He is like another son to me and a great influence on Alex. His home life was terrible, and when he first started coming home with Alex, he looked to us as his second home. I liked that. I liked to think I was the mother he could depend on after losing his own."

Rebecca let her mother's words register. She knew about what they had done before he left for London. "Oh, god. No. You knew? All this time?"

"I'm your mother. Of course I knew. However, your father doesn't know for sure. He only has a suspicion. I think we should keep it that way."

"I think I'm going to be sick," Rebecca said.

"Look, Becca, I know how it is to be in love. You are my daughter, so you love like I do. Your father was with another woman when I showed up to decorate his hotel. Our attraction, the need we felt for one another, was...well...it felt like it was overwhelming at the time. I really thought it was one-sided until he asked me to look at the Liberty Suite with him. I knew something was up on the elevator ride. I only hoped I was right, and I was. I remember hearing the door shut, and then he put the chain on it. The only thing we looked at from that moment on was each other. We stayed for six magical, life-changing hours. After that, he was never with that other woman again. And I never went back to my little apartment. I was in his bed from that night on. And when I found out I was pregnant, we got married. Alex was our first, and we were so excited."

Rebecca put her head in her hands, then laid her forehead on the table. It was too much information. All the things she had believed growing up weren't exactly true. Her parents were very sexual beings. No wonder she was a hound. She got it from them.

She looked up and asked, "You lived with Daddy before you got married?"

"It was so scandalous at the time in my parents' social circle. My father wanted to kill him. Your dad had taken my innocence in the Liberty Suite and made a woman out of me. Yet he hadn't made an honest woman out of me. I mean, it wasn't the 1950s, but to my parents, it was."

Rebecca topped off her wine glass from the bottle sitting in the new ice bucket her mother had purchased the day before. How many hours of therapy would she need to get over her mother's disclosure? How many times would she have to shut her eyes before she wouldn't see her parents knocking it out in a suite where she had stayed many times?

"I'm sorry, darling. Have I shocked you?" her mother asked as she took another delicate bite of salad.

"Yes," Rebecca said and drank the glass of wine as if it were water. Did she have anything stronger in the apartment? If she didn't, she would, posthaste.

"I know it is hard to think about your parents as affectionate, but your father and I still find each other quite attractive and have a very active physical life together. But aside from a little separation when you and Alex were little and we were trying to figure it out, we have been blissfully happy. And I think your father really grew up over those few months. It was either that we walked away or that we made it work and committed in a way we hadn't before. When he came back to me, there was an earnestness about him. I don't know what he did or where he was, but whomever he met, whatever happened, it pushed him to grow up. I have a feeling, of course, that it was another woman, but I'm the love of his life, and there has never been a doubt since he came back."

Rebecca felt sick. It was bad enough to know that her parents were sexual beings, but now her mother admitted her father had been unfaithful, but it was okay because he had recommitted to her. How did she process all this information? Well, she couldn't. Her mother had always been almost formal, a prude, and this new, blunt openness was really freaking her out.

"Mom, please. I'm glad you and Dad are happy, but I don't need to know all the details. I think I might be sick," Rebecca said as she pushed away her salad.

Her mother poured more wine into her glass and asked, "Well, I always thought you were lucky. Mitch is such a handsome young man."

CHAPTER EIGHT

Rebecca

After much thought, Rebecca wore one of the new single-breasted black suits with big baroque pearls on her neck, wrists, and ears. Her hair was up, and she looked like a ball buster. Perfect.

She planned it so that she was early for her first day. Her new boss, Bruce, was expecting her. He was in his fifties, ex-military, and a bit cocky, if she had to put a word to his attitude. He was short and had a crew cut, and she could tell he was always ready for a hostile who might breach the premises of Donovan Security. His suit was too tight, making his muscles appear as sharp lines when he folded his arms. It looked uncomfortable. She wondered if he spent much time in the gym. She bet he did. She wondered if Mitch liked him. She bet he did not.

She had a tablet and paper in front of her to find out what she needed to start with, but the list he gave her was daunting.

"There are some certifications every employee of Donovan Security must get in the first few months. As time goes on, you will have more, but we will start with the basics. Some of them will not feel like they belong in your realm of work but having them means everyone here has the same background. With your education, they should be easy. You'll start with the Intelligence Fundamentals Professional Certification, which is offered in the United States by the Under Secretary of Defense for Intelligence work. You will need a CISCO Secure Virtual Private Networks certificate, then a Certified Electronic Systems Technician certificate for the cyber work that you will be responsible for. We will also want you to have a Security 5 Certification, which is an IT security certificate offered by the EC-Council. Down the road, you will need a Commercial Driver's License. You will also need to complete Certified Computer Service Technician training, earn a Board Certification in Criminal Trial Law, and you must be certified in Homeland Security. Lastly, you will be starting your self-defense classes immediately to make sure you can protect yourself if you are compromised."

Did Mitch have to go through all of this? Alex said he had. In fact, Alex told her he still practiced his taekwondo regularly. No wonder he'd felt so solid when she held him. He could have done a lot more to stop her if he'd wanted to. Heck, he could have probably snapped her neck like a pencil. It was a dark thought she filed away.

"The first dozen classes of taekwondo will be in a group that meets twice a week, then you'll have private lessons," Bruce said, producing a card with an address in Chinatown. "Your first class is tonight at six. Leave a few minutes early if you need to change out of your skirt, which I recommend. I'll show you the locker room and assign you a locker so that you can bring your own workout bag directly to the office from here on out. Physical fitness is a big part of being a member of Donovan Security. We regularly work out in a private gym on the third floor. We are even more into it in New York than they are in London. It is a bit of a competition and a bit of a rivalry. We kick Limey ass all the time. Once a year, we meet and compete, usually in late spring. We met three weeks ago. We've won the last three years in a row. You do not want to be the weakest link. That person is ostracized for a year in between our competitions."

"I wouldn't want that," she said.

"Here's the information you'll need to sign up for your other certifications. It is a source of pride that we all have passed the certifications on the first try. Now, don't go breaking my heart. I need you to be sure before you try an exam. I'm here if you have any questions. Understood?"

"Yes," she promised and felt the first trickle of dread. Yes, they had mentioned that there would be certifications, but this was a little more than she had imagined. She was a computer geek. She had been told there was little chance of her ever being in the field, but maybe that wasn't true. Self-defense class? Well, living in New York, that added defense would make her parents very happy.

That night, for her first self-defense class, she wore a variation of the outfit she usually wore to the gym. She thought she was in pretty good shape. After all, she went to the gym four times a week. She couldn't have been more wrong.

An hour later, she lay face down on the mat, where she had landed like a sack of rocks. The mat smelled of mold and old sweat. When she could find her breath again, she swiped at her running nose, and her hand came away bloody. They were not messing around in this class. It was a bit of survival of the fittest, and they were not mock fighting. She wondered if anyone had ever been killed. She hoped she wouldn't be the first.

If she had gone to work for her father, she would be at her apartment right about now sipping something like a gin and tonic, wondering what outfit to wear tomorrow. There was no such luck with Donovan Security. She wondered if her nose was broken. Some scrawny little girl named Bethany Ann had taken her down. Rebecca needed to get in the game. And if that bitch tried to touch her again, Rebecca was going to punch her, much like she used to punch Alex when he pissed her off.

But then Bethany Ann held out a hand to help her up, with a big smile on her face, and asked Rebecca if she wanted to join the others for bubble tea and sushi at a place called Three Doors Down, she decided to join. It turned out to be a good group of ladies. If she wasn't worried that they could kick her ass, she'd have liked them.

The next morning, Rebecca hurt. Everything in her body hurt as she silenced her alarm and forced her way out of bed. And after a shower to wake her up, where she noticed a few new bruises, she looked in the mirror and said aloud, "Oh no."

Well, at least they couldn't accuse her of not taking her job seriously.

Rebecca Stark—hotel heiress, second in her class at Wharton, wearer of expensive jewelry and designer clothing—had her first set of black eyes, given to her by a Clinique salesperson from Bloomingdales, who chewed bubble gum, said 'like' a lot, thought Paul Newman was a brand of salad dressing, and was named Bethany Ann, which sounded like a coming-of-age perfume that every tween would want to wear to attract their jock boyfriend, who no doubt smelled like a jock strap after a game.

She accessorized her black eyes with a cobalt blue summer silk suit her mother had told her looked "hot" on her. She wore a broach that depicted the sun and put on matching sun earrings in gold that accentuated the tan she was getting on the weekends, when she hung out at her parents' house to lay by the pool. It was odd going home with them spending so much time in Portland, but they still came to their family home in New York, just not as often.

She decided not to try to cover the slightly swollen eyes with makeup. They were too tender to the touch, and it least would show she was giving her all to her training.

The physical stuff would be the hardest, she knew. The book stuff was easy, but physical strength was her weakness, which was a tad surprising.

Bruce saw her as she walked in that morning.

"Damn, Stark. You've got a pair of shiners."

"You should see the other person," Rebecca said.

"That is the spirit. Like it, Stark. Keep it up."

The twenty-person staff that made up Donovan Security New

York filed into the conference room a little before 9 a.m. for their meeting with the London office. Rebecca had hoped she would look better for Mitch, but she also needed to let go of the fantasy that she somehow had a future with him. He was on another continent, for God's sake.

She sat in a chair that was the seventh chair from the left and the seventh chair from the right. She liked the symmetry, but more importantly, it didn't appear to be anyone's "chair," which she had been told was a thing.

One of the secretaries, Shanice, Rebecca knew because she had been nice to Rebecca the day before, telling her where the ladies' room was as well as where to grab a quick lunch (not in their building, but the building next door). Shanice had also told her about the territorial chairs.

The Zoom call began, and they were seeing everyone in London, where it was two in the afternoon. Greetings were made, Rebecca was introduced, and then business was discussed. They went over five clients who spanned both London and New York. Mitch was in a navy suit with a burgundy tie and didn't even look her way, but she recognized the tie. She'd given it to him for Christmas when she was seventeen.

Fine, he was going to pretend that he couldn't see her. Well, two could play at that. One thing she noticed was that he commanded attention. Lucien Donovan was in the room, but it was Mitch's meeting.

An hour later, the call was over, and they all filed out.

Rebecca went to her new office and had picked back up on studying for her first certification when the phone on her desk softly buzzed.

She didn't recognize the number, but they had told her the day before how they wanted her to answer her phone. This was her first call, but the salutation hadn't been rocket science.

"Good morning, this is Rebecca Stark of Donovan Security. How may I help you?" she asked confidently and waited.

"Are you alright?" Mitch asked impatiently.

"Hi," she said.

"Hello," he replied after a long pause.

"I'm working on my certifications."

"Was one of them self-defense?" he asked.

"Yes. A big man named Luther threw me to the ground during my first taekwondo class last night. I smashed into the mat with my face. We had bubble tea and sushi later, so I think he was sorry."

"What the hell, Bex?"

"What are you asking me exactly? I'm confused." She smiled to herself. "Luther" was a good improvisation. She didn't want him to know a chick named Bethany Ann had done this to her.

And Mitch, Mitch was calling her. She couldn't believe it. "I'm trying to do what I need to do, the basic certifications for Donovan Security. Am I doing something wrong? Bruce is mentoring me—"

"You know you can hit back, right?"

"I did a face plant with the mat, right on my nose. Luther wasn't trying to hurt me. He just got the upper hand, and I went down hard." Bethany Ann had been trying to hurt her. And Rebecca intended to punch Bethany Ann if she tried it again.

"I will talk to Bruce today about getting you out of that class. You shouldn't be hurt. The class is meant to keep you from getting hurt. Your eyes look painful."

"Please don't. I've got to start somewhere. And Bruce would think I complained to you. He would make my life harder. And if I'm not mistaken, you learned taekwondo when you started at Donovan Security."

"I'm a guy. I don't want you to ever need it. You will not have to do that kind of work. Not on my watch. Your work will involve a computer screen in a plush office in New York."

"What if they need me in the field?"

"Over my dead body," he said.

"You sound like a protective older brother, but it's not your decision. I live in New York. It might be good for me to know a little self-defense. I'm not a delicate flower, Mitch."

"We both know I'm not a brother to you. And you should avoid dangerous situations. Bex, you don't need to purposefully scare me. I'm too far away to help."

"For the last six years, I've walked in the dark, cavorted with edgy men, taken a few of them home to ravage me, drank too much, driven too fast, and I even smoked to look cool, and I survived. Where were you then?"

"I don't want to know about the other men, okay? It bothers me. Just because we didn't talk then, we are talking now, and I feel very protective of you."

"What? You've been celibate for six years? Try this shiitake on your fiancé. I'm not your concern. You made that abundantly clear."

"Shiitake? Like the mushroom?" he asked.

"It is my nice way of saying shit in the workplace."

"Damn it, say shit," he said. "You're an adult."

"Well, then you can fuck off. How is that for being an adult? Goodbye." She hung up on him then. She tried to get back to studying, but she couldn't concentrate as she needed to. Mitch had called her.

When she got home that night, she put an ice bag on her face and drank a gin and tonic while she relaxed in her big, comfy chair. She had almost fallen asleep when her cellphone started vibrating. She didn't feel like talking, but the caller was Donovan Security, so she picked up.

"This is Rebecca Stark," she said.

The caller at the other end sighed and then said, "It is Mitch. I'm sorry. I called to tell you that."

Rebecca looked at her watch. "It is after midnight in London."

"I couldn't sleep. I was thinking about you."

"What did you tell Lily when you got out of bed to call me?"

"Why would I tell her anything? She lives with her parents."

Rebecca hung her head and said, "Well, if I was her, I'd be in your bed." Why had she said that? Maybe because it was the truth.

"That's where I'd want you."

"What are we doing here? This call…"

"I don't know, but I miss you. I just didn't know how much until I saw you again. Now I can't get you out of my mind," Mitch said.

"I know the feeling. Tell me about life in London. I've been curious for six years. Tell me everything, because I want to know."

They ended up talking for two hours. And when they finally said goodnight, neither of them wanted to be the first to hang up.

CHAPTER NINE

Rebecca / One Month Later / Late July

Rebecca held out her hand to Bethany Ann and helped her up off the mat.

"Damn, Starky. You have really gotten better, and you fight kind of dirty, not that it is a bad thing."

"Thank you, my friend. I hope I didn't hurt you. I pretended you were my brother. How about some sushi and bubble tea, or maybe something stronger? My treat."

"Yeah, I'd love it. Should I round up the gang?"

"Yes, that would be great." There were six ladies who liked to go out after class. Thankfully for Rebecca, they had pulled her into their clique after her first class. She had worked hard at her taekwondo and even hired a personal coach for a three-hour weekend session. It was starting to pay off.

A week earlier, Rebecca passed the Intelligence Fundamentals Professional Certification and received her CISCO Secure Virtual Private Networks certificate. She also passed her exam for a Commercial Driver's License. She became a standout star at Donovan Security, not only for how quickly she'd passed the exams but also because she had such high scores. Bruce hadn't needed to worry. She was setting the bar very high. Contrary to how he had treated her in the beginning, he was now in awe of her. She was his golden girl. He liked to brag about her, which bothered her—unless he was saying it to Mitch, which she kind of liked.

She got home a little after nine that night and wondered if she'd missed Mitch, but he knew it was her night for taekwondo. Besides, these calls could not continue. He'd called her almost every night. In two months, he'd be married to someone else. Then she'd have to deal with a broken heart. She felt sorry for Lily. They should talk as easily as she talked to Mitch. He should want to tell Lily about his day, not a woman he'd once had a lot of sex with over a two-week period six years earlier. But damn it, she looked forward to these calls like nothing else in her life. Codependent much? She had to pull the plug.

Despite all she had done, despite her accomplishments, it took little to make her cry. She just needed to think of Mitch. The tears flowed easily. Maybe she should be happy that she was currently in the shower because it masked how many tears she shed. But she was still crying after the shower. She didn't know what to do. Should she fly to London and confront him in person? At the end of the day, he'd proposed to someone else. He was marrying Lily Donovan. And he knew Lily is wrong for him but wouldn't break it off.

Rebecca was still crying when the phone rang at ten o'clock. It had to be her brother, great. She had come close to telling him about Mitch, but she didn't want to hurt his relationship with his best friend.

"Hello," she answered, trying to sound cheery.

"Hi," Mitch said softly. At the sound of his voice, she started crying. It was three a.m. in London. This had to stop.

Mitch could tell. "Bex, are you okay? Darling, what is wrong?"

"You. You are calling me every night. You are calling me Bex. You are calling me darling. I can't take it. You are marrying the wrong person. Why can't you see what is before you? I'm here. Do you talk to her like you talk to me? I doubt it. I've loved you for ten years, yet you are marrying some little girl because her daddy wants you to. What is wrong with you, Mitch?" Then she did what she should have done weeks earlier. She hung up on him before he could answer.

She stared at the phone for a long time, but he did not call back. She doubted she'd ever hear from Mitchell Wilder again.

Mitch

Mitch didn't sleep. Becca said words he had said to himself, but she'd added a few that were hard to ignore. He kept running them over and over in his mind.

I've loved you for ten years...

It wasn't one-sided. Okay, so he'd tried to forget the kiss in the Windsor bar. Well, the more he wanted to forget it, the more potent it became. He wasn't wrong, but if he didn't do something, he would be making, yet again, the biggest mistake of his life. He knew what he needed to do, and he knew it would be the hardest thing he'd ever done. He didn't want to hurt Lily. She was innocent in all of this. If anything, she was too good for him. He needed someone who was edgier, not so innocent. Someone like Rebecca.

If he didn't do it now, there would come a day when he would do something that would compromise his vows. He would be true to himself and how he felt about Rebecca. He'd never forgive himself.

He called in sick to work the next morning. He was an executive, but he didn't care. He wanted a day to himself, and he didn't want to be bothered. It was something he hadn't done in six years. He spent the morning walking in Kensington Park. It was a warm day, and the park was filled with tourists, but he scarcely noticed. He ended up at a pub that afternoon.

His cellphone buzzed. *Lily.*

Shit. He sat on one of the wooden benches in the back garden area behind the pub and answered his cellphone.

"Hey, Daddy said you called in sick today. He couldn't believe it. I can't either. What is wrong with you? You have never called in sick. You're an executive."

He wanted to fast forward his life a few years to see how it came out.

"I just needed a day to myself," he said.

"Really? That doesn't sound like you. Usually, you tell me if you need to think about something," she said, sounding concerned. "I'm a little upset you didn't think of my feelings. Daddy really counts on you, and you just disappeared today. It is kind of embarrassing."

"I'll work for a few hours from home tonight. I just needed to think."

"Whatever Mitchell. Sometimes, you are just too American, all into your feelings. Next, you'll start doing yoga and going vegan. Sometimes, I wish you were more like Daddy. Or thought about someone else besides yourself."

"Yeah, I'm a jerk. I'll talk to you later," he said and disconnected.

He had never felt worse than he felt in this moment. A small part of his brain announced, *"Just wait."*

Lily tried to call him again, and he let her go to voicemail.

He had a lot of money in the bank. He had great work experience and a solid resume. He was getting a little tired of London. Maybe it was time to go home.

Later that night, he appeared at the Donovan's house without an invitation. He knew from past experience that they did not like to be disturbed in the evening, even if he was a future son-in-law. The maid, dressed in a black dress and white apron, masked her surprise as she informed him the family was still having supper. She showed him to the study and told him that "Miss Lily" would be in when she was finished with supper. No wonder this hadn't worked. They were still formal with each other. They should have been so in love they had to be with each other every moment. Hell, she should be living with him, but it hadn't happened that way.

Ten minutes later, Lily bounded into her parents' study,

where he waited for her. She was in a pink sheath dress and wore pearls. She looked like she was late for a tea at the Ritz. Scowling at his appearance, she didn't approach him for a kiss, which made everything he was about to say much easier.

"Well, this is a surprise. Or did I forget we were getting together tonight? I thought, with your need to be alone, I wouldn't hear from you for a few days," she said, a little anger in her tone.

"No. I needed to talk with you, so I came over."

"Alright. Would you like a drink? G&T?"

"No, I don't think so," Mitch said. Once he said what he had to say, she wouldn't want him to sit back and finish a drink. He'd drink at home. With any luck, he'd get stinking drunk.

"You sound so serious. Should I sit, or can I stand? Mums and Daddy want to watch a movie at eight, so I don't want to keep them waiting. Spit it out, whatever it is," she said.

She didn't invite him to watch the movie, which was not a big surprise. But shouldn't she want to spend that kind of time with him? Come to think of it, they hadn't done a lot of hanging out, just the two of them. There was always someone else with them, like her parents. It was kind of shocking, actually.

"Lily, I think you should sit," he said and looked at the elegant rug that perfectly fit the room.

"What is this? You are scaring me, Mitchell," she said, the light and happiness gone from her.

Just wait, his brain screamed.

"I don't know how to tell you what I need to say, but it is my hope that someday you will be thankful I did."

"Oh my god. You don't want to marry me," she said.

He didn't realize it, but he was subtly nodding his head. "You are kind and lovely. I love you, but I think I'm in love with someone else. Someone from my past. I can't marry you when I have feelings for her. I can't do that to you." He loved Rebecca. He regretted his words immediately. A woman didn't want to hear about the other woman in her fiancé's life. Why had he mentioned another woman? Well, he *was* constantly thinking about her.

"You bastard," she spat. "You are ruining everything."

That was the first time he'd ever heard Lily curse. He had a feeling she did a lot of things that would surprise him. Before Rebecca was hired, he'd have cared. Ironically, he no longer did.

"I am a bastard, but better now than at the wedding or the day before. And thankfully, the invitations haven't gone out yet."

"Oh, how kind of Mitchell to call things off before the invitations went out. Do you want some sort of award? Americans like to give awards for everything. Maybe I should give you a ribbon."

"I'm sorry. I feel awful, and I don't know how to explain it."

"I bet she slept with you. Is that it? I need to let you screw me, then you'll be in love with me? Huh? Answer me, you bastard."

"No, Lily, it isn't like that at all. But this woman is someone I thought I'd never see again. When I did see her, it was like I was overwhelmed. I can't explain it. But if I was in love with you, the way I should be, I shouldn't feel that way."

"You are talking about that little Irish hotel slut, Rebecca Stark. Daddy told me all about her, with her green eyes and how she threw herself at you."

"She didn't throw herself at me, and she isn't a slut. I went to school with her brother. He is one of my closest, best friends. He was going to be my best man. Their parents are like second parents to me. Rebecca is a kind person. She didn't want to do this to us. In fact, she doesn't know I'm here. She might not reciprocate my feelings." And where did Lily's father get off talking about Rebecca as if being Irish was bad? His last name was Donovan. And if Mitch remembered correctly, Donovan was an Irish surname. Stark was actually German and English.

"Oh, that would be so sad for you. Daddy hired her, and you can't say no to her. Maybe you should just screw her and be done with it? Know this: If you do, I won't be here when you come to your senses. Husbands having lovers used to be the norm in this society, but I don't accept it. Well, maybe Daddy can just fire her, and all this confusion will go away."

"Maybe he should fire both of us," Mitch said. "The bottom line is that I can't marry you when I feel this way about her. And on some level, I'd think you'd like someone else for me to have sex with since it seems so repugnant to you."

He needed to stop talking. Now he was just being an asshole.

"Save it, Mitchell. I had a fitting on my wedding dress today. I don't need to hear about how you're in love with another woman. I can't believe you'd walk away from all we could have for some old flame. You're so weak. I took you for someone with a brain, but I meant what I said earlier. You are no better than a humping dog. How pathetic."

"I deserve that," he said. Rebecca was his Kryptonite. He didn't mind at all.

"Is sex all you want? Because if that is what she is offering, I'd like to throw my hat in the ring. Come on, we will go up to my bedroom. I'll pull up my dress, and we can be done with it. I'll let you screw me. Would that make it all better?" That sounded about as passionate as a root canal. And he didn't want to touch her with a ten-foot pole. Not with Rebecca back in his life.

"Lily, please. I haven't had sex with her in over six years. It isn't about that. We kind of grew up together."

"I cannot believe you are lying to me. You want to screw the hot slut over me. Do you know how many men would love to trade places with you?"

It all crystallized for him at that moment. He did want to make love with Rebecca, but it wasn't all he wanted. He wanted everything with Rebecca. A life, children, heck, even a dog and the white picket fence, as long as he could come home to her every night.

"Well, I think you should invite one of them to date you because I don't think I can give you what you need. There are a lot of men out there who would. I'm stepping aside so you don't ruin your life on me. You deserve to feel the way I do when I'm with Rebecca."

Poor choice of words. He was acting like an asshole. The heavy crystal glass barely missed his head as it sailed past him, hit the wall, and smashed into a hundred lethal shards behind him. It almost sounded musical.

He wasn't as lucky when it came to her engagement ring. It hit his forehead and one of the prongs made a small cut, which started bleeding immediately. And although it was Mitch who was bleeding, it was Lily who screamed until her father arrived and escorted Mitch to the front door. Mitch judged that Lucien really wanted him to put up a fight. Anything so that he could hurt Mitch. But that wasn't the way it went down. Mitch left quietly.

CHAPTER TEN

Mitch

I t was over. He was going to the office to clean up his desk, even though he still didn't know if there was anything worth it to go in for. Well, he'd like to get the Mont Blanc pen Victoria gave him years ago when he started the job.

Lily's engagement ring was in his pocket. Why? He didn't know. Maybe he'd give it to her father to give back to her. Mitch didn't want it. He thought it wasn't just big, but it was gaudy. Maybe Lily could sell it and buy something for herself, like a watch. Something she could look at every day and remember what an ass Mitch was and what he'd done to her. Yeah, maybe she could just donate the money. She'd like the recognition she'd get from things like that.

He had to warn Rebecca. Lucien might fire her, too. He was stupid if he did. She was excelling. Mitch had expected no less of his Bex.

The scene with Lily could've been worse. They could have been married with children, and he could have cheated. Lily could have been pregnant. That would be worse. Yeah. Who was he kidding? He wasn't getting Man of the Year anytime soon. This behavior was not a good look for him.

He sat in the back of a cab he'd hailed in front of his flat and looked at the rain while the cab driver vaped. They weren't moving. They would be stuck in this traffic, him in this muggy, smoke-filled cab for hours. He was going to be late for work, but he was in no rush to get there. Yet he felt pretty good. Last night he'd taken a big step that had changed the course of his life forever. Below the guilt was a sense of relief.

He did it for himself. His happiness. He did it to be with Rebecca, but he wasn't even sure she would want to be with him. Yet he was sitting in the back of a damn cab a continent away. Why? Why was he here when he should be with her, discussing what he hoped would be their future?

Mitch unfastened his seatbelt and tapped on the glass that separated him from the driver but did little to protect the passenger from the smoke.

"New destination. Could you please take me to Heathrow?"

"Heathrow Airport?" the man asked as if he hadn't heard Mitch the first time.

"Yes, I'd like to go to the airport, please."

"That will take an hour," the man announced. "Cash or credit?"

Mitch held up three fifty-pound notes and said, "Cash," which unlocked a certain joviality in the driver, who replied an enthusiastic, "All right, sir."

"I'll tell you which airline in the next few minutes." He had never been so thankful as he was at that moment that in his briefcase he had his passport, which was with him due to a trip to Paris earlier in the week.

Mitch leaned back in his seat—self-consciously touching the sore spot on his forehead where the thrown ring had gotten him —and started checking for the next airplane to New York. There was one, Virgin Atlantic, leaving in three and a half hours. It arrived in New York at four-thirty that afternoon, and they had a seat available in first class. He swallowed at the price, typed in his credit card, and secured the seat. They sent him an e-ticket to his phone.

He said to the taxi driver, "I'm flying on Virgin Atlantic going to New York."

"Coach or first class?"

Still wincing at the price, Mitch said, "First class."

"Well, I know some time-saving things to do at Heathrow."

When they got to the airport, his driver went around to the back of Terminal 3, where they drove up to a private Virgin Atlantic / Delta entrance. Mitch added Lily's engagement ring to one of the inside pockets of the briefcase. Then he handed the driver his briefcase after he removed the passport and the rest of his personal items, all of which happened to fit in his trouser pocket. He handed his driver another two hundred pounds and asked him to deliver the briefcase to his personal office at Donovan Security.

Ten minutes later, Mitch had cleared security, had a paper boarding pass, and was walking through the duty-free mall on his way to the Virgin lounge. He realized he needed to pick up a few things so Rebecca wouldn't think he was a bum.

He purchased a carry-on and a small toiletry bag in the duty-free mall. He then purchased a comb, toothbrush, toothpaste, dental floss, deodorant, disposable razor, and shaving cream. At one of the perfume shops, he bought his cologne and a bottle of Bulgari perfume he thought Rebecca might like. It was dark and sexy, just like her. He put them all in the toiletry bag. Then he bought a couple of paperbacks and a charger for his cellphone that would work in America. He even bought a few pairs of underwear and socks, two shirts, a lightweight cashmere sweater, and a couple pair of designer jeans that were completely overpriced. Who needed to pack when you had a credit card? He had stockpiled money for a rainy day. Well, it was storming in his world.

He sat in the Virgin lounge and tried not to freak out. He took a long sip of his screwdriver. He didn't know why he'd ordered the drink, but it sentimentally reminded him of another time when he was nervous and excited in a hotel room at Times Square in New York. Mitch then sent an email to Lucien that he was taking a week off starting today for a personal emergency.

Then he sent a text to Rebecca.

No matter what you hear, please stay in NYC until you hear from me. I need to talk to you, Bex.

It was about four in the morning in New York, but it couldn't be helped.

She replied immediately:

What is going on? Are you okay?

He replied:

I'm sorry it is so early. I'll explain everything later today. I'm flying to NY. I love you.

His phone started to vibrate. He almost let her go to voice-mail, but he wanted to hear her voice. When she hung up on him two days earlier, it had been a gut punch.

"Mitch? Are you okay?" Rebecca asked. He could hear the sleep in her voice.

"I'm great. I think I'm better than I've been in years. And I love you. I. Love. You."

There was a pause as his words registered, then, "Mitch, honey, you are scaring me. Where are you? Are you okay?"

"Do you love me?" he asked.

"Yes," she said, her voice breaking. "I love you. You know that. I'm totally, completely in love with you."

They called his flight.

"I needed to hear that. You might want to call in sick today. I'll explain everything tonight. I'm coming to see you. I'm flying to New York," he said. "They are calling my plane now."

"Good," she said.

"I'll see you soon," he said and ended the call.

As he waited in his large seat on the airplane, he sent a text to the Donovan Security's HR manager.

Rebecca Stark's home address, please.

Rebecca

Rebecca sat up in bed, tears streaming down her face, sweet tears. Had she just had a dream? Had she called Mitch? It was almost seven in the morning. She looked at her phone: *I love you.*

He loved her.

He *loved* her.

She tried to call him back, but her call went to voicemail. Because he was flying to see her…

You might want to call in sick today. I'll explain everything tonight. I'm coming to see you… I'm flying to New York.

He'd said that. Yes, he had. He was coming.

She looked down at her pajamas and over to the rumpled bed. It took only a few seconds for her brain to connect the dots. She picked up her phone and left a voicemail for Bruce.

"I wasn't feeling well after I went to the gym last night, and it is worse this morning. I think I have the flu," she said flatly. "I'll check email and keep studying, but I'd better not come into the office."

She called Mitch's phone again, but it went to voicemail. "I took a chance and told the office I have the flu. I don't. Tell me where you are, and I'll come to you, or you can come here. Do you have my address? I'll text it to you. I love you, Mitch."

Rebecca didn't poach. Mitch knew that she would never get close to another woman's fiancé, but she had a feeling something had changed. She checked Facebook, where she had a recent habit of stalking Lily Donovan. Lily had deleted all of Mitch's photos, and her status was single. Something had happened. Up until two days ago, he was all over her Facebook page. It was kind of sickening.

Her mother, Victoria, would have said that the other shoe had dropped. She could live with that.

Rebecca cleaned her apartment and went shopping for all the food she knew people liked to have on hand: eggs, bacon, bagels, champagne, orange juice, cheese, crackers, potato chips, coffee, chocolate, and ice cream. She wasn't thinking very logically, or she would have picked something up for dinner.

She shaved her legs carefully. She bought candles. She took a cab to Saks Fifth Avenue and bought lingerie. Silky, lacy things she had seen in the windows but always walked by until today. Everything was either red, emerald, or black.

By four, she was showered and dressed in a skirt and blouse, waiting for the unknown. She didn't know what she should be waiting for, so she felt edgy. Was he coming? Had she misunderstood? What if he was coming to tell her that although he loved her, he was still marrying someone else? Maybe he just wanted one last fling with her to get her out of his system. Until he told her what he had to say, speculation could only upset her.

She checked her internet for flights from Heathrow to London. She knew how long it took to fly from Heathrow to New York. Damn it. She tried his cellphone, and it went to voicemail again.

By four, she was pacing.

If she kept this up, she'd need another shower.

Her cell buzzed at 4:45, and she almost had to peel herself off the ceiling. *Mitch.*

"Mitch," she answered.

"I just landed at JFK. Should I go to my hotel? I have a room at Stark International New York—"

"Cancel the room and come here," she ordered. "On second thought, don't pause to cancel the room. I'll take care of it."

"I want to shower, shave, and change. I look rumpled."

"I like you looking rumpled, and I have a shower. Mom bought me these wonderful towels...I'm rambling. Do you know where I am?"

"HR gave me this address for you, and I have your text." He rattled off an address.

She said, "That is it. I'm here, and I'm waiting for you."

"I'll be there as soon as I can. I think it is rush hour."

"It is, but I'm here waiting for you."

"Good," he said.

One hour and twenty-three minutes later, he buzzed her from the lobby of her building. She let him in and waited.

She heard the elevator doors open around the corner from where she stood at the open door to her apartment. And then he was there, looking tired but excited. He wore a suit he had worn on the airplane and carried a small suitcase, which he dropped when she jumped into his arms.

CHAPTER ELEVEN

Rebecca

M itch broke away from their kiss long enough to ask, "Have I told you lately that I'm an idiot? That I've been an idiot? That everything you said was right?"

"No. But then I was an idiot, too. I've never felt the way I feel about you, about anyone else. I'm in love with you," she said, and he kissed her.

"I'm in love with you too, and I'm scared to death," he said.

"Take me inside. We will talk it out until we are no longer scared."

He carried her over the threshold of her door and set her down. He grabbed his slight luggage, tossed it to the side, and shut her door, then he paused to grab the chain and lock the door.

"Welcome to my home," she said, and he lifted her into his arms and kissed her again.

"It is gorgeous," he said, his eyes never leaving her face.

"Victoria Stark went a little crazy."

"Vic loves her daughter."

"I think she likes you a little bit too. She thinks you like me. And she knows you were my first."

"So much for all of our carefulness, our stupid cloak and dagger,"

"She had a spy at the Marriott. She told me when I moved into this apartment."

He walked with her in his arms until her legs hit the edge of her mattress.

They fell onto her bed, the red comforter whooshing as they sunk into it. Her hands disappeared into his hair, and he held her by her hips.

"She's very perceptive and if it had really bothered her, she would have mentioned it at the time or told your dad. Geez, he doesn't know, does he?" Mitch asked.

"No, he only suspects. But in light of the fact we are on my bed, and you came to see me, he is going to figure out that something went on or is going on."

"Something is going on. I hope you don't mind that I decided to come for a visit on short notice," Mitch said. "I'll look better after a shower and shave."

"I think you look pretty good now," she said with a smile.

"Would it be too forward of me to ask if you would like to shower with me?" he asked.

"No, but I'll decline. I spent an hour on my hair and makeup, so you'd think I looked good, so I'll have to pass. However, there is always tomorrow morning."

"I'm going to hold you to that. You always look good to me. Always."

"Can I ask you something?" she asked as they faced each other on the duvet, their faces less than an inch apart.

"Before you do, I should explain that Lily and I are done. I wasn't being fair to her, to you, to myself. I told her I was in love with someone else," he said and then showed her the bruise on his forehead. "This is where her engagement ring hit me."

"I'm very sorry," she said. "For Lily. You got off lucky. I'd have hurt you much worse."

"I hope you'd fight such a declaration like an incensed lioness. She's not you. I think she knew something was wrong with us. She deserves to be loved by a man the way I love you."

"No argument there," Rebecca said.

"My hope is that she has that kind of love someday."

"So that little boo-boo on your forehead looks pretty fresh.

What? You broke up with her yesterday and flew to see me today?"

He nodded, kissed her, and said, "I'm a decisive man. I haven't been in the past, or I've ignored what I should have done, and it hasn't served me well. Besides, we have a lot to discuss. I was on my way to work this morning when the need to be with you, to see you, to hold you in my arms like this overwhelmed me. I couldn't spend one more day without seeing you, without being honest about my feelings. And I had my passport with me, which I took as a sign. Seriously, is it okay that I'm here? I could check into your hotel."

"Your reservation has been canceled. You are not going anywhere. Yes, I'm glad you came. Hell, I'm glad you came here to my apartment. And by coming to see me, you had the added benefit of not having to face Lily's father at the office."

"He found out last night. He suspected something after your interview in London. He could see it. He wanted me to deal with it. Deal with you. Well, I did. Now, I might be unemployed, but damn it, another chance with you is priceless."

"Sounds like I might be unemployed too," she surmised. "I'm not sure that I care either. So many certifications. Such crap."

Mitch nodded and said, "I'm sorry for the certifications, the job, everything."

"I don't think I am. I've shed a lot of tears over not being with you, Mitch. Don't go away again. I don't think I could survive it."

"You could because you are strong like all the Starks, but don't worry, I'm not going anywhere. To be honest, I don't think I can ever live without you. I need you. I've lived a half-life without you. I'm done."

"Just because we met early doesn't mean it was wrong."

"I remember seeing you that first time, and do you know what I said to Alex?"

93

"What did you say?" she asked with a small smile.

"You were in a green V-neck sweater and a long navy pleated skirt down in the front garden, picking the last of the fall roses. You'd pick one and then sniff it before putting it in a basket at your feet. I was speechless, then I found my voice and asked Alex, 'Who is that?'"

"I remember that very clearly. I was picking roses for the dining room table because Alex was bringing a friend home from school, and Mom wanted pretty flowers for the table."

"Alex punched me in the shoulder, hard. Then he said, 'That is my sister, you asshole.' All I could think is that when you grew up, you were going to be gorgeous, and you are."

"Thank you," she said and kissed him.

"Does Alex know about our phone calls?"

"No one knows about them."

"Good. I mean, you could tell people, but I like that you kept them to yourself."

"They were special to me," she said, and he kissed her.

Finally, he said, "Isn't my razor burn bothering you?"

"Not at all. I like having you kiss me."

"Your cheeks are red," he said.

"I'm blushing. I do that a lot around you, in case you hadn't noticed," she said, but then he reached out a finger and touched her lip. "Maybe a little bit is razor burn."

"Let me shower and shave. I'll feel better being in your presence then."

"Can I watch?" Rebecca asked.

He narrowed his eyes and smiled as he said, "You want to watch me shave and shower?"

"Yes," she said with a smile. "I don't want you out of my sight."

They left the bathroom door open as Mitch slowly took off his clothing. First off was his suit jacket, then his shoes. He turned on the shower as he unbuttoned his white shirt. Rebecca sat on a dining room chair she'd moved into the bath for the occasion and took each item of clothing as he disrobed. When he got down to his silk boxers, he looked over his shoulder at Rebecca.

"You are enjoying this a little too much," he said.

"I've seen you naked before," she said as she held up her hands. "And I have a very good memory, but you look a little different."

"I have more chest hair now," he said.

"I noticed," she said. "And more defined muscles on your chest and arms. The taekwondo."

He turned around and kissed her. "And I work out three times a week. Are you sure you wouldn't like to join me? I bet you have some new muscles I'd like to see and feel."

"No," she said. "We have things to talk about. And I can't talk if I'm naked. I'd just want to rub against you or have you touch me."

He shucked out of his boxers and stepped into the shower as he said, "You're killing me. And for the record, I will be touching you when I get out of here and have shaved."

"I'm counting on it," she said, taking in each inch of his flesh. She wanted to feel him rub against her. She remembered how it felt when he was inside of her—the feeling that Mitch, her Mitch, was part of her. She had to try to hold it together. The idea to join him, to rub against him, was overwhelming, but it had been six years. She needed this to be slow and unfold as it was supposed to. "I want to touch you too. I've missed you."

"Then it sounds like we are going to have a very good night," he said.

"I think we are, and I cannot wait."

She watched as the water sluiced over his skin. Aside from the chest hair, little had changed except the muscles on his chest. He had a lot of lean muscle on his legs that she knew he got from jogging. He had an impressive body, then and now.

"Where do you run in London?" she asked, trying to maintain her breathing. She was so glad she had bought the lingerie that she was wearing under her skirt and blouse. She hoped he liked it.

He stuck his face out from behind the confetti curtain of her shower. "You remembered."

"Of course, I remembered," she said.

"Green or Hyde Park, sometimes Kensington Gardens, but it is a little touristy at this time of the year. I don't like to jog along the street. The cobblestones and the pavement are uneven, then there are the taxis to compete with. You know, this is a big shower. Why don't you strip down and join me? I'll scrub your back or front, whatever you prefer."

She wanted to, but it would be too fast, too quick, and if there was one thing she had promised herself was that if she ever had the opportunity with Mitch again, they would take it slow and savor each moment.

"I have a very plush towel waiting for you after you finish... your shower."

Within two minutes, he turned off the water and stuck his hand out for the towel in her lap. She considered not letting him have it but drying him herself, but that would definitely get her wet and in need of a shower herself.

She handed him the ruby-colored towel and waited as he buffed every part of his body while she watched. When he emerged from the shower, the towel was tied low on his hips. It disappointed her. She hadn't quite had enough time to examine every inch of him, but she would...later.

One lone drop of water traveled from his shoulder down his chest. It was all she could do not to push him against the wall and follow the path of that moisture with her tongue. He used the small travel shaving cream and lathered up his face. Then he shaved it off. And when there was just a little foam here and there, he took the towel from his waist, moistened an end from the faucet, and removed the last traces of lather.

Rebecca swallowed hard. This man was the original proto-type for every other man she had ever dated or let make love to her. It looked like she was about to get a chance at the original once again. Good for her. Her nether regions were already beating along with her heartbeat in anticipation.

He then replaced the towel around his waist, combed his wet hair, and opened the box of aftershave from his new toiletry kit.

"By the way," he said, returning to the kit and extracting a red and white box. "I bought this for you because I liked it, but if you don't, you don't have to wear it." He handed her what turned out to be a box of Bulgari Allure Baciami.

Rebecca took the box and read it. She smiled. "Do you know what 'baciami' means in Italian?"

"No. Something good, I hope."

"It means kiss me," she said as she opened the bottle. "I love it."

Mitch capped his cologne, put it back in his kit, and then he crossed to Rebecca and kissed her. She raised off the chair to kiss him back.

"Better?" he asked.

"Yes," she said and added, "Kiss me again to make sure."

He kissed her, the knot on his towel loosening, causing the towel to fall to the floor. He reached for it, and she kicked it out of the way.

"Really?" he asked.

"Most definitely. It has been a long, lonely six years," she said and spent a little time looking at his naked form. He was already erect. She'd make good use of that.

"I agree. See anything you like?" he asked.

"Yes," she said and rubbed the back of her hand from his calf to his chin—a nice contrast to all his warm skin—and purposely avoided his erection. She watched as he shut his eyes and sighed. Oh, how she had missed this man. No one compared. There had been other men in her life, but no one like Mitch.

Mitch

Enough of this tease. He needed her like he had never needed anyone. He grabbed Rebecca's hand and led her out of the bathroom. Six years ago, he hadn't been as demonstrative. Well, they were both older now.

He led her to the red bed where they had laid and kissed. He grabbed the edge of the covers and pulled them back. Then he climbed into her bed, naked, and reclined on the pillows as she stood, fully dressed, next to the bed and waited.

"I'm a patient man, but I need you, Bex."

She smiled, and said, "Look who is sleeping in my bed."

"You have too many clothes on. Take them off and join me."

She smiled and kicked off her shoes.

"Your turn or my turn to see what I've been missing?" he asked.

"I've waited for this for six long years," she said as she unbuttoned her green silk satin blouse and tossed it aside, her emerald eyes never leaving his. He couldn't stop looking at her. Holding himself back from touching her wasn't easy.

Her large breasts threatened to spill out of the sexy black lace bra she wore underneath her blouse. She untied the wraparound black silk skirt. It fell to the floor in a pool of inky blackness. She stood by the bed in bra, panties, and her gold jewelry, which seemed to glow against her beginning summer tan.

The pain of his erection had started when he had taken off his clothes for his shower, and it was now throbbing in protest.

"You are the most beautiful woman I've ever seen," he said.

She smiled and looked down at him as she slowly removed her jewelry and placed each piece on the nightstand starting with her bracelets and ending with her earrings.

There was only one thing that would satisfy him. He wondered if she was going through a similar battle. If she wasn't, he'd take her there. He knew her body, knew how to play it like a fine instrument. It might have been six years, but he remembered everything when it came to bringing out Rebecca's passion.

Before he could offer to do it, she reached behind her and unhooked her bra, her breasts spilling from the confines of the lacy material. They were bigger now than they had been when she was eighteen, and it was all he could do to keep from reaching out to touch her. Her figure was lusher. He wanted to get lost in all that was Rebecca. Her panties were next, and then she was as naked as he was. The anticipation that they were about to consume each other was almost more than he could take. He pulled back the covers a little further and extended his hand to her.

She took his hand, and she slipped between the sheets and into his arms, the skin-to-skin contact making him take a deep intake of breath. "This is oddly familiar."

She stretched like a cat and said, "I love this. I love the feel of you."

"At least this time, I don't have to worry about hurting you," he said.

She smiled softly, and said, "I don't know if I ever thanked you for being so kind and gentle that first time. You made it wonderful for me. I never look at that as an awkward experience because you made it so lovely."

"Is that how you'd like me to be tonight? Kind and gentle?"

"No. Not the first time. I want you to show me how much you've missed me. I want you to take me. I want you to take away any doubt about how you feel about me. I'm yours to make love to…"

He didn't need to be asked twice. He rolled her onto her

back as she smiled up at him. And when he kissed her, she nipped at his lower lip.

How he had missed her. He didn't know where to begin. He could see for himself how much she wanted him, and the feeling was mutual. He liked touching her. He liked the way her eyes became heavily shaded as she moved toward his touch, wanting more. He liked the way her breasts bounced as he drove into her. He liked the taste of her, the warmth of her body, the way she gripped him when she climaxed.

His hand slipped between her legs, to the warmth she held there. She was warm and wet, nearly dripping for him to enter her. He slipped a finger inside of her and then another.

"Please," she said. "I want you inside me, but with something else besides your fingers."

He didn't make her ask a second time. He just spread her wide enough to accommodate him, and then he guided himself into her warmth and sighed.

When he was deep inside of her, she looked into his eyes and said, "I missed you so much."

He pulled out of her and then sank in again, which made her cry out in pleasure as she said, "Mitch...Mitch, it has always been you. This is where you belong."

"I missed you...I love you, Bex."

It was like no time had passed. They knew each other. Their bodies recognized each other. He knew just how to touch her and bring her pleasure. His body responded to hers as if it were coming home.

They had been apart for a long time, but nothing compared to being with her. He couldn't believe he'd denied himself for so long when she was all he wanted. He loved her. There would never be another for him. Everything began and ended with Rebecca.

He pumped into her, making the bed move, watching her

body bounce as he drove into her, heard her gasp as she smiled up at him and then asked him for more.

"Faster, harder…Just don't stop."

He couldn't have stopped if the ceiling fell in on him. He just wanted this woman. All his thoughts were for Rebecca. Then her eyes narrowed as she screamed. "Mitch!"

The orgasm that pushed through her body came in waves of pleasure, and he was relentless, keeping up the pace she had asked for. And when his own body took over, he rode the wave with her and screamed out her name as he spilled himself deep within her.

CHAPTER TWELVE

Rebecca

I n the night, Rebecca turned over and bumped Mitch with her knee. His warm body spooned her from behind, and she had definitely awakened him, but he didn't seem to mind as she kissed him in apology.

"I'm sorry," she said. "I didn't mean to bump you."

He kissed her cheek and then her shoulder, then his arms tightened around her. Smoothly, he rolled her body so that he was on top of her and then took possession of her mouth.

"I don't mind at all. I like being touched by you," he said as he began kissing and nuzzling at her breasts. "Do you realize this is the first time we've officially spent the night together?"

"I don't know if I can spend a night without you ever again. I like having you next to me in bed."

"Good, so you'd better get used to me, Bex," he said, sucking on her nipple.

Before long, she had wrapped her legs around him and guided him inside of her. Soon, they were making love again.

"Fast or slow?" he asked as he began a gentle rhythm.

"Slow, because I want you to be there a long time. I don't think anything in the history of my world has ever felt as good as you do when you are inside me," she managed.

"That is where I want to be. I love you, Rebecca Alexandra Stark," he murmured.

"I love you too, Mitch Wilder," she managed as he thrust into her. "Oh...oh...promise me this isn't some wonderful dream."

He nuzzled her neck and said, "It is real."

"I don't want it to end," she murmured.

"It doesn't have to. Let's make this permanent. Will you marry me, Rebecca?"

"Yyyyyes," she said and then was lost to her in her climax. He joined her in the release. So much for slow. They were still a little too ravenous for each other to enjoy a slow session of lovemaking.

Minutes later, she rested her cheek against his shoulder, her fingers running through the hair on his chest.

"When?" he asked as he pulled her closer.

"Tomorrow or later today?" she asked, thinking that he couldn't possibly mean getting married, but if he was, she was game. The years apart had almost killed her.

"Okay," he said, running his fingertips along her spine.

"I'm serious. I've wanted to marry you since I was fourteen. I'd marry you anywhere, any place, any time. I want to be able to call you, my husband."

"I'm serious too," he said, as he stopped moving his hand from the patterns he was making on her skin. "I'd like to marry you later today. I want to be your husband. I want you to be my wife. Enough of this bullshit. I love you. Those last few years have almost killed me too. Not one more day without you, without this. I want you in my bed every night. I want to make love to you every night, and I want to make it legal. I want the world to know that you are the woman I love."

"You're serious," she said, raising her head off his shoulder. "But we live in different countries."

"Pick one you'd like to live in, and I'll follow you there," he said. "I don't care where we live, just that we are together."

"You're serious," she said again. He really had decided that they were to be together forever.

"Rebecca, I've been lost since I left for London. I can't tell you how many times before I left that summer after graduation that I almost turned around and drove to your house. I was obsessed, and I told myself it wasn't real. Then I got this gift of having another chance. I won't blow it. I'm not letting you go. I'm not letting you out of my sight ever again."

"Good. I don't want to spend another day without you, but I think there is something I need to tell you," she said, placing her hand on his cheek. She paused, then got up her courage to tell him something she had told no one.

"I hope it won't make a difference, but I need to tell you. It happened a long time ago, and I'd deal differently with it today than I did then. I need you to know that. I could have handled it better, but I'm telling you now because I don't want secrets between us."

"You have a boyfriend? It better not be that Luther guy who took you out for sushi," he said as his arms tightened around her.

"No, you kind of set the standard, and it hasn't been easy to find anyone I like as well as you. You are it for me. And I have a confession to make," she said with a laugh. "I made up Luther. A very nice lady named Bethany Ann kicked my butt that first night. Later, I kicked her butt."

Mitch laughed and said, "I was jealous."

"Good. No, I need to tell you about something that happened when I was eighteen."

"Okay, six years ago. Is it something to do with me?" he asked as he snuggled against his pillow and looked at her.

"I should have told you," she said. "Well, one person knows, but I haven't seen her in years. This involves the two of us, and I'm sorry I didn't tell you at the time. I'm sorry. I was scared. Hell, I was terrified."

"It is okay, just tell me," he said.

"I had an ectopic pregnancy that ended with an emergency surgery because I was bleeding internally. They had to remove the damaged fallopian tube, but I still have one. It is just that it might not be easy for me to conceive a baby."

He sat up and looked down at her. "What? When? Was it our baby?"

She was silent for a long time. She had promised she would never tell him, but circumstances had changed. She said, "Yes."

He sighed, placing his hand over his eyes. "I'm so sorry... I don't know what to say. When did you find out? You could have told me. You didn't need to go through that alone." He looked at her then, his face pained and worried.

"I should have told you. It was in August, after we were together that June. I was an intern at Stark International in New York for the summer between my freshman and sophomore years at NYU."

"I remember," he said moving closer to her.

"Mom and Dad were in Portland thinking about moving Stark Headquarters to the Pacific Northwest, and Alex was off learning the hotel business in Canada somewhere. I knew you were just starting a new job, and I didn't want to bother you. Besides, I knew you couldn't do anything from London. I had this intense pain, and the head housekeeper, who I had gotten pretty close to, well, she took one look at me, got a cab, and went with me to the hospital. I had to have emergency surgery because the tube ruptured. By the time the family all met up at the house two weeks later, no one knew what I'd been through, and I didn't tell them. I'd recovered, but I was still a little pale from the blood loss. I told the family I'd gotten a bad summer flu, and they believed me, but I lied. I broke their trust."

"I'm so sorry...I...thought you were on the on the pill. I remember we talked about it that first day. I had condoms, but I really didn't want to wear one. I was worried it would hurt you, then you told me you were on the pill."

"No birth control is 100%. And if you remember, we made love a few times over the two weeks before you left."

"A few is an understatement."

"Well, yes," she said with a little smile.

They made love at every opportunity they could find, which wasn't easy with Alex as Mitch's roommate and Rebecca living at home for the summer in between her years at college. She had started the internship, but she was with Mitch every evening. They lied to her family so they could be together, and they were—every night of those two weeks before he left. And on the weekends, Rebecca told her mother she went shopping with friends but never returned with any shopping bags.

"I'm so sorry. I wish I'd known." He looked tortured.

Rebecca sighed and said, "You didn't know. It just happened."

"What would you have done if you had found out you were pregnant, and the baby was okay? What if you had carried the baby to term?"

"I've thought a lot about that," she said. "I keep picturing this big coming together of the family. I think I would have told my family and you first, of course. I hoped we could have all come together and come up with a plan calmly, rationally, and civilly. Probably wouldn't have exactly come together that way, but I'd have done anything to keep our baby."

"I'd have married you," he said without hesitation. "Right after your dad and brother killed me."

"Mom wouldn't have let them. You'd have asked to marry me, and I always would have wondered if you were doing it because of the baby or because you loved me."

"Well, I was in love with you then, so I'd have worked hard to convince you of my feelings."

"I wonder if we would have lasted, being so young," she said.

"We'd have lasted," he said as he moved closer to her and held her hand in his. "I'm just so sorry you went through that."

"I've had a lot of time to think of this. I've found my peace. Now you have to. I might never have children. I'm sorry."

"It isn't your fault. Most of your happiness in life is who you marry. If we are blessed with children, we will be doubly lucky," he said and kissed her. Then he said, "I'm really sorry about the baby."

"I'm sorry I didn't get to see what we could have made together," she said.

"I know. I wonder if it was a boy or girl."

"Too early to tell, so they told me. But those are the kinds of thoughts it isn't easy to let go of."

"I should have asked you earlier, but I got a little distracted. What should we do about birth control? Should we use it? Do we need it?"

"I've used it sporadically, and I've never gotten pregnant," she said. "I don't want to use it with you. If we get pregnant, it would be a second chance."

"Wouldn't that be something? Our baby."

"You have to be okay with me not ever getting pregnant," she said.

"I want you more than anything else. It is hard for me to think that there were other men after me," he said. "I need to deal with it, but it is hard."

"Not too many, and if you are it from here on out, I'll be happy," she said. "Besides, I got to see one of your lovers in the flesh. I didn't do that to you."

"Lily?" he asked with a sad laugh. "Lily and I were never lovers. She wanted to wait until our wedding night. She was a virgin. And I was very frustrated. I wondered if she'd ever come close to being like you, but I had a feeling she wouldn't. I had a feeling she'd never enjoy sex, which is a tragedy."

Rebecca laughed harshly, "What is this power you have over women, Mitchell Wilder? We all want you to be our first. You're like the great de-virginizer!"

"Maybe women think I'll be gentle. I don't know. Did you?" he asked shyly.

"I really didn't think about it. I just wanted to have sex with you. I wanted you in a kind of carnal way. It was like, he's your man. Now go get him. And when we actually made love, I was very happy with myself for choosing you."

"You always appeared to enjoy yourself, even that first time," he said. "It made me happy."

"You knew how to make it good for me, and it was good every time."

"I wanted you to enjoy it, although I was still in shock that I got to see you naked," he said. "And you had the perfect little body." He leaned forward and kissed her breast, then her lips.

"That was kind of thrilling seeing you naked that first time. You were my first naked man that I got to explore," she said, reaching down to stroke him.

"Well, you're the only one with whom I've been the first. But now I want to be the last, okay?" he asked as his hand rubbed her breast and moved lower to touch her in the way she was touching him.

"I like the sound of that."

They kissed, and their bodies played together again under the billowy red sheets. And when at last she was laying on him, sated and sleepy, she said, "First time I saw you, I knew."

Rubbing his hand over her butt, he said, "We just needed to grow up a bit."

They talked about the first time they'd seen each other. They talked about how hard it had been to say goodbye.

As hard as it was, she told him about Ken and why she'd left him after two years. Mitch told her about Lily, and then they agreed to never talk about their exes again.

They talked about their dreams for the future. They were living their biggest dream, being together.

"I don't need to stay in New York," she said.

"I'm tired of London. I want to come home. I will be anywhere you want to go."

"Maybe it is time to see if there are any opportunities at Stark. Would that be okay with you?"

"I could be a valet. I could park cars," he said with a smile.

"I'm thinking of something a bit more corporate for both of us, but we can talk to Dad about it. He might need a manager at a hotel, and we could have a lot of fun with that."

"Like Barbados or Thailand. Someplace we could get a private beach and frolic."

"Frolic?" she asked.

"Yeah, preferably naked."

Rebecca laughed. "Even if we aren't asked to manage a hotel that comes with a private beach, I think we will do alright with just a bed."

"Actually, any flat surface will do," he said with a wink.

Mitch

Rebecca swirled in the mirror as Mitch watched from the edge of the bed where he sat. They had a fun shower that morning that had a lot more to do with a bet they had about seeing if he was strong enough to hold her against the tile wall and make love. Her feet never hit the marble floor. He thought he'd won, but Rebecca countered that she was really the winner.

He felt a little dazed and confused. A sexual haze that was all about Rebecca.

"Well," she asked, "What do you think?"

She was in a white Chanel summer suit, a few strands of family pearls, and a pair of high heels made of cobalt blue silk. She had borrowed a five-pound note from him that she had tucked in her bra. She had sprayed on her new perfume, which made him want to rip the suit off of her. She had to be the most gorgeous woman he'd ever seen. He had come so close to marrying the wrong person it made him shudder a little.

"I think it is perfect, but I prefer you out of it. Come here," he said and held out his arms. He didn't have to ask her twice. She sat on his lap and wrapped her arms around his neck. He did not deserve to be this happy. His thoughts turned to their future children, if they'd be so lucky as to have them. She had been through a lot because of him. He needed to make it up to her and find out if there was any way they might have a child together. Maybe they would need a surrogate. He didn't know, but he knew they would have a baby somehow.

"Let's get a move on," she said. "I wonder if there will be a line."

"Are you sure this kind of wedding is okay?" he asked. "We could get rings first, tell your parents. Maybe invite them to be our witnesses."

She shook her head. "Tomorrow, we can get rings. I want to get married to you today. I've wanted to marry you since I was fourteen. There wasn't a day that went by that I didn't cry a little that I'd lost you. I think I've waited long enough."

"I know exactly how you feel," he said. "Well, I'm a dude, so I didn't cry every day, but I thought of you every day."

"I'll count it," she said as she kissed him and then jumped off his lap.

"How mad do you think the family will be?" Mitch asked as they left her apartment.

"Mom can throw us a big reception. She always prefers a party to any other event, like a wedding or a funeral. As long as she can decorate or plan a menu, she is good."

There was a line at the courthouse, but they were third, so their wedding happened by ten thirty with the two of the clerks for the judge acting as witnesses. They signed the documents and then it was time to go.

As they walked down the courthouse steps after getting married, they stopped, smiled at each other, and then kissed.

"Well, how does it feel, Mrs. Wilder?" he asked.

"Wonderful," she said, then dabbed at a tear as she added, "I have a husband."

He hugged her and asked, "Are you hungry?"

"I could eat," Rebecca said with a smile.

"We need you to keep up your energy. How about Katz to commemorate our first date?"

"Only if I get sex later," she said with a smile.

"I think you can count on that."

When they got back to her apartment, they made a beeline for the bed, where they stayed for several hours that afternoon.

"Wow," Mitch said as he pulled Rebecca close. "We really did it, Mrs. Wilder."

Rebecca laughed and then hugged her new husband. "You're my husband. I cannot believe it! Finally, damn it, finally! And we consummated it!"

"That really was the fun part," Mitch said and kissed her.

"We are married! Married sex is fun!" she exclaimed.

"Tonight, let's have dinner here. I'll make some pasta. We will drink some champagne, get a little drunk and then have drunken sex."

"Wait, you cook?" Rebecca asked.

"Yes, but I only make pasta when I want to impress someone. And in this case, I want to get lucky. So, we are having pasta."

"You are going to want to sleep with me when you get a load of what is in my kitchen before you even start to cook. It is quite the aphrodisiac."

"When it comes to you, Bex, I'm kind of in a permanent state of arousal. Your kitchen might do me in."

"Well, if it gets too much, I'll be right at your side to render aid. I'm very well appointed…"

Rebecca's cellphone chimed with an incoming text from her mother, interrupting what was turning into a very interesting conversation.

Rebecca read the message, looked up at him, and said, "Holy shit."

"What?" Mitch asked as his hand gently kneaded the warm skin of her breast.

"Mom knows. She wrote: *Really, Rebecca, a courthouse wedding? Call me. Now.*"

"How did she find out?" Mitch asked.

"I don't know, but the cat is out of the bag."

"We haven't even gotten our rings yet," he said. "She won't be happy. Alex said she takes jewelry very seriously. She told him that if he ever gets married, he needs to buy his wife a big ring, and it has to hurt him a little. Considering how much he makes, that is going to be a big ring."

"Ergo, the way she has my dad get her a bigger diamond with each five-year anniversary."

"I love your mom. Vic has always been kind to me," Mitch said. "Get ready because, tomorrow, I'm buying you a big ring. I don't need your mother upset, and I want it to hurt a little. Sweet, hot pain. And I'd like you to be the one to make sure I hurt a little." He kissed her breast and gave the nipple a gentle tug with his lips. She arched toward him and, at last, moved away.

"Remember where we were. Right there. Now stop, because I've got to call her," Rebecca complained.

"Put her on speaker, spoilsport," he said as he reached for her butt and gave it a little squeeze.

Rebecca shook her head, "Stop that. I've got to act serious, and that is hard to do when I want to respond in kind...or just... jump you and screw your brains out."

"After the call, you can jump on any part of me you want," he said, and she made an attempt to push him away, but not too strong. "I'm always up for a good screwing."

"Shhh…" she whispered as she called her mother and put the phone on the mattress between them.

"Rebecca?" her mother answered.

"Yeah, it's me—"

"I'm here too, Vic," Mitch said and smiled at Rebecca, who shook her head.

"Am I to understand correctly that congratulations are in order?" Victoria asked, her voice softening.

"Yes, Vic. We got married a few hours ago," Mitch said. "Have I told you that I'm in love with your daughter?"

Rebecca punched his shoulder playfully.

"See, Rebecca? I told you so," Victoria said. "Welcome to the Stark Family, my sweet boy. You know that I always thought of you like a son, Mitch. And your words are music to my ears. Treat my baby well. Keep her happy."

"I will do everything in my power to keep her happy. Thank you. You know I always thought of you as my second mother."

"Oh, sweetie, I'm so happy you two got married."

"We are too. Finally! By the way, Rebecca and I were talking, and we were wondering…Would you be interested in hosting us a reception to celebrate our marriage?" he asked.

"Oh, I'd love that. We can talk about it tonight," Victoria said.

Mitch and Rebecca looked at each other. Silence loomed.

"Rebecca, you haven't forgotten our plans. We've had dinner on the books for several weeks. We will pick you and Mitch up at six."

"Mom, I'm sorry—"

"Sounds great. We will be ready," Mitch said and smiled.

A minute later, they disconnected. When Rebecca was sure they were off the phone, she said to Mitch, "Tonight is our wedding night. Do we really want to spend it with my parents? Because I don't. I want to fool around."

"Having dinner is the lesser of several evils. We have to eat. Come on, let's make the bed and grab a shower. They will be here in ninety minutes."

They showered together, a little longer than necessary, and then dressed. Mitch wore his new designer jeans from the duty-free shops at Heathrow and his freshly pressed white button-down shirt. Rebecca wore a red halter dress.

"I'm going to need some more clothes if we are going to be social. It is warmer in New York than London, but I do like this shirt." Rebecca rubbed a hand over his chest and smiled as her hand slipped under the fabric and rubbed his chest.

"Do we look like we've had a lot of sex in the last day?" Rebecca asked.

"Yes. We look happy," Mitch said. "Besides, how much sex have we had? Okay, I lost count, but are they so stupid to think we hadn't done the horizontal rumba? I mean, seriously, we love each other. We got married. But stop touching me, or I'll toss you onto the nearest flat surface and have my way with you. A quickie before the family arrives."

"No...we can't. My lipstick is perfect. Okay, seriously, does the apartment smell like a sex den?"

"No, it smells like your new perfume. The bed looks made and perfect, not like it has been used within an inch of its life."

"And your cologne. I can smell traces of it," she said. "Maybe we should brew coffee."

"Yeah, right, because after I came from London yesterday to be with you after six years of being apart and pining for you, we got married today...and all we could think about was sharing a cup of joe?"

"I...damn it...my parents will know we've been having sex. Let's just have the windows open anyway."

"We are married. It is okay," Mitch reassured her as her

parents buzzed from the front door. He pulled her close, kissed her, and said, "Let's make it an early night. I've got jet lag."

"I'm sorry. Are you tired?" she asked with concern.

"No, I just want to have more sex with you, but you bought that excuse, so, good, it worked."

She smiled, untangled from Mitch, and said, "You really must be tired." Then she buzzed in her parents.

Thirty seconds later, they appeared. Her mother, Victoria, glowed with happiness for her daughter and Rebecca's father, Garrison, gave Mitch a stern look. He offered Mitch a hand as Victoria hugged Rebecca.

After Mitch shook hands with Garrison, Victoria hugged Mitch and kissed him on the cheek, then said, "I knew you'd come to your senses."

Mitch gave an "aw, shucks" shrug and said, "I think I've been in love with her since the first time I saw her."

"I know," Victoria said, patting his cheek. "I remember the moment it happened. I thought, yes, that is the way it should be."

CHAPTER THIRTEEN

Rebecca

Her parents' driver, Mr. Jensen, drove them to a new restaurant called Platinum that supposedly took months to get into.

"How did you swing a reservation here?" Rebecca asked her mother.

"It is owned by Prudence DeLong. I went to college with her, so I simply called. Her son, Landon, is the head chef. I suggested that I knew we'd have a good time and intended to tell all my friends and our hotel concierges just how spectacular the food was when we dined there to celebrate my daughter's surprise wedding."

"How did you find out about our wedding?" Mitch asked.

"Simple. I was driving by the courthouse on my way to my aqua aerobics class, and I saw you walking down the steps, holding hands. And you," she said, looking toward Rebecca, "were wearing the white Chanel, you know, the one I brought you back from Paris a month ago. Remember what you said when I showed it to you?"

"It looked wedding-y," Rebecca said. "See? I was right."

Mitch grabbed her hand, brought it to his lips, and kissed it.

"Good call, Vic," he said.

"I cannot believe you didn't call us," her father complained. "I didn't even get to walk my only daughter down the aisle."

"I'm a modern woman. I might not have let you anyway,"

Rebecca said. "I don't like the idea of being given away like chattel."

"I don't care how we got to this place, only that we are here. I'm very happy for you both," Victoria said. "It has been a long time coming."

They both thanked her and let the driver help them out of the now-stopped limo.

"Your brother will be shocked," her mother said to Rebecca.

"I'm going to let Mitch tell him," Rebecca said, smiling at her groom.

"We are going to tell him together," Mitch said. "We will call him tomorrow."

"Oh, you don't have to," Victoria said. "He is meeting us here, but I didn't tell him. I figured it was your story to tell."

And Alex was waiting at the table for them, a scowl already on his face. He smiled when he first saw Mitch, but then he figured it out, and the scowl reappeared.

Maybe her parents didn't look at her funny, but her brother Alex had given her the evil eye as soon as he saw her with Mitch.

"What? You never write, you never call, and then you appear with my sister? What gives?" Alex asked.

Rebecca answered before Mitch could.

"Careful how you talk to my husband."

Alex looked from Rebecca to Mitch and asked, "What?"

"We got married today," Mitch said.

Alex's father clapped a stunned Alex on the shoulder and said, "We are all shocked. The women are giddy, so just go with it."

Alex shook his head. "But...you didn't tell any of us... I didn't even know you and Becca were dating. I thought I was your best friend."

"I only asked her at about two this morning," Mitch said.

"Besides, I know how protective you've always been of Bex. I am your best friend."

"Two *this* morning? Where were you? No, wait, don't answer that. When did you get to New York?" Alex asked.

"He got in last night," Rebecca said and then smiled coquettishly as she snuggled against Mitch.

"Oh...god," Alex said, sounding annoyed. "I thought you were engaged to some virgin chick you were going to marry in September. Your boss's daughter, wasn't it?"

"I felt pressured, and I never thought Rebecca could be mine," Mitch said, his arm encircling her. "Lucien and I interviewed Rebecca when she came to London, and it rekindled all of these old feelings. I think I've been in love with your sister since you first brought me home to your family. I think my feelings grew and could not be denied."

"Shit, I need a drink, my best friend and my sister? Shit..."

The waiter magically appeared, and Victoria asked, "Gary, darling, shouldn't we have some champagne to celebrate?"

Garrison looked at his wife. "Yes, darling. I've got it." Then, turning to the waiter, he asked, "You got any Dom, '95 or '96?"

"Yes, sir," the waiter replied.

"Bring us two bottles to start and keep them coming until I tell you otherwise."

They sat at the round table and Rebecca said, "I'm so happy."

Mitch kissed her cheek, and they both laughed.

"This is just so fast," Alex said with a shake of his head.

"You've not been watching. To those of us who have, it isn't fast at all," Victoria said.

Garrison asked, "If I'm understanding this, you just broke off your engagement on...?"

"Tuesday night," Mitch replied. "It didn't go well."

Garrison prompted, "And on Wednesday morning..."

"I was on my way to the office in London, stuck in traffic,

and got to thinking that in a few hours, I could be in New York. I wanted to see Rebecca, be with her, tell her how much I loved her, so I asked the taxi driver to drive to Heathrow."

"You were an unengaged man for only about twenty-four hours?" Alex asked, tag-teaming with his father.

"I knew what I wanted," he said and smiled at Rebecca.

"Alex, Dad, leave Mitch alone. Look at his jet lag. Poor baby can barely stay awake. It isn't fair that you are ganging up on him," Rebecca complained.

"You know Mitch is like a brother to you, Alex, and a son to us. Now, it is just official," Victoria complained. "I'm so happy. And look at Becca. She is glowing."

"She certainly is," Alex agreed through narrowed eyes that looked from Rebecca to Mitch. "She looks very...content."

As appetizers arrived, Mitch told them his plans to live anywhere Rebecca wanted.

"You have enough experience. You can get whatever job you want," Rebecca said and smiled at her husband.

Between their first and second course, Victoria asked, "What kind of engagement ring are you going to get?"

"Something big and impressive, but really, whatever Bex wants," Mitch said and gave her hand a squeeze.

"As it should be. If you will permit me, I have a suggestion. And just so you know, you don't have to take it, but when I suggested it to Gary earlier this evening, he liked it. Didn't you, dear?"

"I did," he said and gave his wife one of his rare smiles. "I like anything that makes my Vicki smile."

"What is your suggestion, Vic?" Mitch asked.

"Since you were twenty, we've gotten to know and love you. You are like the child we didn't have. I have something special I'd like to give you that you can give to your intended should you choose."

Rebecca sat up straighter in her chair. "You're giving him a ring to use as my engagement ring? Wow."

"Not just any ring. Your father gave me the ring after we could see that you had his emerald eyes. With Alex, we had just gotten married, but when you came along, it was six years later, and it hadn't been easy to have you. You were a much-wanted child. And there you were, a beautiful raven-haired little girl with beautiful green eyes."

"Thanks," Alex said softly.

"The emerald? The big emerald? The one I always loved as a child? You are giving it to Mitch?" Rebecca asked her mother.

"Only if he wants it," Garrison said.

Mitch was speechless. Rebecca turned to him and said, "I love the emerald. Ever since I was a little girl, Mom and I would talk about how Dad gave it to her for having me. It was now what they call a push present."

"Well, at the time, it was just very romantic," Victoria said.

"I was in the delivery room. Your birth wasn't easy on your mother," Garrison said. "I felt guilty for getting her pregnant. Then you arrived, and you were beautiful. My little girl."

"I'm so overwhelmed," Mitch said. "I don't know what to say. Victoria, Garrison, I'm so proud that I've gotten to know you. I think of you as my parents more so than my in-laws. Victoria got up from her chair, circled the table, pulled Mitch to her bosom and gave him a tight hug.

From a quick glance around the table, Rebecca could tell that everyone, even Alex, found it hard to speak. Once Victoria had retreated, Mitch leaned toward Rebecca, and then he whispered, "Is this what you want for your engagement ring? I'll get you anything you want. I just want you happy."

"Yes, yes, I want the emerald," she said and started crying. "Just like I've loved you for a very long time, I've loved the emerald since I was a little girl."

Mitch gently dabbed at her tears with his linen napkin and then pulled her into his arms, where she stayed until Victoria gently placed a red leather Cartier ring box next to his champagne glass.

Rebecca heard the box open and Mitch's exhalation of breath.

She turned to look at the ten-carat perfect emerald-cut Colombian emerald framed by two, one-carat triangular-shaped diamonds all set in platinum.

"This is stunning. It is the exact color of Bex's eyes," Mitch said as he freed it from the box and examined it. Then he looked at Rebecca and asked, "Rebecca Alexandra Stark Wilder, will you wear this ring to signify my love and be my wife?"

"Yes," she said as he slipped the cool platinum over the third finger of her left hand. It fit perfectly.

She waggled her fingers and smiled, then gave Mitch a look that needed no explanation. He kissed her in front of her family. Sometime during the kiss, she realized she had moved to his lap, and the entire restaurant was cheering.

Mitch

He was touched. He had always felt very close to Garrison and Victoria but had never voiced his thoughts. It felt good. He was a mushy, in-love guy, and all his emotions were bubbling to the surface. Hell, he couldn't stop touching Rebecca. He couldn't believe she was really his wife. He was so, so damn lucky. He had almost made the biggest mistake of his life. Thankfully, he hadn't.

"How did it go over with your boss that you were dumping his daughter just two months before the wedding?" Alex asked.

Mitch set down his fork. He still felt horrible about how everything unfolded. His intention had never been to hurt anyone. In the long run, he hoped Lily would find the man of her dreams. It was definitely not him. He grimaced before answering. "He's rightfully upset. Better this happened now than at the altar or later. I didn't want to inflict pain on anyone, but at least she now has a chance to meet someone who will feel about her the way I feel about Rebecca. The marriage would not have lasted. I'm certain about that."

"You mentioned finding a new job. Do you still have a job?" Garrison asked.

"If he doesn't fire me, I will give two weeks' notice when I return next week. I hope Rebecca can come with me. I'd like to show her my place and where I like to hang out in London," Mitch said. "Heck, maybe we will start our own security business. We have the time and funds to really think this through."

"She will probably be fired, too," Alex said, looking at his sister. "Collateral damage on her first job."

"Stop trying to be an ass, Alex. It is over, done. Mitch and I are together as we should have always been. I like Mitch's idea, or I will find another job. I really don't care. The only reason I looked into Donovan Security was to be close to Mitch," Rebecca said.

"That is not what you said when you were packing before you went to London," Alex said.

Rebecca looked at her brother and said, "I lied."

"Did you go to work today?" her father asked.

"No, I called in sick."

"So, you want to live in New York?" Garrison asked Mitch.

"I really am finished with London, but I'm open to whatever Rebecca would like to do.

I've had six years to establish my career, but it is up to what she wants now," Mitch said.

Victoria laid a hand over her husband's. Something passed between them, and he nodded. Victoria smiled and said, "You know that we've moved the corporate headquarters to the Pacific Northwest?"

"Portland," Garrison added.

"Yes, something about tax advantages," Rebecca said.

"It is pretty, and you can get a lot more for your money there. Besides, it is centrally located. Closer to Asia. You can be there in four fewer hours," Garrison said, "And it is away from New York. You can still drive easily in Oregon."

"What are you thinking, Dad? I can almost see the wheels turning," Rebecca asked.

"I know what he is thinking, and I approve. Jed Barlow is retiring in a month," Victoria said. "It is causing some concern for the company."

Mitch looked to Rebecca, who was smiling slyly. She turned to Mitch and said, "Jed is the Head of Security for Stark International. It is literally the perfect position for you."

"That is what I was thinking," Garrison said. "It might be too big a job for one person considering how we have expanded. We might need a team of two people. And that way, you could be ambassadors for the family."

"Are you making us a job offer?" Rebecca asked.

"Maybe I am."

"I think we just got a job offer," Rebecca said to Mitch and smiled. "But what about Spencer? Does he have a say in this?"

Spencer Whitlow. Mitch had spent some time with this family cousin because he was a little behind them at Wharton and joined their social circle. Mitch liked him. After Spencer's parents retired, Spencer had stuck a foot in here and there but really hadn't asserted the fact that he was a silent partner in several of the hotels. He seemed to be happy to have Alex and their other cousin, Adam, look out for his interests.

Victoria had been a Whitlow before she married Garrison, and the Whitlows had been involved in the Stark Hotels starting shortly after Victoria married Garrison. The marriage and the business union had been very beneficial. Spencer was a smart man, but Mitch knew he preferred to work with cattle than difficult hotel guests. He was also a horrible Monopoly player.

"Spencer idolizes you, Gary. He will approve whatever you suggest," Victoria said.

"Well, we have mutual trust. You see Mitch, it is yours if you want it," Garrison said. "And whatever you are making at Donovan, just double it. And as for you, Becca. Same consideration. Family looks out for family."

"Hey, now," Alex protested.

"Be happy we didn't hire Becca to be your partner, son," Garrison said. "She did better at Wharton than you did. And I think she'd keep you on a tight leash. And this way, if for some reason you don't head up the company one day, she will be in a position to take over. I have every confidence in her ability, as well as in Mitch's."

"That shut him up," Rebecca said, and Mitch had to chuckle.

CHAPTER FOURTEEN

Rebecca

There were lots of hugs and well wishes as Mitch and Rebecca were dropped off at Rebecca's loft.

"Well," she said when they were alone in the elevator. "I think that went better than I thought it would."

"Alex and your father look at me as if I'm evil incarnate. As if I have violated you in eighteen different ways."

"A girl can wish. I think we are only up to fourteen," she said as she put her arms around his neck, sinking against Mitch as the elevator doors opened. "And I know you are tired, and jet lagged and ready to get to bed. Besides, we've already consummated our wedding, so I won't be expecting you to satisfy my needs tonight. Tomorrow is a different story, however."

She used her key to open the door, and then Mitch swung into action, throwing her over his shoulder, to her delight.

He locked the door and deposited her on the bed. Then Mitch tossed off his clothing in less time than it took to comprehend. Rebecca sat up on her elbows and smiled.

"And here I thought you really were tired."

"No, I played that up to make it an early night, so I could get you back here and be naked. I hope you don't mind."

"I don't," she said. "And I don't need you to be gentle. My need for you... well... I'm kind of ravenous."

They ended up on the rug next to her bed, but Rebecca didn't know how they ended up there because they had started on the bed. Now, they both had rug burns on their backsides. As she panted—straddling his lap, her legs wrapped around his waist, his body still deeply rooted inside hers—she said, "I think I might have passed out for a few seconds there."

Mitch swallowed hard, leaned against the side of the bed, and held Rebecca to him as he said, "It was very intense... And very, very good. Damn. I've never..."

She rested her head against his shoulder and let him rub her back as she said, "I know... It is like our bodies were made for each other. We know just what to do."

She had never fit so well with a man. He was a good ten inches taller than she, but their bodies were made to give each other pleasure. It was such a remarkable thing. Her other lovers, well, she hadn't had that many, but none of them could satisfy her so completely. The orgasms she had with Mitch left her entire body trembling. They weren't a feel-good moment. They were a feel-good hour. She wondered if it was just the fact Mitch was making love to her. To look up and see his face. To know it was Mitch sharing the experience, the feelings, and the passion. That helped everything along, but it was a combination of Mitch and his perfect body.

"I'm not done with you yet, but if you're tired..."

"No, I'm not tired. I'm just getting warmed up," she said. "I'm not done with you yet, either."

"I love you," Mitch said as she smiled, and he kissed her damp cheek.

"I love you too," she said as he grazed on her chin and then found her lips.

Picking her up as he stood, he placed her on the bed and leaned into her so that she would sink into the mattress, their lips meeting again.

This second time they made love was slower, gentler, and much more sensual compared to the satisfying, primal need of their first mating, which had more to do with action and satisfaction than emotion.

Later, she handed him a bottled water, cold from the fridge, as they lay in the tangled sheets.

They each drank deeply from their bottles, and then Mitch asked, "Would you really be okay with me working for your family business?"

"I think I'd love it," she said, looking at Mitch's face and noticing the way it softened. "I think we'd have a ball."

"Good, because it sounds kind of interesting," he said, setting the water on her nightstand and reaching for her.

Mitch

The next day, he wondered if he had channeled some ancient ancestor who proclaimed, "Mine," when his woman was beside him. Mitch could not explain it, but when the jeweler showed him a diamond eternity band for his Bex—and he slipped it on next to the emerald, and it not only fit but looked nice—he relaxed a little.

"It is gorgeous," Rebecca gushed.

"I like that it looks like a wedding band to anyone who would look," he said.

"What?" she whispered, "So people will know I'm taken? That I belong to you?"

He didn't have to think at all before responding. "Yes, damn straight. You are mine, and I am yours."

"Then you will understand why I want you to wear a ring. My ring," she said, as her right hand discretely lowered and cupped his butt. This was what he liked about his Bex. She could be naughty, which he loved.

He kissed the tip of her nose and repeated, "Yes."

She turned to the jeweler who was staring at her engagement ring and said, "Now then, something for my husband, something in platinum. How about some diamonds?"

"No, you get to wear the diamonds. I just want a smooth, plain band," Mitch said.

"A big, thick one," she said with a straight face.

After a few minutes of looking, they settled for a plain platinum band that she slipped on his finger.

"Why are you smiling like that?" she asked.

"I guess this makes it real. We belong to each other," he said and earned another kiss from her.

The jeweler looked uncomfortable. Mitch thought he should. He was the third wheel in their intimate moment.

"We will take them," Mitch said, his eyes never leaving Rebecca's face.

"The total is going to be—"

"Just put them on my card," Mitch said, handing the man his platinum credit card. It seemed right to use a platinum card. "We'd like to wear them out because we are already married."

"Well, congratulations! Might I say I love your emerald. What a gorgeous piece. I know we don't have anything like it in the store. Where did you get it?" the jeweler asked.

"Mom gave it to me to give to her," Mitch said, still looking at Rebecca, who smiled and let Mitch pull her close for another hug. "It is a family piece."

"Your mother must have thought you chose well," the jeweler quipped.

"She thinks of my Bex as a daughter," Mitch said, making Rebecca laugh.

CHAPTER FIFTEEN

Mitch

M itch watched as Rebecca moved around his London flat carefully. They had been married exactly a week, and she had agreed to come back with him as he extricated himself from Donovan Security. He liked to think of their time in New York as a mini honeymoon. They were tourists for a week, doing everything from visiting the Statue of Liberty to dining in Tribeca.

They had also talked again to her father, Garrison Stark, about their new positions. They would be starting to work at Stark International in less than a month and be based out of Portland at the new company headquarters. Mitch's head was spinning with all the changes, but in a good way. He hoped to take Bex on a real honeymoon if they could squeeze it in, but every day and night, when they found out more about each other and different ways to bring pleasure to each other, it felt like they were already on a honeymoon.

"I feel bad for blindsiding Bruce. He asked me if I was feeling better," Rebecca said. "I said yes because technically, I'm feeling a lot better than I was because I'd had some major life changes. Then I told him I was quitting and asked him to check his email for my resignation letter."

"And then what happened?" Mitch asked as Rebecca paused to look out the window at the Thames.

"He guessed that we were together, but at least he was decent about it. He said, 'Well, I heard a rumor that you were with Mitch Wilder.' I didn't want to add to the gossip. I just said that my parents wanted me to work in the family business, and he said I could go when I wanted but that he was disappointed to see such a promising candidate leave. I thanked him, and I said my security badge, laptop, phone, etc., were on my desk in New York. He said, 'But you are in London.' I didn't know what to say to that. How did he know I was here? Did they chip me sometime when I was asleep?"

Mitch looked contemplative. "That's actually not a bad idea."

"Stop it," she said.

"Kidding," Mitch said. "But seriously, when I go into the office today, they are going to see my wedding ring. Tongues are going to wag, but I don't regret anything. And I don't want to hide the ring."

"Good. I bet Bruce told Lucien I was in London. The cat is out of the bag. I feel bad for Lily, but I would not want to change places with her. In a way, before you came to see me, I was her, the woman in love with someone who was promised to another."

Mitch came up behind her, wrapped his arms around her from behind, cupped her breasts, and said, "I'm sorry. I didn't handle it well, but then I don't know if it could ever be handled well."

"I don't think it could," she said and leaned back into Mitch.

"Better now than a year from now," he said and kissed her neck. It would be hard to be away from her today.

"What do you think will happen when you go to the office today?"

"I'll give two weeks, but Lucien will more than likely want me to clean up anything that is pending. Unfortunately, I've got some nasty shit on my desk that needs tidying up. What will you do while I'm at work?"

"There are a few things I've always wanted to see that I didn't see when I was here with my family. I want to go to the Tower of London, the National Gallery, maybe have tea somewhere. Plus, Dad asked me to visit Stark International Hotel and give him a detailed report as to anything I see that is concerning. When I was here for my interview, I did mention a few things. He wants me to do a follow-up. One thing that stood out was the food from the room service menu, which was bland and heavy. I need to look into that. On the whole, I thought the hotel looked a little dated, maybe dirty."

"Garrison Stark's daughter. The apple didn't fall far from the tree. It sounds like you have a few projects. What did he say about Alex?" Mitch asked as Rebecca turned in his arms to face him.

"Alex will be in London next week on his way through Europe. Hopefully, we can grab dinner, as long as he doesn't threaten to kill you."

"He just needs some time to get used to us being together. His best bud and his sister are doing it right under his nose." He continued to nuzzle her neck as she giggled, and then he said, "We could invite him here for dinner. One last dinner party before we move back to the States."

"That would be nice. Heck, we could even cater. Will you miss London?" Rebecca asked.

"I'll miss some of the people, but I'll be glad to be away from some of the others. And I'll miss the parks. I love the parks here."

"Could we take a walk in your favorite?"

"Kensington Gardens. And yes, I'd love to show you around, especially my favorite park. Next weekend, we can visit Windsor Castle on Saturday and Kensington on Sunday." Mitch kissed her and then glanced down at his watch. Then he said, "Okay shoot, I'm going to be late because my sexy wife is distracting me."

"I'm sorry," she said.

"I'm not," he said and kissed her deeply, then he leaned his forehead against hers. "You realize this is the first time we've been apart since we got married?"

"Yes," she said and added, "I don't know what I'll do with myself."

"Be careful, and leave me a note or send me a text if you go anywhere, okay?"

"I can do that," she said.

"You should go back to bed and rest up," he said with a half-smile.

"Maybe I will, but I'll miss you. I'll be lonely in that big bed all by myself."

"That's how I felt every night before we got married. I'll try to come home at lunch, but I don't know what is waiting for me at the office," he said. "I don't want you to wait around for me."

"I'll see you at six," she said.

"Yes, you will. And I hope you will be well rested, Mrs. Wilder."

"Count on it," she said and gave his butt a playful squeeze as he kissed her goodbye. It would be so much easier to stay with her all day. Maybe another cuddle in the bed and then act like tourists for the rest of the day. But this was what being an adult meant. He had to go to the office and do this the right way.

Walking into Donovan Security was like crossing into enemy territory. What had once felt so comfortable and a place he considered home now felt odd and different. Everyone, from the security guard to his assistant, gave him what he would liken to the evil eye. They knew. And where he was once on the inside, now he was on the outside.

He walked by the desk of Sally, his secretary, and she was curt, more curt than usual, when he offered his customary, "Good morning, Sally."

"Lucien wants to see you as soon as you arrive," she answered coldly and handed him a stack of messages. Maybe he'd be joining Becca on that little walk in Kensington Gardens earlier than anticipated.

His briefcase was sitting on the center of his desk blotter. The taxi driver had done as he asked. He spun the dial, entered his code, which happened to be Rebecca's birthday, and opened the case. He found Lily's engagement ring in the pocket where he'd left it. He would give it back to Lucien.

Then he looked at his desk and gauged how many things he'd have to take with him when he left for good. Everything that was important would fit in his briefcase. He turned over the framed the photo of Lily. He wanted to give it back to her father, but no way would that go well, so he faced it backward and set it on the credenza so he couldn't see her.

Time to face the firing squad. He left his office, didn't speak to Sally as he walked past her, and made his way to the office at the end of the hall that Lucien had always said would be Mitch's one day. No, it wouldn't.

Lucien's secretary wasn't at her desk, so he knocked on Lucien's office door and waited until he heard a gruff, "Come in."

He entered and saw the other man's eyes narrow at the sight of him. This wasn't going to be good.

"You're back," Lucien said.

Mitch had spent a little time each day he was in New York working from Rebecca's apartment.

"I'm sorry. I really needed to get my head straight."

"And that involved disappearing for a week after you broke my daughter's heart?"

"That wasn't my intention. Things just happened, as you know," Mitch said as he took the chair on the other side of Lucien's desk. "I'm sure Lily will find the right man, someone who is hopelessly in love with her. That is my hope, my wish for her. Regardless, I thought it was better than marrying her when I didn't love her the way I should."

"Well, after you broke my daughter's heart, what exactly did you do?" Lucien was angry. He was barely holding it together. Mitch wasn't sure he could blame him.

Up until a week ago, Lucien was going to be his father-in-law. Mitch was being groomed to take over this company, but he walked away from it all for Rebecca. And although she was totally worth it, he didn't expect Lucien to understand.

"Even you noticed how I tried to ignore my friend, Rebecca Stark. I wanted to love Lily like I love Rebecca, and I tried. I tried every time I saw her, but instead of getting closer, we grew further apart. It was not a surprise to Lily, not really. She was increasingly frustrated with me because I wasn't the man she needed me to be. She deserves to have someone who really loves her. I truly, truly hope she finds someone who loves her the way she deserves. I'm sorry. I'm not explaining myself well. But I think it would have hurt more if we'd tried to make it work, and it hadn't. Because I have to tell you, I don't see how it ever would have worked, not while Rebecca was in my heart."

There was silence as Lucien silently rocked in his chair, then he let out a large breath and said, "This is obviously not the way I wanted things to work out. And here I was planning on turning over my business to you. Well, that isn't going to happen. You really messed up, Mitch. You hurt my girl."

"I didn't want to, Lucien. This isn't the way I thought things would go, either. I'm glad we stopped this before we made a huge mistake. And, I think it would have been a huge mistake."

"Well, at least you didn't do it right before the wedding, like the week before or after marrying her. I think it would have been worse. It is bad, but it would've been a lot worse if you were married and then had taken that Stark girl as your lover."

What if he hadn't seen Rebecca? Would he have married Lily? He hoped not, but there was no way to know now.

"I'm very sorry," Mitch said.

"I have a very upset daughter at home who has a wedding dress and no groom."

How upset could she be? Mitch knew she had been unhappy with him for weeks.

Mitch said nothing more. In time, they would come to see that this was best for all of them, but at the moment, it was too soon.

"I should have never interviewed Garrison Stark's daughter," Lucien complained.

"It was a matter of time, Lucien. If it hadn't been Rebecca, I hope Lily or I would have come to our senses and spoken about our fears. I hope one of us would have called it off before we walked down the aisle. Rebecca just sped it up a bit, but it isn't solely her fault."

"I'm just not sure how we go forward from here. I heard that Rebecca Stark quit yesterday. I think that was probably for the best."

"Yes. I think it would be best if I quit, too," Mitch said.

"You are a valued, if not the *most* valued, member of the team, but you've broken my trust, and I can't forgive that. Regretfully, I've come to the conclusion that I think it would be best if you and Donovan Security parted ways."

"I understand that in light of the circumstances. I don't wish to bring additional pain to Lily."

"I noticed the ring. Did you do something stupid, like marry Rebecca Stark?" Lucien asked.

"I thought about removing it, but I'm trying not to deceive you. We did marry last week in New York," Mitch replied.

"That is quick," Lucien said. "And a bit surprising. You really know how to screw up your life. You've ruined everything in less than a week. I bet you didn't think about that when you were sleeping with Rebecca Stark. No one will hire you, not in this industry." The man was baiting Mitch. It was harder than he thought not to say anything. He'd always thought Lucien had an ugly side. Well, he was seeing it.

"I'm willing to take that risk," Mitch said, barely controlling his anger. His hands were balled into fists. How dare he speak about Rebecca that way? It was everything Mitch could do not to stand up, haul Lucien out of his chair, and punch him in the face. But Mitch and Rebecca already had better jobs and each other. Wasn't that all that mattered?

"I'm just sorry I had *Mrs. Wilder* fly over here for an interview, but I didn't think anything would happen, like you turning into some kind of over-sexed, brainless lunatic. It turned into a shambolic situation and really showed your true colors."

"If there isn't anything else, I'll clear out my desk and email you my letter of resignation," Mitch said. The desire to hit Lucien still loomed large.

"Lily deserves much better than you."

Mitch realized Lucien wouldn't let it go. He wanted his pound of flesh.

"Yes, she deserves a lot more. Sven in accounting likes her," Mitch said. "He was always looking longingly at her, and he is a nice guy."

"He is a nice guy. She could do much worse. Well, she already has, thanks to you."

"Believe it or not, I want Lily to be happy. I've found my happiness. It is her turn."

"I'm already working on your replacement."

"Good. I'll wrap up the transactions on my desk and leave."

"We have some very important meetings coming up," Lucien said.

"If you'd like, I'll stay for those and then make my exit, or I will leave today. Your call."

"Don't be civil for a letter of recommendation. I won't be writing you one. But I need you to clean up the mess on your desk. You'll need to stay for the two weeks as outlined in your employment contract, and you are not to discuss Lily in any way. Do not call, text, or email her. I want you to stay away from her. And please, *please* violate your noncompete. I'd like to drag you through the mud and sue your ass."

"My intentions are to go into the private sector. Who knows? Maybe one of our clients is hiring." *I'd love to have them fire Donovan Security.*

"Get out of my office," Lucien spat, like a spoiled child who hadn't gotten his way.

"Love to," Mitch replied. He should have just left. But he had never been raised to leave a job half done. He would finish out the two weeks and then leave for good.

Rebecca

Okay, Rebecca thought. She had watched her mother make lasagna for years. She had visited the Tower of London and then actually stopped at a little Italian grocery store near where Mitch lived and purchased everything she needed to make her mother's specialty. Okay, some of the items were a little random, but she thought they would work. That, and two phone calls with her mother later, the lasagna was in the oven, and she had opened the first bottle of chianti and was well into her first glass.

At a little after six, the door opened, and Mitch arrived with a smile. He dropped his briefcase, took off his coat, and made a beeline for Rebecca, who handed him a glass of wine and gave him a kiss.

"Welcome home," she said and wrapped her arms around her.

"After six years of coming home to an empty, quiet apartment, it was wonderful to have you here, waiting for me," he said and kissed her. Then he said, "Something smells wonderful, besides you. Are you cooking?"

"Well, I'm trying to make Mom's lasagna because I know you like it. It is going to be something. I mean it is cheese, sauce, and pasta. How bad can it be?"

"I don't know if you have ever looked sexier, wearing your little apron and holding a glass of wine."

"Keep that talk up, and you are going to get lucky tonight, maybe more than once."

"I think I'm going to get lucky anyway," he said.

He kissed her again and she said, "I need to pull that lasagna out of the oven in ten minutes or turn the oven down to warm while we do whatever we might want to do in the bedroom to celebrate your return."

"Turn the oven down to warm now," he said, and then, "On second thought, allow me." He went to the oven and did it himself. Then he returned to Rebecca, grabbed her hand, and led her into his bedroom.

Later, after their bodies had been reacquainted after a day apart, they lay together, snuggling under the covers as she rubbed her bare breasts against Mitch's chest. She was enjoying how his chest hair tickled her nipples as she said, "How was your day, dear?"

He laughed and said, "Bad. Lucien is a serious jerk. This afternoon, he sent me a memo that he wants me to deliver a few things to Iraq next week, and then I'll be done."

Rebecca sat up, pulling away from Mitch.

"What?" she asked. "What did you just say?"

"I've done it before. It is no big deal. We have a military contractor in Iraq. We are delivering two helicopters to this American at Collins Industries. He's making a mint on military contracts. The government pays a lot, so I have to go to make sure everything happens smoothly because the contract is worth a lot of money to all parties concerned. Nothing ever happens. There really isn't a need for a security detail on this mission, but Lucien is being an ass, so we are pulling out all the stops.

Delivering these helicopters after rolling out the red carpet for them."

"Then why do you have to go? Why can't someone else go?"

"Because I'm the one who has been negotiating this deal. The military contractor, Jake Collins, is my client. It will end things on a pleasant note, which is a positive change, as we did not have a good conversation about my leaving today. But at least I can do this and end things cleanly. I want to end this position with integrity."

"I don't want you to do this," Rebecca said. "I'm really worried. I don't want you going to Iraq."

"Bex, I used to do this kind of thing all the time when I began at Donovan. Maybe six times a year. You should see my passport. It is covered with visas and stamps. Heck, I was just in Iraq two weeks ago, and the visa is still valid for another two weeks. It is no big deal. You just didn't know about it. I even speak a little Farsi, which is very helpful in hotels and restaurants," he said with a chuckle. "Let's just say I can order lamb vs. camel."

"This isn't funny. It is Iraq," she said. "There is always crap going on over there. I really don't want you to go."

"Let's sleep on it and see how we feel over the next couple of days."

"Um, I have no say in this, and I know there will be no changing your mind or mine. You are going to do it because you feel guilty, and that is bullshit, Mitch. This is dangerous. Please do not do this. Just walk away. Screw integrity."

"Honey, my Bex," he said, pulling her into his arms. "Do you think I'd do anything that would take me away from the woman I've been in love with for years and have just now finally gotten together with?"

"I don't know, but I hope not," she said and leaned against his shoulder. "You might not see it coming. You don't know what will happen."

"I do. We have it planned. And as for us, we are at the beginning of our story. Once this is over, you'll realize it was nothing. No big deal. I wouldn't do it if I had any concerns."

"How long will you be gone?" she asked.

"Three days, maybe four at most."

"Okay…okay…Can I go with you?" she asked.

"No, not to Iraq. It is safe for me to do this, but if you go with me, there becomes an added danger. Some of the men refuse to deal with women. It is a different culture. It would not work."

He must have surmised how she felt because he pulled her close and said, "I love you. This is standard operating procedure. It will be alright. I'll come back in three days. We will pack up this flat and fly to New York as planned. After we've done the same to your place, we move to Portland. We will find a house, an actual house, and we will pick out things like wallpaper and colors. Then, if you want, we will have a honeymoon. Wouldn't that be fun? We will get a damn dog. Whatever you want. Heck, we could ask Vic to help us. I like how she sexed up your apartment with all that red."

"All I want is you," she said and looked up at him, her face crumpling. His face softened.

"Honey, please don't cry."

But she couldn't stop. They ate lasagna at the kitchen bar and drank wine, but Rebecca leaked tear after tear. She couldn't stop. And even when he took her to bed later that night and held her, she still cried.

The next night, he came home with a definite departure date. She felt his words like a knife to her gut. She did not want him to go.

As they lay in bed that night, Mitch spooned Rebecca and kissed her bare shoulder before he whispered in her ear, "I have a little surprise for tomorrow."

"Damn, I was hoping it was something like, 'I'm not going to

Iraq after all'," she said and turned to face him, their noses brushing in the twilight.

"Iraq is going to be fine," he said, pulling her tighter to him. "You won't even miss me."

"I will miss you. I already miss you," Rebecca replied and when he said nothing more, she asked, "Okay, what is the surprise?"

"I was able to get us tickets to Windsor Castle. Our entry time is 10:30 am, which is unbelievably lucky. They are sold out for the next three weeks. Tomorrow, we will take a cab ride to Windsor and then have a wonderful lunch and return. Does that sound good?"

"We will be tourists," she said, smiling in the dark. "I'm excited."

"It is almost like a date," he replied, and kissed the tip of her nose.

"I wish we could have done more of that," she said.

"I'll make it up to you," he said, "Married dates. I think we are going to have lots of fun."

They held hands as they walked through the castle and then through St. Georges Chapel. The weather was beautiful, the bright summer sun making a rare British appearance.

"Who are your favorites?" he whispered as they walked inside the cool chapel past vaults that held various sovereigns.

"I'm partial to George V and Queen Mary," Rebecca replied in a demure whisper.

"Okay, why? They've been dead since before you were born."

"They loved each other. I like to think they had something special," she said giving his hand an extra squeeze.

"We definitely have something special," he said. Then he looked around to make sure they weren't about to get run over by eager tourists and kissed her. They took photos of each other and then someone offered to take their photo together.

They stopped in little souvenir shops and bought a Bobbie bottle opener for themselves and a bobblehead of the King for Alex.

On the ride back to London, after a lovely lunch at one of the small hotels near the castle Rebecca looked at her phone. She vowed that the photo of the two of them with Windsor Castle in the background was suitable for framing.

On their last night together, they had a quiet dinner with candles, wine, and ginger ale for her. She didn't know what to say. She had something to tell him, but she didn't know how he would take the news.

"Are you okay?" he asked.

"No, I'm a mess," she said and started to cry.

He got out of his chair, walked to hers, and pulled her up close. Then he held her and said, "I'm sorry, but this is no big deal. Once I deliver these helicopters, I'm done. With any luck, I will only be gone for two nights, three tops."

She cried in earnest then and said, "I need to tell you something. Maybe it will make a difference to you."

She didn't know how he would react to this. She hoped he would be as excited as she was.

"What?" he asked.

"My period should have started two days ago. I'm either really stressed or pregnant. I don't know. I think I might be pregnant. I know it has only been a couple of weeks, but we've really had a lot of sex."

She waited, then Mitch smiled and pulled her close and said, "A baby, wouldn't that be something?"

"I bought a test, but I'm too scared to take it."

"Bex, take it. I want to know."

"But what if I'm not?" she asked, looking up at him and seeing the hope in his eyes. "A month ago, I didn't know if I could ever get pregnant, so I put it out of my mind. But now there is hope. I will be upset if I'm not pregnant."

"And what if you are?" he asked and smiled.

She lowered her head and said, "We can't get our hopes up. It happened so quickly."

"Well, we can hope you are, and it isn't like I've just met you. We've known each other for ten years," he said. "When are you going to take the test?"

"I could take it now," she said and opened a drawer in the kitchen that held a bag from the local pharmacy. She took the kit out of the bag and reread the directions she'd read that afternoon.

"How can I help you?" he said as he wrapped his arms around her.

"Try not to be disappointed if the answer is negative," she said, and he kissed her.

"Either way, it is okay," he said. "I just like to think that all our lovemaking resulted in a baby. It is kind of exciting. If it did happen, I bet it happened on the afternoon we got married."

"Yes, that was particularly spectacular," Rebecca said with a wink. Then she pulled away from him and walked to the bathroom.

"And if you aren't," he said as she walked away, "I think we should keep practicing a lot. We will get there eventually."

She smiled at him over her shoulder, then shut the door. He made practice a lot of fun.

Five minutes later, they were both looking at a stick that showed two pink lines.

Mitch looked at her and said, "I love you. And I guess I knocked you up."

She smiled, remembering some of their more intimate

moments. "I love you too, and I would agree. I think you made me pregnant."

They turned and smiled at each other, and then they hugged and kissed.

In between kisses, he said, "I'm telling you. It was the afternoon we fell off the bed. I just know it."

"That was a pretty fabulous time," she said, remembering it was a standout orgasm that she was pretty sure people on the street below could hear.

"Shall we recreate it?" he asked as he slipped his hand inside her blouse and cupped her breast. His body always ran a little warmer than hers. She enjoyed the warmth of his fingers as they sought and found her nipple. Then, he began to knead her flesh in a suggestive way that he knew she liked. She needed his mouth where his hand was, and she knew he wouldn't mind her request.

Rebecca moaned at his touch and managed to say, "The couch is right over there. I don't think I can make it to the bedroom. I want your mouth where your fingers are."

"I can think of a few places I'd like to put my mouth," he said as he led her to the couch.

They made love in front of the fire. There was a different tone to their lovemaking now that they knew they were pregnant. They kept smiling at each other, and Mitch placed his hand on her tummy several times and then kissed the space where his hand rested.

As they lay cuddled under a blanket on the floor, having ended up there after starting on the couch, he asked, "Boy or girl? The first thing that pops in your head."

"Girl," Rebecca said, and added, "with your dimples."

"And your green eyes," he said.

"Not to get ahead of ourselves, but what would you like to name a little girl?" Rebecca said.

"My mother was Emily, which I've always liked, but if you

don't, that could be a middle name," he said. "Or some version of it."

"I like Emily. And if it is a boy?" she asked.

"Well, Rebecca Alexandra Stark, can you think of two birds with one stone?"

"No, we are not naming a son after my brother."

"It is after your middle name," Mitch countered.

"No, no, no. I'd be more apt to do Mitchell Junior," she said.

"No way," he said.

"Okay, we still have some work to do," she said.

"I'll think about it on my trip," he said.

She tensed, and she knew he felt it because he held her tighter and said, "It is going to be okay."

After dinner, he packed a small bag for Iraq while she watched silently from the bed where she sat and worried.

CHAPTER SIXTEEN

Mitch

S aying goodbye to Rebecca was harder than he thought it would be. He would only be gone two to three nights at most, but she was upset, so upset, he could not ignore it. She cried and clung to him at the door as he prepared to leave. For the first time in six years, he was a little worried about this delivery himself. He had done this kind of thing at least a dozen times before, so he didn't know why this bothered him, but it did. Possibly it was because he knew what waited for him back home, and he didn't want her to be alone. Or it was because his gut was telling him not to go.

"Will you be able to call me?" she asked, her arms around him as he looked down at her tear-streaked face. He felt awful for hurting her. She had been employed by Donovan, so she knew the rules.

"No, Bex, I'm sorry. We adhere to radio silence to keep security tight. I'm sorry. I'll just be home in three or four days. I know it is too soon for us to be apart."

She nodded and said, "I really hate this."

"I'll call you before we take off from Heathrow and then when we land back in London if I can. Remember, this is one and done. When I finish with this, I'm done with Donovan Security. In a week, we will be in New York cleaning out your apartment. In two weeks, we will be in Portland and starting to look at neighborhoods. So, try to think of more pleasant things while I'm away."

"Oh sure, that will be easy. I wish we could fast forward to

New York," she said as he dabbed at her tears with a silk hand-kerchief.

"Me too, Bex." He kissed her a final time and said goodbye.

Mitch went to the airport and boarded Donovan Security's private jet bound for Saudi Arabia with three other colleagues. The helicopters were already in Saudi Arabia, having been shipped there and waiting at the shipper's point of entry. They would inspect the helicopters and ride two hours with the pilots to deliver them to the client in Iraq the next day. One helicopter that belonged to Donovan Security would bring them back to Saudi Arabia, where, after delivery, they could then fly back to London.

"I really hate this part of the job," one of Mitch's coworkers said.

Mitch agreed. "This is my last delivery. It's my last anything with the company."

"I heard you got married," said Jeff, one of the security personnel.

"I did," Mitch replied.

"I thought you were marrying Lily Donovan."

"No, we broke up. It was for the best."

"I bet that really pissed off Lucien. No wonder you are leaving the company."

"Yeah, well, she will find the right guy, but I wasn't the one," Mitch said.

They flew to Riyadh, Saudi Arabia. The flight took the better part of seven hours. It was still light enough when they arrived that they were able to inspect the helicopters. Then, they all went to the local Hilton hotel where they were staying for the next two nights. They had dinner at the hotel restaurant named the Lotus.

Mitch thought about calling Rebecca, but he wasn't kidding with what he told her. As a precaution, when on a delivery, they were not allowed to communicate with their families. Until they were back in London, it was radio silence. She was five hours behind his time, so when he got ready for bed, he thought of her probably having dinner.

His floor-to-ceiling windows had a wonderful view, but he was uneasy. Without Rebecca, with the delivery still ahead, he felt a great deal of apprehension. He needed to get a grip. This was an easy babysitting job. Why he was so upset, he didn't know, but he needed to let it go.

Sleeping alone in his king-sized bed didn't feel right. He reached for Rebecca more than once in the night. He missed her, but he was very glad she wasn't with him. He thought of her back at his flat by herself, which was good. He didn't like that she was so worried, but there wasn't much he could do about that.

They left at six the next morning, wearing the black uniforms that Donovan Security wore when delivering equipment. It was referred to as "Ninja Wear," and Mitch would be happy to give it up.

He rode with a pilot in one of the new helicopters. He preferred it when they worked directly with the military. As it was, they were hired by a military contractor. In their contract, the client was supposed to let the military know their plans for delivery of equipment. Did he trust Jake Collins to do it? Nope.

Donovan Security personnel rode inside each of the helicopters with the pilot, who flew in military formation prearranged by the pilots.

Everything on the two-hour journey was smooth--until it wasn't.

Everything changed in an instant. They heard a noise like a shriek, but before Mitch could even ask about it, he knew. The helicopter that was in front and slightly to the right of them seemed to shake. Before they could even comprehend what they were seeing, it exploded into a massive fireball. Surprise turned to horror as they grasped what had happened. The shriek was a missile breaking the sound barrier.

Mitch could not believe his eyes as the aircraft was there and then simply gone. He felt the heat of the fire and had to shield his eyes from the brightness, despite his sunglasses, as he tried to comprehend what he was seeing. Had it exploded because there was a bomb onboard, or had someone shot at it?

It took Mitch several moments to understand, but then he became aware that something had hit the side of their aircraft so hard it threw the helicopter off balance, and the pilot was swearing as they dropped rapidly from the sky. The last thing he heard was the pilot speaking to someone on the radio, issuing what he knew to be a mayday.

He thought of Rebecca and their unborn baby. Then everything went black.

Rebecca

When the call on her cellphone read, "Donovan Security," Rebecca smiled. Mitch had found a way to call her.

"I thought I wasn't going to hear from you—"

"Rebecca?"

It wasn't Mitch. In fact, it sounded like Lucien Donovan.

"Lucien?" she asked.

"I'm afraid I have some upsetting news."

Rebecca sat down on the couch and felt her heart beating in her chest.

"We had an incident with the helicopters. There is no easy way to say this. They were shot down en route to the client. It was a total loss. There were no survivors."

Rebecca didn't speak. She didn't move despite noise she could hear in the background. Later, she would find out it was someone knocking on the door of the flat. It got louder, but she didn't hear it as she ended the call and tried to stand. Instead, the floor ran up to meet her. She fainted. That is where her brother found her, after he had the building manager open the door to the flat.

She opened her eyes and saw her brother. Alex had come to see them in London after all.

"I heard you inside, but you didn't answer, so I made the manager open your door," he said, the concern evident on his face.

"Mitch died," she said and started to cry as she held up her cellphone.

Alex grabbed the phone, hit redial, and heard the news again from Lucien Donovan.

Hours later, Rebecca sat on the couch in Mitch's flat with a blanket wrapped around her and watched as Alex started trying to find answers. She hadn't eaten, nor had she slept. The call from Lucien Donovan had been adamant. He'd had reports from the client who was supposed to get the helicopters. There were no survivors. Alex wouldn't believe it, and Rebecca had never been more thankful for his stubbornness.

Alex sat at Mitch's desk with a laptop and his cellphone.

He started with a number a friend had given him for the U.S. Embassy in London. The friend had a connection. Rebecca listened as he explained this, but she didn't care what they had to do to get answers.

She did offer, "How about someone directly from the State Department?"

"If we strike out here, that is my next call."

Rebecca watched, feeling a desperate chill in her bones that didn't want to go away despite the down comforter she'd taken from Mitch's bed. She had ceased to care about anything the moment she'd gotten the call from Lucien Donovan. Maybe she was in shock, but she hoped, she prayed that she would wake up from the worst dream of her life.

After two hours, Alex was telling Mitch's story for the fifth time to another person, and this time, it appeared he was getting somewhere. He paced as he talked. This time it went on for a half hour, and then Alex ended the call and joined his sister on the couch.

"What did he say?" she asked.

"He is going to look into it. He was aware of the helicopter crash. I guess he monitors contractors in Iraq. London, or the U.K., seems to be the hub for contractors who want to work in foreign countries. Here is the thing: If he confirms that Mitch is dead, the story ends. We must move on and let it go. Those are his words, not mine. If Mitch somehow survived and was injured or was captured by someone who might want to ransom him, this man, Nathan Kelly, well, then he steps in. In fact, he takes over. He would be the person who manages the negotiations or keeps us informed of how the negotiations are going. He wasn't exactly clear on that."

"Kidnapped?" she asked, her hand going to her mouth.

"It happens, Becca. I think it would be better than a couple of alternatives."

"It is all bad," she said as tears trickled down her face. "What is he doing now, this man you talked to?"

"He starts talking to the contacts he has in Iraq. You've seen the news about prisoners and people that are held for ransom. You know that there is a lot of intervention when this happens. Lots of unnamed sources. The politicians, maybe even the president get involved."

"It takes a long time, but at least there would be hope, which is something we can't count on," Rebecca said.

"No, we can't. I'm sorry, Becca. I hope there is news. I hope we get something definitive, but I think we have to prepare for the worst. It is the last thing I want to say to you," Alex said and then grew frustrated. "What was Mitch thinking? You hadn't even had a honeymoon yet. Why did he go?"

"He wanted to leave with integrity. He felt guilty about Lily. He wanted to make up for it."

"I wish he had less integrity," Alex whispered.

"I tried to stop him," Rebecca whispered and then started to cry. "I wish I'd tried harder."

Alex sat next to her, pulled her close, and held her tightly to him.

"I'm sorry, Becca. It isn't your fault. Hell, Mitch thought he was doing the right thing. Ending his time at Donovan on a high note. I just can't believe it. I'm here for you."

"If there was ever a time I needed my big brother, it is now," she said.

They sat around the flat and waited. They didn't sleep. They barely ate. Alex paced. Rebecca cried.

The call from Nathan Kelly came two days later, and it wasn't good news.

Alex ended the call and sank to the nearest chair. His hand covered his eyes as he struggled to process whatever the man had said to him.

Rebecca silently cried as she sat down in the chair next to her brother and felt his arms go around her in comfort and shared grief.

"What did he say?" she asked.

"They lost five men in the attack. The State Department has requested the return of what they found, but it is complicated because several of the men were British, so now it is a joint negotiation. This isn't the news we wanted."

"Which means Mitch might never come home," Rebecca said.

"If they are able to identify his remains, it will take time. They aren't sure that Iraq will cooperate."

"Then they are sure that he didn't survive?"

"The man started the call by apologizing for our loss."

Rebecca crumpled, and Alex held her as they mourned the man who had meant so much to both of them.

After four more nights, Alex left. He asked her to come with him, but she had what seemed like an overwhelming list of things to do. Alex needed to stay busy and volunteered to start calling Mitch's friends. They needed to have some sort of service for him, even if his body was never returned. She couldn't think of a final goodbye to her husband and asked Alex not to mention it again until she returned to Portland.

Mitch's apartment was filled with his life. A life she had only recently started sharing. What would he want done with it? She had to talk to a lawyer. There were things to dispose of, and her life was in shambles.

A week later, she was checking tasks off her list. She went to the Donovan Security offices and was escorted into Lucien Donovan's office, where he sat behind his desk and rose to greet her. She was still in shock but aware enough to know that she didn't want him to hug her. She stuck out her hand and shook his.

"How are you holding up?" he asked. His question was flat, emotionless. Was he upset about losing Mitch and four other employees? She didn't think so, but to her, it wasn't business. It was personal.

"Not well," she said as she sat down.

"You must be wondering if you are in the middle of a nightmare," he said as he perched on the edge of his desk. "Have you found any additional information?"

"I don't wonder. I know I'm in the middle of a nightmare, and I'm angry. My brother talked to the embassy, but they couldn't tell him much. I feel abandoned," she said robotically, thinking about how in the last week, she hadn't slept more than two hours a night. One moment, she was a happy bride who was going to have a baby in a with the love of her life. Now, she was a shell of herself. Life outside had turned pretty awful. And this man, this horrible man in front of her, had sent Mitch to his death. A part of her wanted to hurt him.

"It has been grim around the office, as you can imagine. Many sad stories."

She nodded but said nothing.

"We got a few of Mitch's things from his desk and office that I thought you'd like to have," Lucien said as he got up, moving to the side of his desk and producing a small cardboard box.

"Thank you," she said as she glanced in the open box. Looking up at her was a photo of Mitch and Lily, obviously at an outdoor garden party. Mitch had his hand around Lily's waist, and she was looking up at him longingly. It was probably taken a month or two before Rebecca and Mitch found each other again. Silently, she turned over the photo, so they weren't smiling up at her. She also noticed a black pen with the telltale white star top, the Mont Blanc that her mother had given to Mitch. It was all she could do not to break down at that moment.

"We hope to have his luggage and personal items that were with him in the hotel in Riyadh returned in the next few weeks. Would you like to have them back?" Lucien asked.

"Yes, of course, but I'll be in the United States. Can you please send them to me?"

"Yes, just give me an address," he said, placing a tablet and pen on the desk in front of her and next to where he sat.

"Thank you," she said and had to think of the address before addressing it to her mother and father's penthouse in Portland.

"I just have a few papers for you to sign," he said.

She set down her pen, not understanding, and said, "Excuse me?"

"Every employee of Donovan Security has a two-million-pound life insurance policy in case of something like this. It goes to the surviving spouse. It is above and beyond the Defense Base

Act that will also be offering you compensation for foreign contract workers because Mitch was an American. Odd. Did you know the Defense Base Act is actually an extension of the Longshore and Harbor Workers' Compensation Act, which provides coverage to private employees who are engaged in paramilitary overseas activities? So, finances won't be a problem for you."

What? She should be celebrating her windfall? Rebecca didn't remember standing. One minute she was sitting, and the next, she was face to face with Lucien Donovan. "How dare you say such a thing to me after I lost my husband?"

"I'm just stating the facts," he said, holding out his arms in mock surrender. She saw something in his eyes she didn't like. Glee.

"As far as I'm concerned, you can shove that money up your ass. I'm not signing a thing. Mitch only did this because you asked him to. He'd be alive if it weren't for you. I'll never forget what you did to him and to me." She didn't mention the baby. It wasn't his business.

She turned and walked away. Rebecca would let her lawyer know about the life insurance, and then she'd put it in a trust fund for her baby.

She took a taxi back to the flat and sat on the couch, holding the Mont Blanc pen, and trying to hold it together. But in the safety of Mitch's flat, she realized she didn't have to hold it in. She let herself cry. All she needed to do was think of the baby, and the dam burst.

As Mitch's wife, she became the owner of all that was his, but they hadn't been married long enough for that to feel comfortable. Many of the possessions he had accumulated happened when she wasn't a part of his life. She knew that everything she touched had sentimental value to Mitch, but she hadn't heard the associated story, and now she never would. It was heart-breaking in a whole new way. There were a few things that looked older. That evening, after her horrible day, her solution was to call her brother and see if he knew the backstory of some of Mitch's possessions.

"I'm looking at an old stuffed animal dog, which appears to be a black lab," she said. She held the dog to her and wondered how many times Mitch had done the same thing.

"His grandmother gave it to his mother when he was born," Alex said.

Rebecca put it in the box to keep and thought about giving it to their baby in a few months. Then she said, "I don't think you ever told Mom and Dad that you and Mitch went to Puerto Rico in college."

Alex chuckled a little. "That brings back some memories. We went for spring break senior year. What did you find?"

"Photos, lots of incriminating photos," Rebecca said, looking at a photo of Mitch and Alex drinking something that looked alcoholic under a Bacardi sign on a beach that announced: *Welcome to Puerto Rico!* Mitch was so handsome. Had she ever fully appreciated what a wonderful person he was inside and out?

"Would you please put those someplace safe and bring them home to me?" Alex asked. "I'd like to have them."

"What? I can't show them to Mom?" she asked.

"No, Mom still thinks we stayed home and studied. Let's not ruin her illusion."

"Yeah, right. I wouldn't bet on her not finding out. That woman has eyes in the back of her head," Rebecca said, placing the envelope of photos next to the stuffed animal. "I just wonder what else I will find that speaks to your bad influence on my sweet husband." Her voice was thick with emotion.

"Seriously, Becca, do you need any help? I could fly back over and be there tomorrow."

"Thanks, Alex, but I'm fine. You were here in the beginning when I really needed you."

"Keep telling yourself that, and you just might start to believe it."

"I'm just trying to tie everything up here and get home. Then, once I get to Portland, all bets are off. Buy stock in Kleenex."

Thankfully, as she continued to clean out Mitch's flat, she learned more about her husband. She delighted with each new discovery. He followed baseball while in England. His love of history showed in the books he read. She knew all of this to be true, but to look at his books and see the memorabilia he'd collected, well, she was happy there were no surprises, and that was okay by her.

It took her four days to clean out Mitch's flat, which had to be the most painful thing she had ever done. Her mother offered to fly to London to help, but it was something Rebecca wanted to do on her own. It had taken a lot of convincing to get Victoria to stay home.

Her family was worried about her. Rebecca was a little worried about herself too, but that had to go on the back burner. She had things to do.

"Are you alright?" her brother had asked the next night when he called her. "I really worry that I left too quickly." It had felt really lonely after Alex left, but she couldn't have him stay with her indefinitely.

"No, but I appreciate how long you did stay. I'll do what I have to do here. Then I'll come home. I have no idea what to do with the rest of my life."

"Becca, you don't have to decide anything next week or month or year. It isn't like you need money. You have a trust fund. You are a very rich woman. Take your time. We are all here for you."

"Thank you. I will take my time," she said to her brother as she walked around Mitch's empty flat. How had this happened?

Why? Why? Why? They had wasted six precious years from the time she was eighteen.

"Mom really wants to fly to London," he said. "Please tell her it is okay. She is pacing."

"Really, I'm okay," she lied.

"Would you prefer if I came? I could reach out to one of your friends from school."

She hadn't told them she was married yet. She didn't want to have to explain everything to them.

"Alex, thank you, but no. I'll be home in a week, and then I will need all of you to take care of me. I'm going to be a mess." She stifled another sob. He didn't need to hear just what a toll this was taking on her.

"I know you are holding it together until you get home, but how are you now?"

"I'm keeping a handle on it for a moment or two. If I ever let that guard down, I'm not responsible. Let's just not get too mushy, okay?" She didn't want platitudes. She didn't want to hear that she'd feel better in time. Everyone could shut the hell up.

Alex understood. "Call anytime. You know, he was my best friend, too." Alex was dealing with his own emotions. This wasn't a time she could be there for him, but she tried.

"I'm not the only one suffering, and I know it. How are you?" she asked.

"I miss him. I should have been nicer when we had dinner with Mom and Dad. I mean, here is my best friend marrying my sister. It is wonderful. You were perfect for each other, even though it wasn't easy for me to think of you together."

She gave a sad laugh. "Thank you for that."

Later, when she was cleaning out Mitch's nightstand, she found the tissue with her lipstick on it from that ill-fated kiss at the Windsor bar. It was from the day she interviewed and saw Mitch for the first time in six years. Holding it, she cried anew.

He had kept the tissue. She was part of the story of his life. Part of what was left behind.

The flat felt like it belonged to a stranger, not her husband. Heck, since they had returned to London after getting married, she had spent more time there than he had. Cleaning it out felt like a betrayal. It was so final. He was never coming back, and she had years ahead to live by herself and remember that he was gone for every day of the rest of her life. How was she going to do it?

She hadn't been back in his life long enough to really have made an imprint on his space, but what she had done was give his life a new direction. And there was still a part of him that was alive, their baby. She would do anything she could to protect their child, her baby...Baby Wilder.

Cleaning out his closet had to be the worst. She could smell traces of his cologne, and there were pieces that she recognized, the burgundy tie he'd worn to her first Zoom call with the company. She saved the tie after rubbing it to her cheek and then holding it close. She refused to admit how many of his suits she had hugged, but she couldn't help it.

He had an old fleece from Wharton, and she couldn't believe he still had it with the frayed edges and faded coloring. She kept it, along with a leather jacket, all his photos, even the ones Alex wanted, and any personal item she thought might have sentimental value. The photos he had of Lily were placed in a separate pile. She didn't know what to do with them.

It broke her heart to donate all his clothing to different charities. And in the end, once she'd gotten rid of his clothes and the furniture, she was left with six large plastic bins with lids. She would ship them home and keep them for their baby. She had yet to tell her family about the baby. It was still only her and Mitch's secret.

The empty space now echoed with each footfall. Mitch's life was broken down to only six boxes. Nothing broke her heart like seeing those six lonely boxes that summarized such a big life. She bundled them with tape and luggage belts for good measure and then sent them to her parents' penthouse in Portland.

Now, just two weeks after she'd kissed Mitch goodbye, it was time for her to go. She grabbed her last things to make her way to the Stark International Hotel, where she would be staying tonight in the corporate family suite before heading home tomorrow. It had felt much different to arrive with her luggage than to leave. Who could have predicted such a horrible ending to such a beautiful love story?

When the landline rang while she was in the middle of cleaning a spot on the kitchen floor for the final time, she almost ignored it.

"Hello?" she answered, thinking that if it were her parents or brother, they would always call on her cell.

"Is this Rebecca?" It was a woman's voice, and Rebecca had a feeling she already knew who it was.

"Lily?" she asked.

"How did you know it was me?" the other woman said, sounding surprised.

"I just had a feeling you might want to talk to me," Rebecca said. "I found some photos that you should have. I was going to mail them to you."

There was silence and then Lily spoke.

"What are you doing this evening? Would you like to meet for tea at Claridge's? Say six?" she asked, as if they were two civilized women who hadn't been in love with the same man but maybe were old boarding school friends who were reconnecting.

Rebecca took a taxi to her family hotel, checked into the corporate suit, showered, dressed, and tried to look her best before she took a taxi to Claridge's with a Harrods canvas bag filled with things that belonged to Lily. Much of the bag was filled with photographs and a couple of books Lily had made to document their dating life before they were to get married. Rebecca had quickly looked at a couple of the pages and gotten a feel for what they were about, but she didn't linger. Torture was torture, and she had been through enough. Rebecca had been there first, but Lily had been with him a long time. This was the hardest and kindest thing she could do for another woman who had been in love with her husband.

Rebecca had never been more thankful that Lily hadn't been a frequent guest at Mitch's flat. He'd told her himself that Lily never slept over and hadn't left anything behind, which Rebecca found to be true. It was a bachelor's apartment, through and through. It was just another way that Lily and Mitch were not compatible. The truth was, they didn't have the connection that he and Rebecca did. She knew it in her bones.

The air inside the taxi was sweltering. It was raining outside, yet the heat of late summer was still hanging on and creating something like sweaty steam room inside the small space. This was not a meeting she wanted to arrive at feeling like she was melting, but she did.

Claridge's was elegant as usual as she stepped inside one of her favorite hotels, which was next in favor when compared to her family hotel.

The black and white marble floor spoke of another time and place, as Claridge's had been around a lot longer than her family hotel. She admired the décor—the huge chandeliers, the coved ceilings. She made some mental notes to share with her father because he would ask, but today everything hurt a little. One of the helpful staff asked her if he could help direct her to a location, and she wondered momentarily if he thought she was in need of help. Instead, she told him that she was there for tea. A moment later, she was standing by a hostess who showed her to a table on the left side of the room, off the main path but regardless, a place to be seen. She was the first to arrive and would easily see Lily when she arrived a few minutes later.

Pillars that were kissed with gold leaf, mirrored walls, and tall, coved ceilings paid homage to the calming cream-and-gold space. The table was set with the signature muted sage green and white tea service edged with gold, but Rebecca didn't think she would be able to have a bite of anything. When was the last time she'd eaten? Yesterday? She recalled eating a bagel. Maybe it had some butter or cream cheese on it. She couldn't remember, but it was something creamy. She had glanced at the tea menu, but nothing looked remotely appetizing.

Lily breezed in five minutes late in a lime sherbet-colored suit in summer silk that clashed with the fine interior of the tearoom. She wore a white Birkin bag on her wrist along with strands and strands of baroque pearls. She looked happy. Rebecca wanted to like the other woman, but she couldn't. She was just doing what needed to be done.

"I'm so sorry I'm late," she said, in a swirl of that familiar sickly-sweet perfume Rebecca had smelled on the day of her interview. Lily smiled a sweet smile that Rebecca wasn't sure she'd ever be capable of doing again. She wanted to slap the smile off of Lily's face. How could she claim to have loved Mitch and be able to smile so easily and so happily so quickly after his death?

"No problem," Rebecca answered and even let the other woman hug her. "Traffic was a mess."

"How are you?" Lily said quietly, lowering her voice, as if she remembered this was a sober occasion as she arranged her napkin on her lap.

She wondered what Mitch saw in Lily. It really didn't matter now. Neither one of them had him now.

"I'm managing," Rebecca said, and happily, their waiter arrived to explain in great detail what their tea would consist of. Why had Rebecca agreed to this? It was going to take two hours, and then what? Why hadn't she agreed to meet her on a park bench in Hyde Park? Hand over the goods and leave? Hell, she could have dropped off the stuff at Mitch's office. Well, at least there was a bit of a performance to the whole civilized tea thing. Tea selection, sandwiches, scones, and dessert. Okay, each step got her closer to leaving. By tomorrow at this time, she'd be on a plane home to the United States.

At the waiter's suggestion, they ordered additional beverages to go with their tea. A glass of champagne for Lily and a ginger ale for the widow. Even if she could drink, she wouldn't touch champagne. It wasn't appropriate for the occasion.

"I don't know how I feel. My feelings around Mitch are complicated," Lily said, and Rebecca slowly raised her eyes to meet the other woman.

"I imagine you don't," Rebecca said. "I would bet you are quite confused. I'm sorry for what you went through with Mitch. I know he wanted to minimize your pain, but it was still an awful situation."

"I'm sorry too, but you know, I've had some time to think of everything."

Rebecca wanted to ask, but also knew she shouldn't. She just hoped Lily wouldn't feel the need to unburden herself. It would be too ugly and make Rebecca wish she hadn't agreed to this meeting.

She felt for and touched the emerald and diamond ring, which was still on her left hand next to her diamond wedding band. Rebecca hadn't even considered taking them off. And with a baby on the way, she knew she never would.

"Mitch was an amazing man, but I don't know if we'd have been happy in the long run. We were very different. I'm starting to come to terms with that," Lily shared. "Believe it or not, I haven't cried. Isn't it crazy? You'd think I would. But the company lost so much that day, people from the company. It has been so morbid."

Where was the waiter with her ginger ale? Rebecca tasted

bile in her mouth. She didn't need to hear about Lily and her revelations. She needed to get through this.

"I'm sure it has been hard," Rebecca said.

"Mitch...just, well, he was a nice person, but he was American, and I don't know how to say this because you are American. They are different from the British men I usually date. They don't know the way British women expect to be treated. I'm sure you get along better with him because, like him, you are an American," she said with a bright smile, "I've started dating an old friend I went to school with ten years ago, and we are much more on the same wavelength. The way he dates me, his expectations are more in line with mine. So, in a way, I'm thankful Mitch and I were no longer together."

"I'm happy for you," Rebecca said. Lily was going to get her happily ever after, after all. Funny how things happen.

"There is just a way we do things in England. Roland understands."

In retrospect, Rebecca was pleased to hear this. If Lily had cried or proclaimed her love for Mitch, Rebecca didn't know what she would do. As it was, Lily sounded like she had found someone who was perfect for her.

Rebecca's thoughts flashed to how Mitch hugged her to the point she said, *"I'm real. I'm not going away."*

And he replied, *"You don't know how wonderful it is to just hold you, to touch you anytime you want."*

"I like it when you touch me."

"Music to my ears, Mrs. Wilder."

A physical relationship was important to Mitch. That worked because a physical relationship was important to her. What if they had grown old together and not been able to have sex? Well, he could still hold her. She could hold him. They could hold hands. And she didn't think there would ever come a time when she wouldn't want to kiss him.

The tea was awkward, as expected. She and Lily had little to say to each other that didn't involve Mitch, and Mitch was a tender subject. They talked about Roland, Lily's new boyfriend and what his flat was like. *It needed a woman's touch, and she could not wait to help him!* Then, Lily talked about London and the sights to see as if Rebecca were a tourist, not a twenty-four-year-old widow.

"I love the city of Windsor and Windsor Castle. You have got to go there," Lily said.

Rebecca didn't tell her they had been there the weekend before Mitch left on his last trip. She just had no idea it would be the last time they went anywhere together. They had walked around, had a lovely lunch, and toured the castle and the chapel. Ironically, they had talked about an extended honeymoon, visiting several exotic locations that also had Stark Hotels. They had narrowed it down to Paris, Rome, Saint Barts, the Cook Islands, and Hong Kong. But it was all a dream. Instead, they had looked at all the crypts of the kings and queens. How morbid to know that Mitch had joined the dead so soon after that visit, and their honeymoon was yet another sad dream.

Rebecca tried to eat the neat little sandwich delicacies they placed before her, but they tasted like sponges with fillings that were unpleasant. This, she knew, was not true. They were filled with wonderful ingredients—the best, freshest ingredients the chef could find—but today, they were making her nauseous. She was more interested in drinking her ginger ale and the end of her horrible time with Lily. Realizing that the only thing that would move the tea along was eating, Rebecca forced herself to do so.

Bite.

Chew.

Chew.

Chew.

A sip of ginger ale before you spit it out or vomit.

Swallow it down.

Repeat.

Rebecca managed to do this with the majority of the sandwiches before her, the scones with clotted cream, and the desserts. She drew the line at the figgy pudding. Even the scent of it threatened to push her over the edge of control.

Lily continued to drone on about her adventures with Mitch. She dabbed at her eyes to catch unshed tears that might have been nonexistent. Rebecca felt no need to cry for Lily. Her tears were for herself and her baby.

Rebecca reached under the napkin in her lap and felt the flat stomach underneath the fabric. She rubbed her tummy for reassurance. She wanted this baby more than she wanted to breathe. She was doing everything she could to be careful and take care of herself.

At last, it was time for the check to arrive. Lily insisted that she would pay. Rebecca gave a half-hearted fight for it and then let Lily do the honors.

Lily hugged her for too long as they said their goodbyes. It was a pathetic hug and lacked sincerity, but it was also filled with pity and waves and waves of nauseating perfume that threatened Rebecca's ability to keep the tea sandwiches in her stomach. And more than anything, Rebecca didn't want Lily's pity.

Rebecca poured herself into a taxi in front of the hotel, feeling sick and a little dizzy as she went back to her family hotel. Now, she wanted to cry.

"You never have to do this day again," she said to herself as she got in the elevator and rode up to the floor that housed her suite.

At the door, she struggled to find her keycard in her purse when the door suddenly opened, and her mother stood in the doorway.

"Mom?" she asked in surprise and then fell into her mother's arms. And then another set of arms was around her: her father. They had come against her wishes, and she was never so happy in her life to see them.

Her mother held her on the couch while she cried. Before long, she broke free and ran to the nearest bathroom, where she purged the contents of her stomach. Once that was finished and she had brushed her teeth, she went back to the couch and sat between her parents who formed a protective border around her.

"Was the tea that bad?" her father asked, trying to lighten the mood.

"No," she said and figured that she had nothing to lose. "I'm just a little bit pregnant."

Mitch

Everything hurt like a hundred little paper cuts. Mitch was having a hard time wanting to breathe. The air was heavy, warm, and stank like an open sewer. He didn't need to open his eyes to know he wasn't in friendly territory.

"Khayin," the voice said, then louder, "Khayin!"

Mitch knew enough Arabic to know someone was yelling about a traitor, which was probably him. Whoever was screaming was close to him, and the sound hurt.

He just wanted to go back to sleep. He hurt, and the bed was more of a cot, but he wanted to stay on it forever. He had a chill, which he recognized as being a fever. It wasn't good. An infection could kill without the proper medications. At least he realized he was alive...for now.

His eyes were shut against the light in the room around him. And he didn't mind everyone thinking that he had passed out. Occasionally, there would be a warm breeze, and he could hear lots of shouting and cars in the distance.

He needed to know if it was safe to engage, but from all the information he had gathered in the last thirty seconds, he didn't think so. Better to appear more injured than he was. Well, who was he kidding? He knew he was injured, but thankfully he still had both legs and arms. His fight-or-flight reaction had been triggered. But something told him it would be prudent to hide in plain sight. Pretend to be out of it. Well, he didn't need to pretend much.

Where was he?

The last thing he remembered was the helicopter pilot letting out a string of expletives before the machine dove toward Earth. They had crashed. He remembered the ground coming up to meet them. Then pain. Then nothing.

They were delivering helicopters to Collins Transport. Their client provided the soldiers with medical supplies, the ultimate military contractor. They hadn't balked at the price of the helicopters, but they should have. Lucien was making money, but so was Collins. He wondered if Congress knew what they were about to be charged for helicopters...

He was delivering them, two of them, to Collins with the promise of four more in the next year. Mitch was riding in the second helicopter, but the helicopter in front of them had blown up before his eyes. He'd actually felt the concussion of the blast and the heat.

Their helicopter was next...

Why was this happening? It was supposed to be an easy delivery. What had gone wrong?

He wasn't supposed to be in any danger. This was strictly a handoff of equipment.

Rebecca had been right. It was far more dangerous than he thought it would be. Why hadn't he just listened to her? Would he ever see her again? The baby! She was pregnant.

"Khayin!"

The man was back, and this time, he was closer. Mitch felt the man's breath on his cheek. Something told him that if he opened his eyes, it would be very bad for him.

He had read that the same anti-American factions who chanted "Death to Americans" also called individual Americans "The Great Satan" or just good old "Khayin." He was in the worst possible place he could be, aside from death.

He could barely move. Possibly, the best course of action was to continue to play passed out. A moment later, the man had touched one of Mitch's injuries, and he didn't have to hope to pass out. He had.

CHAPTER SEVENTEEN

Rebecca flew to New York with her parents. Their personal plane was getting serviced, so they flew commercial. It was a horrible flight. Even though they flew first class, which offered her a suite area on Delta One, it wasn't like traveling on the family plane. When she was given permission to do so, she closed the little door that defined her suite, lay her head on her pillow, and cried for the duration of the flight. Her mother had once said that life was filled with good, bad, and so-so, but she'd never had to navigate anything like this. Rebecca thought that when Mitch might marry someone else, her life was over. This was so much worse than she had ever thought possible. There was no chance he would come to his senses and find her. No, he no longer existed on this planet. It was a loneliness like nothing she had ever felt.

Was she only supposed to get a brief taste of happiness, and that was it? She had been married only a few weeks, and now she was officially a widow. How did that happen?

Several times during the flight, when she was supposed to be asleep, she saw her mother looking over the partition to see if she was awake. Each time, she smiled up at her mother, who blew her a kiss. Rebecca's life, which had been so ravishingly happy up in the last few weeks, had become a scattered trailer park after a destructive twister. And nothing short of Mitch could restore it to its prior happiness. How was she going to go on?

She had come up with a plan, but no one liked it.

"Why on Earth would you want to do that? I could see New York. You have girlfriends in New York, and we could easily put your old apartment back together there, but I think in your condition, you should stay close," her mother said when Rebecca shared the plans she had decided on the night after they had arrived home in Portland. Her parents just stared at her.

Her mother had paid someone to pack up her New York apartment. The boxes and furniture had been driven across the country to Portland while she had been in London. All the possessions had been unloaded and set up in another suite on the same floor her parents occupied at the Stark International Hotel in Portland. She had asked her mother to do it, but now she realized she no longer had a home unless she wanted to move into the suite. Instead, another idea had formed.

"What is wrong with my plans?" she asked.

"Your family is in Portland," her father said as he joined the conversation, "And yet you want to move three hours from here. Are you running away from home?"

"I'm running to the family beach house. A place I've been going for years. Is that really running away? I'm just asking to borrow your house."

"It is in the middle of nowhere," her father said.

"It is in the middle of a small community," Rebecca argued.

"We are just very worried about you, Rebecca. If you are three hours away, who will you call if there is an emergency? Don't you see you are putting yourself in danger?" her mother asked. "And you have the baby to think about."

"I'm well aware of my baby, Mother. I need this baby like I've never needed anything. I'm putting myself in time out," Rebecca said, and when they said nothing, she continued. "Look, if you don't want me to use the family beach house, I'll buy one. Thanks to your hard work in starting a very large hotel chain, I can buy a little place at the beach this afternoon if I want to. It is what I'm going to do. Living in a big city, well, that is a problem for me. Too many people, too many questions. I just want to hide for a bit. Surely you can understand that? I want to go where there isn't news, where no one knows me. I want to disappear and come to grips with what I've lost. Do either of you understand that? I loved Mitch for ten years. I don't know what it is to be an adult and not be in love with Mitch. I'm beside myself with grief, and I don't know who I am without him in my world."

"I guess we just didn't know how long you and Mitch were involved," her father said, giving a glance to her mother.

"I've had a crush on him since I was fourteen. We didn't get involved until I was eighteen, and he was scared of your reaction. He said I was too young, but I convinced him to be my first lover. I kind of put him in a no-win position. I told him if he wouldn't have sex with me, I'd get drunk at a frat party and sleep with someone I met that night. I didn't even care if I knew their last name." Why was she telling them this? She wanted them to know that they had loved each other for a very long time.

"Oh my God, Rebecca. I can't listen to this," her father said. "I thought we raised a lady. How could you put him in that position? My god, what else are we to learn about our daughter?"

She ignored his reaction. She didn't have time for his drama when she had so much of her own to deal with.

"What I'm trying to say is that it wasn't a casual thing. We were deeply in love with each other for a very long time. If he hadn't been so worried about what you thought, we might have had six years together. Instead, I had a few weeks of happiness. I regret I didn't stand up for myself and for Mitch."

"So, this is our fault that our twenty-four-year-old daughter is pregnant and a widow?" her father said, his jaw setting in an ugly line.

"Okay, let's all take it down a notch. We don't need to be doing this to each other. Let's stay in the present. We all loved Mitch, but I understand your need to get away from everything for a bit," her mother said, trying to calm them all down. "This is a terrible time."

"Thank you, Mom," Rebecca said.

"And for the record, Gary, I would feel the same way if you were taken from me," Victoria said to her husband as she put a hand on his arm and gently rubbed it. He soon warmed up and gave his wife a tentative smile.

Then he said, "I love you, Vicki."

"Sometimes, I wonder," she teased.

Rebecca was always happy her parents were so in love, but seeing it today hurt. She and Mitch would not have any of those intimate moments in the future.

Victoria wrapped an arm around Rebecca.

"Darling," she said, addressing Rebecca. "I'll get you the keys and the alarm code to the beach house. Would you like me to send someone down to Yachats and stock the fridge, maybe clean up the place a bit?"

"No thanks, Mom. I can do it all myself. I just need to buy a car, and I'll be on my way tomorrow morning."

"You could take a hotel car," Victoria offered.

"A black Mercedes with a Stark something license plate? In Yachats? No thanks. I'll buy one. I want something of my own that is a little less recognizable."

Victoria turned her attention to her husband. "If either one of us had lost the other, we'd feel the same way."

"I'm sorry, Rebecca," her father said. "It is just that you are so young. You are still my little girl."

"I'm sorry too, Dad," Rebecca said.

"You know, I feel I need to say this to reassure you. In time, you'll meet someone else," he said. "Women like you do not spend their lives alone. And your baby deserves a father."

Rebecca shook her head and turned away from her father. "Dad, not exactly the time or the place. Mom, I think I want to go to the guest room and not talk to Dad for a few days or weeks. Maybe you can find his sensitivity gene. He obviously lost his." The thought of going to the suite that held her things wasn't anything she could bear at the moment.

"Forgive him. He says stupid things when he doesn't know what to say," Victoria said as she looked pointedly at her husband.

He rolled his eyes, and Victoria punched him in the arm, hard.

"Ouch, Vicki," he said.

"Be glad I didn't show you how angry I really am," she replied.

Rebecca knew her parents were trying to help, but nothing anyone could say would really help her at this time. The only thing that consoled her was the thought of the baby. She had thought of not telling Mitch until he returned from Iraq. Thank goodness she hadn't waited.

Mitch

He opened his eyes for the soft-spoken doctor who touched his hand gently.

"Welcome back, Mr. Wilder."

The man was small and bald, and reminded him of his orthodontist from childhood, Dr. Klein, except that he was wearing fatigues and looked like he might like to kill people for the heck of it.

"Hello, sir," Mitch said, thinking that paying the man a little respect wasn't a bad idea.

"You have a broken leg, a concussion, and potentially a lung injury," the man said in perfect, if not heavily accented, English. Where was he? Was he still in Iraq?

"Thank you for taking care of me." He was confused and foggy. It was like the worst bender he'd ever had with Alex times ten and add pain.

"When you can walk, when I've determined you won't die, they will move you to different accommodations," the doctor said. Mitch thought this guy needed to work on his bedside manner. He might die?

"Where am I?"

"That is not your concern, Mr. Wilder. We just want to make sure you will live. Then we will parade you in front of those capitalists who will pay for your safe return. Then, if they do what they are supposed to and you stay alive, our business will be done."

Done? Was that going to end well for him? He didn't think so. He'd been kidnapped and was being held for ransom? Well, he might not be in Iraq, but he was still in the Middle East. Did anyone know he was there? What happened? Rebecca? How long ago had he seen her?

The man that Mitch came to think of as Dr. Klein turned his back and walked away.

He was alone in a tent, on a cot. It was stiflingly hot, and he was sweating, but thankfully, his fever had broken. It probably made him more alert, but he was far from thinking clearly. Glancing down at his leg, he was first of all happy to see it was still there. He saw the crude splint meant to keep it straight. Great. One blood clot from the break just needed to break free and run to his heart or his lungs, and he was a goner.

The other leg was concerning for a different reason. It had a shackle on it. Did they really think he'd try to escape? He was in no condition to try something like that today.

He heard the wind start up, and it blew through the tent with ferocity. No wonder he felt grit everywhere. It was sand. He was definitely in the desert. Where the hell were they?

The rest of his body was a roadmap of bruises. Heck, he had stitches on his arm and on his shoulder. He remembered getting none of them, but they weren't fresh. They were at least five or six days old.

He was alone in the space and was indeed on a cot. He still wore part of the black shirt from Donovan and part of the matching pants. He figured parts had been ripped away to render aid. Did that mean that his left side was basically uninjured? It didn't feel like it.

The ground was covered with battered canvas, sand and unknown debris that was partly dried mud, partly dead branch that had probably blown in and dirty dressings that had no doubt come from him. He tried not to think of what kind of infection might be settling into his body, just waiting to attack and finish him off.

A battered bottle of water was sitting on a little table next to him. With stiff fingers, he grabbed for it, although it felt heavier than it should. The action showed just how weak he was. He broke the seal and drank several long sips from the bottle and tried not to swallow the whole thing at once. It hit his stomach like a sledgehammer, and he had to close his eyes and concentrate on keeping it in his body.

A glint caught his eye. His wedding ring was still on his left hand where Rebecca had placed it when they got married. It no longer looked new. The platinum was scratched and battered. He knew what it would take to damage platinum, and it gave him pause.

"I love you, Bex. You were so right," he said aloud, wondering if he'd ever see her again. Did she know he had been captured? Did she know he was alive? If they killed him, would they return his body to her? What about the baby they had conceived? He had loved her for as long as he could remember.

CHAPTER EIGHTEEN

Rebecca bought a two-year-old black Audi in Portland the next morning. It wouldn't stand out and would get her where she wanted to go. An SUV that was roomy and not too big, but most importantly, it was a very safe car. Her father had offered to go with her, but she wanted to do this on her own. She bought the car without anyone's aid. There was something she enjoyed about negotiation, especially when it came to things like cars. The main thing was, she didn't care. If they couldn't come to an agreement, she didn't mind walking away. Thankfully, they wanted to sell it to her at a price she wanted.

Despite the comfort she had once gotten from knowing Mitch was going to be her partner in life, she was slowly digesting the reality that he wasn't going to be there. She was going to raise their child, and she was going to do it on her own.

Her parents had almost an entire floor to themselves at The Stark Hotel in Portland. She knew her mother wanted a house, but her father enjoyed this kind of urban living. Besides, he always countered that they had the house in New York and the beach house. Her mother wanted something with grass and rose bushes, and the rooftop garden at The Stark didn't do it for her. Rebecca would have to start thinking where she wanted to live.

Rebecca pulled the Audi into the valet area of the hotel.

"Would you like us to park it, Miss Stark?" they asked. She could see their eager, wide eyes to try the new car. She hated having to valet park.

She turned and said, "It is actually Mrs. Wilder."

The valet almost turned himself inside out with embarrassment, but she held up her hand and said, "It is okay, no worries. I will be leaving in an hour. Please keep it close, like right over there."

Ten minutes later, she was piling her luggage by the front door of her parents' foyer. Included in the mix were Mitch's boxes. They had arrived from London quickly, and she wanted to take some time to go through them. The baby would want mementos of their father, and she was hoping for some extra photos she could enjoy and, no doubt, cry over.

There were some things she wanted from where her New York apartment had been set up, but she figured she could ask her mother later. It was too soon to see all her things and remember how she and Mitch had spent a magical week in her New York apartment.

Her father rushed to help her with a horrified look on his face.

"Rebecca, please be careful with yourself."

"I'm fine, Father."

"Please be reasonable. Who is going to help you unload when you get to the house? Let one of us follow you down there and get you settled in."

"Thank you, but none of the luggage is over thirty pounds. I was very careful when packing."

Her mother appeared from out of nowhere. "Garrison, I've got this."

Rebecca did a double take at her mother, who was dressed casually in jeans and a sweater set in turquoise blue. Victoria said, "I'm following you down. I'll get you unpacked, make sure the house is fine, and then drive back to Portland. I probably won't stay an hour. Take it or leave it. I changed the alarm code remotely this morning. You can't get in without me."

Her mother played dirty, and she didn't mess around. Victoria Whitlow Stark just took action. Although it annoyed the hell out of Rebecca at times, today she respected it.

She also knew when she was licked. And she knew this was important to her mother. "Okay," she said. "Pack a bag so you can spend the night."

"Already in the trunk of STARK 7. I like that hotel Mercedes, number 7. It has a little extra something."

"Am I that predictable?" Rebecca asked, ignoring her mother's thoughts on the car. "How long has your bag been in the trunk?"

"Oh, only about an hour. You are just so much like me."

"Fine, but I want to stop at Luna Sea for fish tacos in Seal Rock."

"I think that sounds great," her mother agreed.

"There are a few items I'd like from my New York apartment. Would you mind getting them for me? I really don't want to see everything. They have too many memories."

"I understand. I don't mind getting them for you."

Rebecca gave her a list of items, from the red bed sheets to clothing to books.

They arrived in the early afternoon at the beach house Rebecca's parents purchased while she was in college. Her mother, who had excellent taste, had gone a bit crazy hiring an interior decorator from San Francisco, with whom she spent weeks collaborating. They decided the inside should only be decorated in the colors of the beach and ocean, which were sand, mauve, and aqua. The result was a stunning yet calming interior.

Rebecca had spent two weeks there every summer for the last five years with her parents and sometimes her brother, if he wasn't visiting some far corner of the world.

Now that she was back in the United States, in a world that didn't contain Mitch, the beach house was an oasis by default, as she had never been there with him.

And the beach house felt like home. Well, at least until she could figure out where she wanted to raise her child. It would be a girl, she thought. It felt like a little girl, with Mitch's dimples and her green eyes.

Victoria wouldn't let her carry anything inside.

"Mom, I'm not handicapped."

"No, but you are pregnant, and I want you to give that baby the best chance possible. You are my daughter, and I loved Mitch like a son, so this baby, my first grandchild, is very important to me. That means I will do the heavy lifting. Absolutely do not think of arguing with me, Rebecca Alexandra Stark."

Rebecca did as she was told. If her mother knew about the first pregnancy she'd had, she would have never let her come to the beach.

Rebecca sat on one of the plush, overstuffed, sand-colored couches with light aqua silk pillows and watched her mother unload the Audi and then the Mercedes. In the end, Rebecca hadn't packed light. The important contents from Mitch's condo and what she asked her mother to pack from her New York apartment had boiled down to about ten boxes.

"Which room would you like to be your bedroom?" her mother asked.

"The bedroom I always use upstairs?"

"That is probably alright for the first few months, but if you stay here into your second trimester, you will not want stairs. I'd go for the first-floor master if I were you. Your father and I redid all the bathrooms two years ago, but there is something about that shower. It is heavenly. And the master has a lovely view down the beach."

"But don't you want to stay there tonight?" Rebecca asked.

"Darling, I'm your guest tonight. There are four other bedrooms for me to settle into. I might take the bedroom across the hall on the first level or your bedroom on the second. They are all beautiful because I decorated them. I'd prefer not to think about you running up and down the stairs. One slip could be devastating."

"Okay, the main floor for me," Rebecca agreed.

"Have you been to the doctor yet?" her mother asked.

"No, there wasn't time in London, and I've only been back in the country for two days. Heck, I'm still dealing with jet lag. I thought I'd ask around here and see who people suggest. I mean, there have to be women having babies in this area."

"You might have to go to Florence or Newport. Maybe you will want to have the baby in Portland," her mother suggested. "I'm sure we could find the best for you."

"I'm only about four or five weeks along, if that far. I haven't decided yet."

"Take your time," her mother said.

Rebecca ended up driving to Newport to have her first obstetrician appointment the following week.

Dr. Bates was a no-nonsense man, with no bedside manner that Rebecca could find. She didn't care. She just wanted the best care for her baby.

"Mrs. Wilder, does the father want to be part of the birth process?" he asked once she'd had her exam, was dressed, and sitting in his office.

"My husband, Mitch, was killed a few weeks ago in Iraq. He worked for a security company and was delivering helicopters to a military contractor. His helicopter was shot down with no survivors."

It was the most tender spot in all of this. Was there anything left of Mitch to send home? Alex and her parents had encouraged her to do a memorial service to say goodbye. But she hadn't come close to even thinking about it. Was it denial? No, it was self-preservation.

"Mrs. Wilder, I'm so sorry," the man said, breaking the cool reserve she had noticed over the last half hour.

"Thank you. Now you understand why this baby is so important to me. The baby is the last part of my husband that I have. Help me to have a healthy baby, please." She didn't realize she was crying until he handed her a tissue from a box on his desk. Why had she thought he was cold? Now, she saw the caring in his eyes.

"We have no reason to believe you will have anything but a successful pregnancy, but we want to be careful. Stress isn't good. We have a lot of literature we can give you on meditation. And we will want you to eat a healthy diet. We will monitor you closely, and all of those things should help to improve your chances of delivering a healthy, happy baby."

"How about the fact I've had an ectopic pregnancy in the past?"

"I read that in your chart, but I want to have you tell me about it."

She did.

"The chances of having a second ectopic pregnancy if you've had one before are greater, but the risk, overall, is still very small. We will schedule an ultrasound just to be on the safe side."

"When?" Rebecca asked.

"Due to the nature of the situation, let's get you in as soon as possible. I don't want you to stress over it."

"Thank you," Rebecca said.

They were able to schedule the exam for the following week.

Rebecca was worried, but she didn't tell her family, or anyone for that matter, about the ultrasound. She arrived by herself and tried to relax during the exam.

After she got dressed, she waited in her doctor's office for the results.

He came in looking as serious as ever, and Rebecca had to bite back tears. Then he smiled, his first real smile, and she did cry.

"It is okay, Rebecca. The baby looks good. The baby is embedded where it should be in the uterine wall. Looks to be about six to seven weeks along. I put the due date at around May 15th."

"I'm so relieved. May I hug you, doctor?"

The gruff man was soft at heart and gave her a hug as she cried on his shoulder.

Rebecca watched as fall came to the beach, offering some of the most gorgeous sunsets of the season. Her parents let her go about two weeks between visits. Yet again, she felt the relatives were on a rotation. If she wasn't seeing her parents, it was her brother Alex. At one point, her cousin, Spencer, dropped in because he was "in the neighborhood," which was a fat chance. He lived in Texas. They spent several afternoons sitting on the deck and reminiscing about Mitch.

"I remember watching you two playing Monopoly that day when he asked you out right in front of Alex. I could feel the tension," Spencer said.

"I think if Alex had picked up on it, he'd have been beside himself," she said.

"I never told you this, but I pulled Mitch aside that night and told him I approved."

"You did?" Rebecca asked, placing a hand on her cousin's arm.

"I liked him. I liked you two together."

Leaning toward him, she kissed her cousin on the cheek. "You are such a troublemaker. I love you."

Everyone seemed to understand that she needed to be treated gently.

When Alex arrived in early October, driving his car of the moment, a Porsche Panamera in black, he brought her takeout in a cooler from an Italian restaurant she liked in Portland.

"You must really feel sorry for me," she said as he unpacked the food from Pastini and started placing it in her fridge.

"I've had practice with Mom. She is a bit inconsolable. I

think Mitch was her favorite child. Forget about us, her actual children. He had dimples or something she just can't forget."

"He did have great dimples," Rebecca said, rubbing her tummy.

"He got away with calling her Vic. Who does that?"

"Spencer calls her Aunt Vic," Rebecca countered.

"But seriously, you seduced my best friend when you were eighteen?"

"Dad told you?"

"He's kind of upset. Every father's daughter is a virgin, and to hear any different is really Earth-shattering."

"Well, I'm married, and I'm pregnant. And for the record, Mitch and I had a lot of fun together. We loved each other, and it was like we were meant for each other."

"La la la la..." Alex said, covering his ears. "Look, I'm glad you two loved each other, but you are still my sister. I don't need to hear about it. Please hold back on the details."

After dinner, they sat across from each other and worked on a jigsaw puzzle. The house had a closet filled with puzzles and games, including Monopoly. She had contemplated throwing the Monopoly game away. It wasn't the same one they had played all those years ago, but it was a reminder of happier times. She and Alex worked on a round puzzle that was a golf course and all green. Rebecca liked puzzles because they helped her to think. Where her mind wandered to was another point altogether.

She had another ultrasound at the sixteen-week mark that determined that her baby was, indeed, a little girl. A name came to her, and she decided on the spot that the little girl would be named Emily.

Mitch

Mitch had never been a fan of curry. It was odd because it

was a staple for many of his coworkers in London. But when he was given what he could only describe as curry and rice served in a metal bowl with a large metal spoon, he ate it. About midway through it, he wondered if they had poisoned him. Well, it was too late to think about now. His hunger had overtaken reason. He had to act grateful. It wasn't easy. These were his kidnappers, but despite the horrible conditions, his leg was healing. He couldn't bear to put any weight on it, but it was looking better. He hadn't had any reoccurrence of fever for at least a week.

He'd tried unsuccessfully to ask the staff where he was, but they pretended not to understand him. He was pretty sure he was near the crash site in Iraq.

The brain fog was clearing, and he remembered the mission. Delivery of Donovan Security helicopters. He remembered the blast of the helicopter beside them being shot down out of the air. Then they were hit. He remembered the fall but not the rescue, nor the first week in captivity.

His arms were scarred now from the crash, but he was just happy they healed without infection. He'd seen his stitches, but there were others on his back that he hadn't seen. He was lucky to still have his leg.

The sad-eyed older woman who always wore a Hijab took his bowl away when he'd finished eating, and then the "doctor" arrived, and he wasn't alone.

The polite banter was over.

Yelling at Mitch, the doctor, who reminded him of his orthodontist, shoved a newspaper into his hand. Something he could not read. And by the look of the lettering, it was Arabic. The second man, who was dressed in fatigues and looked like he wanted to kill Mitch with his bare hands, pulled out an iPhone and snapped several photos of Mitch holding the newspaper.

No one needed to tell him what was going on. It was proof of life. The negotiations had begun, but when they took his ring, which had become loose on his finger, he had a very bad feeling of foreboding.

CHAPTER NINETEEN

"You are driving Mom crazy," Alex said to Rebecca two days before Christmas.

"It is not my intention to drive anyone crazy," she said as she stroked her slight baby bump, sat on the couch at her family beach house, and watched the ocean outside. If she wasn't watching a movie, she was reading. If she wasn't reading, she was doing a puzzle. Lately she'd started ordering things online for the baby. Her priority was delivering a happy, healthy baby girl, and the rest of the world could go to hell.

It was King Tide, which meant the water was rough and the waves were big. Alex sounded exasperated on the phone. Poor Alex. He had lost his best friend, but that was overshadowed by her loss. She tried to be compassionate, but it didn't come easily.

"You aren't being logical."

"Let me ask, do you think I give a damn what the family thinks?" Rebecca asked. She knew she was lashing out, and it was not becoming. "I'm skipping Christmas this year. End of story."

"I will feel like our little talk didn't matter if I can't convince you to come home for the holiday," he said, his tone sad.

"Look, I'm sorry. I don't mean to bite your head off. I know the parents put you up to the call. But as for Christmas, I would have to get presents for everyone, show up at the ornately decorated Stark Hotel in Portland, act like everything is wonderful, and make merry when I've lost the love of my life and am pregnant with his child. I can't do it. I won't do it."

"I know it is a big ask, but I think it would be good for you.

No one is expecting gifts, so why don't you just bring yourself, and we will distract you? Or the two of us can distract each other."

"No, I can't do it. You do have an open invitation to come down here. But a big family Christmas in Portland? That is ridiculous. They can have Christmas, sing damn Christmas Carols for all I care, make cookies for Santa, I don't care. I just don't want to be there. I don't want to smile or be nice to anyone, okay?"

"I'm sorry about Mitch, Rebecca."

Rebecca felt bad. Alex had lost his best friend. "I'm sorry. I know you miss him too. I'm sorry I'm being a bitch. You've been great to me. I love you, bro."

"Someday, some year from now, it won't feel so raw."

"Promise?" Rebecca asked.

"Guaranteed."

On Christmas Eve, she drove eight miles to Waldport and bought everything she'd need for her mother's Shepherd's Pie, except she couldn't stomach the idea of lamb or beef, so she bought near-beef. It was supposed to be plant-based beef, but it looked a little disgusting, and even though she hadn't thrown up in a week, all bets were off for the rest of the evening.

She bought a frozen French Silk pie that looked a little processed. Merry Christmas to her.

At the checkout line, she saw a box that contained a string of white lights. She bought it. It would be her ode to Christmas.

Driving home, she didn't think she'd ever felt lonelier. If Mitch was alive, they would be with her family. And wouldn't that have been fun, to have their first Christmas together and share a bed under her family's roof? How many times while growing up had she fantasized about that?

She wondered what he would have given her this year. Probably something to celebrate the baby. They would be thinking about how to decorate the nursery for their little girl. Mitch would want to participate in the decorating because he was that kind of man.

She would have given him a really nice silk bathrobe, a few ties, and one specific Hermes tie with red hearts on a navy background that she had seen when they were exploring London as newlyweds. There would have been a few books and the framed ultrasound photo of their baby girl. He'd have been excited. Their baby would be his first blood relative since his mother died.

He would have made a wonderful father to their daughter. She could see him teaching their little girl to ride a bike, bandaging a scraped knee, and hugging her as she cried. Maybe he'd teach her some of his taekwondo moves so she could defend herself on the playground and in life. She could see him explaining to their little girl in a few years that she was about to have a sister or brother, and it didn't change how much Mommy and Daddy loved her. And later, he'd tell her that her first crush was a jerk and that she deserved better. That hadn't been the case with Rebecca's first crush, but then they weren't typical.

Rebecca had to fight back a few tears. The sun was lowering on the horizon and caught her engagement ring, flashing a red spark, not green as she would have thought it would have.

She hadn't thought of taking off the emerald. It meant too much. Eventually, she should get it sized for her right hand, she supposed. But she wasn't ready. Hell, she hadn't even been married six months yet, and here she was, a widow.

Reflexively, she touched her belly. Their little girl was in there, growing. And in a few months, she'd have a little part of Mitch back. All the fantasies she had about the little girl looking up to her father, being Daddy's little girl, they weren't going to happen. The poor child would never know her father, but the people closest to Mitch would be there to tell stories and try to let their daughter know her father, even though he was dead long before she was born.

Halfway back to Yachats, Rebecca turned on her music. She needed a distraction, and she needed to stop thinking about Mitch, or soon she would be crying too hard to drive.

It was late afternoon when she arrived home, and after she put her groceries away, still having second thoughts about the plant-based beef, she focused on the little box of lights. It had been such a stupid purchase. But it reminded her of the big tree her mother always got for their house in New York. It had white lights on it, not colored lights that Alex and Rebecca preferred because her mother didn't like the garish-colored lights. The white lights, she said, reminded her of the sparkles in snow. She supposed there was a big tree in their suite in Portland. Maybe next year she'd want to see it.

At Christmas, when she was a teenager, before she and Mitch were lovers, they had exchanged gifts because once he started coming home with Alex, he was part of the family. Her mother used to spoil him right along with her other children.

The gifts he gave to her always meant so much. The first year, he'd given Rebecca a small iPod filled with music. She'd almost worn it out, but she still had it. Then, when she'd been fifteen, he'd taught her to drive, given her lessons for Christmas and a bejeweled keychain of a big "R," with faux emerald Swarovski crystals on it. She still had it, too.

Then someone told him that she liked perfume. She suspected her mother. Then he started giving her perfume, Samsara, and then Cartier. Always red bottles. It didn't matter what was inside of them. The bottles were always red, just like the Bulgari he'd brought her from London. Why had she never thought to ask him about the red bottles? The perfume was always wonderful, but still, it was something she could put on her skin. Every time she smelled it, she thought of Mitch.

Without knowing she was doing it, she sniffed her wrist, smelling the Bulgari that was there. At the rate she was using it, she would have to buy another bottle in a month. She'd keep the bottle Mitch brought her. She'd never get rid of it, but she would buy additional bottles to keep the memory of the scent alive.

She thought of the gifts she'd given him over the years. He'd kept them because she found them in his flat in London. Each year, she'd given him books, and because he liked to read, especially about history, until he stepped it up to the perfume, then she'd done what she wanted to do. She'd give him her favorite book of the year, and also something personal. Something that he could wear and think of her. The Wharton fleece had been a gift from her, as were several of the ties he wore during the time he worked in London. They were nice ties when she bought them under the guise that he would need them for his upcoming interviews. They were expensive at the time, but it said something to her that he'd kept them and was still wearing them.

While they'd been in bed after they'd gotten married, he admitted to wearing the Hermes burgundy tie that had little dragons on it with his navy suit during their first Zoom call because he was thinking about her. He hoped she'd recognize it, and she had.

Her landline rang and interrupted her thoughts of Christmas past. She snarled a little. It was no doubt her mother, who called twice a day, morning and night.

She picked up the phone and said, "Hello, Mother."

"Good guess, darling. How are you today?"

"Just as fine as I was fine this morning when you called. Nothing has changed, and you?"

"Well, you will have to forgive me if we lose each other. We are driving in a spotty area," Victoria complained.

"The West Hills, huh?" Rebecca asked, wondering why her mother had not waited until she got home to call. The west hills of Portland were notorious for spotty cellphone coverage.

"No, darling. Highway 101," her mother said.

"What?" Rebecca asked. This was not funny.

"Surprise. If you don't come home to see your family, your family will come to you. Ah, we are just turning into your driveway. See you in a minute." Then her mother hung up on her before Rebecca could say another word.

Rebecca stood and looked out the window that faced the driveway. Yep, two cars were turning into her driveway: one of the black hotel Mercedes, STARK 7, and a black Porsche Panamera. At least her brother had been smart enough to drive his own car.

"Shit," Rebecca muttered under her breath.

She stepped out onto the back porch and gave the arrivals a closed mouth smile.

A moment later, her parents and her brother descended on the beach house.

A flurry of activity ensued as Rebecca stood back and watched. Finally, she claimed her favorite chair and wondered if she was in the middle of some strange live theater production of "Spring Up Christmas."

These people looked like her family, but they were insane. A small tree was erected in her living room, and boxes of ornaments were placed next to it. Presents were stacked on chairs. Food in the form of large, foiled baking dishes were put in the oven, and timers were set. Alex carried luggage to various bedrooms upstairs as if he were a very high-priced valet.

But when her mother arrived next to her chair with a tall glass of cranberry juice over ice and a vitamin, Rebecca lost it.

"Mom, what the hell is going on? What is this pill?"

"It is a prenatal vitamin. I wasn't sure you were taking any."

"Of course I'm taking prenatal vitamins."

"Good dear," Victoria said and walked over to the Christmas tree, reached into one of the boxes, and pulled out several strands of clear lights that she plugged in. She seemed delighted that they all worked as she started stringing them on the tree.

Rebecca watched as her father smiled to himself in her kitchen. Then he poured a bourbon and coke into a highball glass and added a lime wedge. She didn't like bourbon, so she would never have bought it. Besides, she was pregnant. She didn't have booze in the house. And she didn't have any limes. He set down the bourbon next to three or four other bottles of booze. In less than five minutes, her kitchen was a bar, and dinner was cooking in the oven.

"What is in my oven?" Rebecca asked.

Her brother appeared and smiled like a smug asshole as he said, "A bun."

"Duh. The oven in my kitchen, smart ass."

Victoria arranged the lights on one of the branches and said, "That is a prime rib. And in ten minutes, we will add the dish of scalloped potatoes."

So much for her plant-based dinner. You didn't stop the Stark train when it was going full speed. She took a sip of her cranberry juice and wished there was some vodka or gin in it.

"Well, it looks like you're staying for Christmas," she said. "Even though I didn't buy any presents and asked that I be allowed to skip it this year."

"Oh, but you did buy presents. And I really thought you did a good job this year," her mother said with a wink.

Rebecca wanted to cry and relive all the Christmas pasts with Mitch. Her family, specifically her mother, was not going to let her. So much for sticking a fork in the middle of the French Silk pie and eating her way to the edge. Damn it, her mother had also made a red velvet cake, Rebecca's favorite.

After the prime rib, which she found she liked, to her surprise, they sat around and opened presents, as was their preference on Christmas Eve.

Alex gave her a sterling silver rattle from Tiffany's that was engraved with *"Baby Wilder."* She teared up as she hugged her brother.

"And I picked it out myself," he said proudly.

Her parents gave her a large, heart-shaped light green stone to wear around her neck.

Her mother patted Rebecca's thigh as she stared at the large stone.

"It is really pretty. Is it beryl?" Rebecca asked. It would match the emerald. She might even call it a light emerald. Maybe it was a tourmaline.

"It is a rather rare, natural green aquamarine."

Rebecca loved gems, so she knew it was in the emerald family. And it was just like emerald, but it had less chromium and a little bit of iron, which actually made it stronger.

Rebecca waited for the reason. With her parents and jewelry, there was always a reason, just like the emerald engagement ring.

Her mother looked contemplative and then said, "Mitch's birthday was in March. It is his birthstone. I thought it seemed appropriate."

There was the reason. This time, Rebecca did cry. She and her mother had been discussing the potential of a small memorial service on Mitch's birthday to celebrate his life. She tried to put it out of her mind.

Rebecca had sent her mother photos of her ultrasound. The mother and daughter did think alike. Victoria and Garrison loved the framed photos of their first grandchild, which were in silver frames. Rebecca's mother had gotten creative.

"Hells bells, what did I give you?" Rebecca asked her brother, Alex.

"Let's find out," he said as he reached for his gift "from her."

Alex opened the box and sighed.

"What?" she asked.

"It is a bit of a hodgepodge," he said, holding up a box of glow-in-the-dark condoms.

Rebecca didn't think she would ever laugh, not today of all days, but she did laugh. She couldn't help it.

"Mom, I'd have been much more likely to enter him into the bacon of the month club," Rebecca said.

"Well, we will consider that for his birthday in June," Victoria said.

"Gee, I even got a print and digital subscription to *Playboy, Architectural Digest,* and *Oprah* magazines," he said.

"That seems like it will make you well-rounded," Rebecca laughed.

"And, oh joy, what is this," he said, holding up an envelope. Then he read what was inside and got a horrified look on his face. "I'm Bachelor of the Month? April?"

"It's good, it is for charity, for homeless pets," their mother said. "You will be purchased at the luncheon of The Ladies Auxiliary of Portland in April. The charity has already been picked. You know how I feel about animals. The person who buys you will have you for the day. I'm told they really like landscape work because the average age of the ladies is something like seventy-five, and it hurts their knees to bend down. So, remember to wear something you can use to weed the flower beds, but don't be surprised if they have a garage or an attic for you to clean out."

Rebecca couldn't stop laughing, but when she met her brother's horrified stare, she said, "I'm sorry. I'll buy you some spider repellant for the garage and attics."

"I don't know how to weed. That is what you hire gardeners for," Alex complained.

"Victoria, really, that seems even harsh to me," Garrison said and then to Alex, "Don't worry, I'll lend you a gardener from the staff."

"You will do no such thing. I think it will be good for him. I mean, come on, he got a subscription to *Playboy*. I'm not heartless," Victoria said innocently. "But it is important to me that my children are well-rounded and can get their hands dirty once in a while. Alex is a little spoiled."

"Thanks Mom. Care to explain this?" Alex said, holding up a final box within his gift.

"You'll like what is inside of that," Victoria said.

"Cannot wait," Alex said and then opened the box.

He held up a blue sweatshirt with red letters, ironically the colors of Wharton Business School, but it was still something he'd never be seen in. In big letters, it read: #1 Uncle.

"Oh," Rebecca said. "I love it."

Mitch

All Mitch did was wait. He counted the minutes. Hell, he counted the seconds. He could bear weight on his broken leg, so they had moved him from what he called the "hospital" tent to some structure that reminded him of a Quonset hut. It stank of stale death and body odor. And unlike some odors, he never got used to it. Then he wondered if he was smelling himself. He hadn't had a shower in months. He had a cot and a little space to himself behind a locked door. There was a hole in the floor that served as a latrine. Strangely, they didn't chain him up like they had before. Well, the place he was in now felt much more secure. He didn't want to think of how many had come before him. And he didn't want to examine the strange stains on the floor too closely.

Mitch tried to bring order to the information he had. He was captive for ransom. They had all of his identification, knew he was American, and probably by now had a good idea why he'd been in Iraq. Mitch presumed they were holding out for the big bucks. If Rebecca knew where he was, she'd get her father to fund the ransom. He was sure of it.

When he was at his most desperate, he thought of Rebecca. Her gorgeous hair, mesmerizing eyes, cute little nose—and by now, her pregnancy would be showing, that was if she hadn't lost the baby, their baby, whom he was sure was a little girl. He longed to be there with her, to see her belly grow with their child. Mitch prayed she was okay and hoped once again the military was looking for him. He was pretty sure he was the only survivor, though no one told him for sure.

Why wasn't his ransom getting paid? Who were they talking to?

Sometimes, his captors fed him, sometimes they didn't. It was part of their torture. And when they did feed him, he tried not to look like he was ravenous, although hunger never left him. Curry seemed to be the meal of choice for prisoners. He no longer cared that he didn't like it. He needed to survive. He would also get a single bottle of Volvic water each day. Sometimes it was still sealed; sometimes it wasn't. And when it wasn't, he wondered if he'd be dead after he drank it. Then he rationalized that if he was dead, his suffering would be over, but so would his hope of ever seeing Rebecca again.

No, they'd probably just shoot him if they wanted to end it.

Mitch thought it had been weeks, if his count was right, at least six since the photo of him with the paper. But it was hard to tell not only how many days he'd been held but also whether it was day or night. He tried to keep track of the different guard shifts, which he thought happened every six to eight hours.

They'd taken his watch in the beginning and his wedding ring at the time of the photo, so he had no way to measure time. The groove that was starting to develop on his finger from the ring was gone. He touched the place often. The thought of that made him very sad. He thought of Rebecca all the time. *I'm alive, baby. Don't give up hope.*

The slot of his door opened, and this time it was more rice and curry sauce, but also some kind of dark meat that he would have said was goat. He doubted they would give him anything as good as a goat. Then the guards talked too fast for him to understand anything, but he was able to pick up one word, "Chellah." It was what Persian cultures celebrated near Christmas: Chellah Night, the celebration of Winter Solstice.

He'd been a captive for almost four months.

He had to get out of here somehow. Mitch couldn't count on them releasing him. They had to have received the ransom money by now, making him wonder if they were asking for more or if they were asking the right people. They probably had no intention of letting him go free. It was then Mitch realized if he wanted to live, it was up to him. And that's when he decided it was time to get serious.

Mitch needed to get his strength back.

He got out of bed and knew what he had to do. He dropped to the filthy floor and did one hundred pushups, then one hundred sit-ups. Then he repeated the action.

He was going to get out of there or die trying.

CHAPTER TWENTY

Rebecca
March 21st

Rebecca hated this, but Victoria had insisted that it be done. Rebecca had turned over all the planning to her mother, as the mere thought of arranging such a thing made her cry. She didn't think they needed to have a memorial service for Mitch, but that didn't matter.

Donovan had sent Mitch's luggage from the Hilton in Saudi Arabia to the address in the United States Rebecca had provided. Victoria had brought the bag to Rebecca.

Since Rebecca had watched Mitch pack it, it held no surprises, except a couple of photos of her and then of she and Mitch together in New York. It hurt, and although she had copies of the same photos, she liked having the set he had taken with him.

"We must have a memorial service," her mother had said, and arguing with her was futile. Victoria was acting like Mitch's mother so Rebecca knew she couldn't stop it.

"If you want it done so badly, then you can arrange it," Rebecca had retorted.

"Listen, I know you don't want to do this. This doesn't kill hope. It just helps us to move forward."

It would not help Rebecca to move forward.

First of all, they still didn't have Mitch's body. Second, Mitch wasn't religious. Third, what they were doing was morbid. Fourth, Mitch would have hated it.

Rebecca wore a designer black maternity dress that her

mother had purchased for her and stood on the beach next to her parents, Alex, and her cousins, Adam, and Spencer. A handful of Mitch's friends had assembled as well. Alex had sent the plane to New York for them, and Adam had hosted them as they flew to Portland and eventually driven to Yachats. It was hard for Rebecca because she knew most of them, and they were in disbelief that she had married Mitch and was actually his wife. To see that she was pregnant had a lot of them shaking their heads in disbelief.

Victoria had asked a nondenominational minister from the Yachats local community church to officiate and read a prayer from the Bible as they did a little memorial service by the ocean for Mitch. The minister was happy to comply, and Rebecca wondered how much her mother had donated to the church.

They all held white roses that they were going to lay in the surf, which was getting closer with each word the minister spoke.

After he finished, each person said a little something about Mitch.

Alex said, "I remember when we met. I thought Mitch would be a good wingman because he had this great smile. Then we started talking, and I realized Mitch was a heck of a nice guy. He wasn't just my best friend. I came to think of him as the brother I never had. I miss him each and every day. I will be there for Mitch's Bex, who just happens to be my sister. I will make sure the baby knows about her dad—the good things, not the things we vowed never to tell another living soul." His last line elicited a chuckle from their friends.

Rebecca was the last to speak and had a hard time putting her feelings into words.

"To my darling husband, our time together was too short, but I think in those few short weeks, we had the best time of our lives. Thank you for our daughter. I will raise her to know what a loving and kind person that you were. You are in my heart forever, my darling. Happy 31st birthday." She had more to say, but she was crying too hard to get a word out.

Her mother and father hugged her as she cried.

They ended up back at the beach house where staff borrowed from the Stark Hotel in Portland had put together a sumptuous buffet lunch with an open bar that was ready to drown anyone's sorrows.

"I'm glad you thought of that," Garrison said to Victoria as they stood on the deck and enjoyed the rare early spring sun that had decided to grace the day.

"What?" Rebecca asked, holding a glass of ginger ale as she joined her parents.

"I bought out two of the little hotels in town so Mitch's friends and our staff could stay the night instead of facing a three-hour drive back to Portland."

"That was a good idea. I just wanted to thank you. It was a nice service," she said and felt that all too familiar lump form in her throat.

"It needed to be done, and now it is over," her father said.

"I never need to live this day again," Rebecca said.

Each parent wrapped an arm around her, but they didn't speak. They just watched the water and let their own thoughts ebb and flow with the breaking waves.

CHAPTER TWENTY-ONE

May

"I'm huge," Rebecca said to her mother.

"You are glowing," Victoria said as she hugged her daughter.

"I'm tired of being pregnant. I was due yesterday," she said.

"I know, honey," her mother said.

"I've mentioned it a few times."

"Once, twice, twelve times. It is okay," Victoria said. "You are allowed."

Her father stuck his head in the doorway to the bedroom they had fixed up for the baby, which was opposite Rebecca's bedroom on the first floor of the beach house, and said, "The flowers are planted, the lawn is mowed, and the car is washed. What next?"

"The gutters?" Victoria asked.

"Done," Garrison said.

"Could you help us assemble the damn crib?" Rebecca asked.

"We almost have it, I think," Victoria complained.

"Right," Rebecca said. "Sure. And those extra parts?"

She sat on the little couch they had purchased for the baby's room and watched as her parents assembled the crib that would soon be where her and Mitch's baby would sleep. There was also a new rocking chair and changing-station-dresser combo. Victoria and Garrison had hung seashell pink wallpaper. Rebecca was thankful for the help and knew her parents needed a project.

Mitch should have been here to assemble the crib. He should be here to love her, to love their baby.

She must have sighed because her mother stopped helping her dad and said, "Are you okay, Becca?"

"I'm fine. I think I'll go the kitchen for water or something," she said. "Maybe I'll just pace."

"I can get you something," her father offered.

"She wants to move around to start the labor," her mother said.

Ten minutes later, she was leaning against the counter and trying to breathe. The movement had worked. The contractions had started, and they were coming faster than she'd like.

Her parents were on each side of her, and they both looked worried.

"Okay," her father said. "We have to get to the hospital. They are three minutes apart."

"But they are supposed to be two to four minutes apart, and that pattern is supposed to last for two hours before the hospital," Rebecca said. "It has only been about ten...oh...shit...minutes."

"Let's go now," her mother said.

This was a fight she wasn't going to win.

Five hours later, she sat up in her hospital bed and looked down at the little bundle in her arms. Her daughter was perfect. If she did say so herself, she and Mitch had made a beautiful baby.

Their little girl had her father's dimples, and Rebecca was pretty sure she had his smile, too. And her eyes were blue, but she bet in a few months that they would go green. She just had a feeling. This baby was stunning.

Her mother had been in the delivery room with her, holding her hand and offering encouragement. If it couldn't be Mitch, she was happy it could be her mother.

There was a knock on the door, and then her mother appeared with her father.

"Hey, Dad, would you like to meet your granddaughter?"

Her father looked like he might dissolve into tears as he nodded. There was a lot of that going around. She wished she had stock in Kleenex's parent company, because the Stark and Wilder families had gone through a lot of tissues that day.

"Have you decided on a name?" her mother asked.

Rebecca nodded. "Please meet Emily Stark Wilder."

Mitch

He heard the guards change outside his door, and he quickly stopped his exercise routine, which was a mix of basic calisthenics and taekwondo. The less they knew, the better. He tried to appear weak at all times, but he knew he was getting stronger. He was the only one who could get himself free, which had become more evident these last weeks. He knew time was running out. At any moment, they could come for him, take him into the desert, and that would be all she wrote.

The paper and photograph routine had been repeated two times since the winter solstice. But the last time, which was three days ago, there was a little something more. They had brought him a phone connected to none other than Lucien Donovan. Even though the last time they had talked hadn't gone well, Mitch had never been happier. Surely, Donovan would call in the troops in the form of the State Department, the Army, the Marines, Homeland Security...anyone who could get him out.

"Mitch, holy shit. Everyone, including the American State Department, thinks that you are dead," Lucien said, sounding almost like it was a joke. Mitch didn't like the tone of the conversation. Something about Lucien and the way he had responded. Well, he knew the man could be cold, but this...this was so much worse.

"I cannot tell you how honored I am because this means I get to bargain for your life myself. There is no need to bring in the government with all their negotiators and red tape. You look terrible. Your hair...you've got quite a beard."

"Pay them. I'll pay you back," Mitch ordered, dismissing the pleasantries.

Lucien was silent, then he said, "Did you know my little Lily cried over you? It broke my heart to see her like that and to know you were to blame. I think that is an offense you could be sentenced to death for, but I'll think about it."

Then he hung up. He hung up on Mitch's kidnappers.

A trickle of fear traveled through Mitch's body.

CHAPTER TWENTY-TWO

Rebecca

The landline at the beach house rang, and Rebecca struggled to get it. She didn't want the baby to wake up, not after she hadn't wanted to get to sleep last night. Rebecca shook her head. This child was her mother's daughter. Her teen years would be epic, much like her mother's. Rebecca was already worried.

She had been sleeping on the couch, which was convenient when Emily was napping in one of the downstairs bedrooms. The noisy phone was just a nasty interruption. She wanted to yell at the person on the other end of the line, but she was pretty sure it would be her mother, whose life Rebecca had made a living hell in the last year. At least Rebecca had a new sympathy for her parents.

"Hello," she answered, trying to keep her anger in check.

"I'm coming to see you next week," her mother announced.

Not this again. There wasn't even a polite, "Is that okay?" No, now her mother just appeared. There was no asking, no taking no for an answer.

"Mom, I'm fine. You don't need to." Seriously, her mother just wanted to come and hold the baby. And maybe suggest that Rebecca get her hair styled.

In truth, Victoria was very worried about her daughter, and with good reason. Rebecca had something a little worse than postpartum depression. Since Emily's birth, she felt like she had lost Mitch all over again. She couldn't stop crying. She cried every day, and no one was fooled. She was struggling.

Mitch would be so angry with her for not pulling it together. He would want her to get on with life. It had been eleven months. She was trying to accept what was unacceptable. She couldn't if *people* kept reminding her of the worst thing that had ever happened. It's too bad she was the *people* in that scenario. She could not stop thinking about him. Everything reminded her of Mitch.

She wondered what he'd think of her now. Bex no longer existed. She was no longer the confident woman who had boldly told him that she wanted to watch him shower or told him what to do to her when they made love. No, she didn't recognize herself, not this emotional puddle. She no longer looked sexy. She looked like a lactating mother.

Their baby, their precious, sweet little girl, represented the best of their life together. Rebecca had lost Mitch, but she had Emily, and that was amazing.

"I'm just sorry that I couldn't stay with you for longer after Emily's birth."

Her mother had stayed for three weeks. That was enough. Then she visited again less than two weeks later.

"It's fine. We are fine." Well, as fine as she could be. She might never be okay again.

"Well, I haven't seen you or Emily for three weeks. I need to see you both with my own eyes."

Accept what you cannot change. Hadn't that become her mantra in the last few weeks? Her mother had wanted to come two weeks ago, but Rebecca had come up with an excuse, which was lame because it was her parents' house, and really, they could visit whenever they wanted. They had keys and stuff.

"Is Dad coming with you?" Rebecca asked.

"Yes, if that is okay," her mother said.

Well, that would all depend on how long they stayed.

"Is Alex coming?" Alex had become much more important to

her since Mitch's death. Through their shared grief, he had become her closest friend.

In one of their evening phone chats, he had mentioned he was between girlfriends at the moment. Ironically, his last steady was the granddaughter of the woman who bought him at the auction in April. Rebecca didn't know the details, but knowing her brother, well, she just shook her head. Someday, someone would mess with him in a way that he could not ignore. She would mess with his world. Rebecca couldn't wait to see that play out and meet the person responsible. He might have the persona of a playboy, but she knew the sweet person behind the façade.

"Yes, but he is coming in a separate car because he is only staying for a couple of days. Daddy needs him to go to Singapore."

"Okay, what should I get from the store?" Rebecca asked. This was their ritual.

"Don't worry, we will bring everything we need," her mother said. "Is there anything I can bring you from town?"

"I'm about out of lipstick. I was going to go online, but if you could get me something reddish from Nordstrom, I'd appreciate it."

"What brand?" her mother asked.

"Whatever you think will look good. I don't really care, but most days, I only slather on some random color and call it good."

Rebecca could hear her mother sigh at the other end of the line.

"I'll get you a few things and maybe a few things for the baby. Do you have any facial cleanser? Moisturizer? Powder? Eyeshadow? Blush? Mascara?"

"Um...well...don't go crazy," Rebecca said.

"Don't worry, you know how much I like this kind of thing. I'll see you in a few days. I'll call tomorrow morning."

"Okay," Rebecca said with no enthusiasm.

Five minutes later, the phone rang again. "What now, Mom?"

"Mrs. Wilder?" the man asked.

"I'm sorry. Yes, this is Mrs. Wilder," she confirmed. There had been a lot going on with paperwork regarding Mitch's death. Heck, Donovan's insurance company had yet to pay. Rebecca didn't need the money. It would all go into a trust for Emily, but she thought of the other families and wondered what it would take to get it finished.

"This is Matt Jones with the United States State Department in Washington, D.C."

He had her full attention.

"We've been picking up on some chatter that may concern the helicopter crash that killed Mr. Wilder last fall."

"What have you heard?" Rebecca asked, her heart beating through her chest.

"Have you talked directly to Lucien Donovan? I see you were employed by his company."

"I talked to him after Mitch died, after I'd quit the company," she said.

"We would just like to have you take us through your last conversation with Lucien Donovan. Do you happen to remember the date of that interaction?"

She told him everything she knew.

"Is there a chance my husband is alive?" she said, thinking they might be the most important words she'd ever spoken.

"No, I'm sorry, Mrs. Wilder."

She wanted to ask more, but after a few basic platitudes, Matt Jones ended the call.

Mitch

Two Days Earlier

Mitch ran for his life. He hated Lucien Donovan, but damn, the taekwondo had come in handy. He'd been practicing in his cell, keeping what little muscle tone he had left, waiting for an opportunity. Then one presented. He felt bad. He didn't want to think of what he'd done. But when it was kill or be killed, sometimes you had to make the hard decisions. No doubt, they'd found the guard's body by now.

He was closer to a town than he'd thought possible. He wondered if it was friendly or hostile? Now it was just a matter of finding a way out. Hell, he'd escaped. Wasn't the hard part over? And now he was cowering behind some random building.

He heard the shot, felt the pain, and then saw the blood. So much for easy.

CHAPTER TWENTY-THREE

Rebecca straightened each room in the house. It wasn't much, but at least the house was clean, well, sort of. She hoped her family wouldn't look in the corners. Her mother had a staff of maids at her disposal, but that did not stop her from getting on her hands and knees to take care of business when she needed to.

Well, at least she changed the sheets on her bed. She couldn't remember the last time she'd done that, but she had a bad feeling it had been more than a week or two ago. She needed to start paying more attention.

Matt Jones. Matt Jones. Matt Jones.

She had run over their brief phone call at least five hundred times in her mind since it had happened earlier in the week and tried to read between the lines. He had given her nothing but pumped her for every shred of information she had. She didn't know what to think. And what had his parting words been? "I'm sorry, Mrs. Wilder, we are just crossing all the T's and dotting the I's. There is nothing for you to do or think about. Thank you for the information."

Yet what had she done? She obsessed with the information. She needed to take action where she could.

Tomorrow, before her family arrived, Rebecca decided that she would make an effort. It was time to start making plans.

She'd use a curling iron. She'd find her emergency tube of lipstick in a pleasing color instead of the generic drugstore crap she'd purchased when she last bought diapers. Maybe she would try some mascara, if there was any left in the tube she had. When was the last time she'd worn mascara? April? She was looking forward to her mother's little care kit that would no doubt be chock full of goodies, like expensive lipstick and baby clothes for Emily.

What did they say? Fake it until you make it? Maybe she was ready to make an effort.

It was a get-busy-living or die-with-Mitch moment, and she had decided she had wallowed long enough. Her baby needed a good mother who was present and moving forward in her life. Life was hard enough.

She lived for Emily. She was so thankful for her beautiful, perfect baby. She was a blessing, and Rebecca thought the baby had done a lot to get her through the last year of her life. Maybe, when the weather started to turn a little nasty at the beach, she should think about moving back to Portland and possibly think about getting a job. She could get a nanny, but more likely, her mother would want to have Emily with her if Rebecca went to work.

What would she do for work? Ask her father for a job? She'd come a long way by even exercising this conversation in her head. It was enough for now, but it had started the wheels turning. She found mascara and lipstick and applied it. She brushed her hair and used some of the perfume Mitch had given her. She saved it now for special occasions, but it was called for today because this was a scary conversation to ponder, and she was brave to have it. It deserved to be considered special. Small, baby steps, but significant in their own way.

Before the baby woke up that afternoon from her midday nap, Rebecca stepped onto the deck and let the sun hit her face. Yes, it was a beautiful day, and they could walk on the beach. Rebecca wanted and needed the exercise, and she thought Emily liked it, too. At least Emily liked to smile when they were outside.

The walks on the beach had become something Rebecca

loved. The Pacific, with its power and majesty, would never disappoint.

When the baby woke up, Rebecca said, "Okay, baby girl, guess what? It is beach time!"

As was her ritual, she slathered them both in sunscreen, baby sunscreen for Emily. It was probably unnecessary, but if there was a chance of sun exposure, she wouldn't risk it. She wore a big hat and made sure the baby was covered up.

Placing Emily in her stroller, Rebecca locked the house's main door and pocketed her keys and phone. Then they took a ramp to the beach, a block away from their house. Normally, when she used to come to the beach before Mitch, she would have traversed the cliff right in front of the house, but not with the stroller and its precious cargo.

"Here we are, baby girl. The beach is ours to explore."

The noise of the waves breaking on the beach was calming to Rebecca as different thoughts entered her head. She realized her first wedding anniversary would be in a little over a week. It seemed like ten years ago that she and Mitch had run to city hall and gotten married. At the moment, she didn't think she could fit into the Chanel suit. Not like she'd ever wear it again, but it reminded her of one of the best days of her life. Maybe someday Emily would wear that suit.

Rebecca couldn't look at Emily and not feel the joy of having their baby, even though, in the end, Mitch wasn't a gift she could keep. She had become reticent. She was now happy for the time they had together. Lots of people never knew that kind of love. She had been lucky.

She felt cheated they wouldn't be growing old together, but it wasn't meant to be. Currently, there would be no picket fences and no father to walk Emily down the aisle when she married one day. Emily would never know Mitch. She would be told stories from every member of the Stark family, but it wouldn't be the same. Emily, as well as Rebecca, would always carry a hole in their hearts for Mitch.

Then and there, she decided her daughter would grow up in a house with a white picket fence. Rebecca would have that for Emily. They would live in a big house with a white picket fence and rose bushes in the backyard in a neighborhood where all the kids ran around on their bikes. She could give that to her child.

There would be a lot of men who could walk their daughter down the aisle. Alex, Spencer, and Adam came to mind. But maybe it would just be Emily and Rebecca. Nowhere was it written that it had to just be the father.

She often thought of what she should have said to have prevented Mitch from going on the trip. She had asked him nicely. Well, if she could turn back time, nice wouldn't have been an option. She'd have been unrelenting and forced him not to go. She'd have threatened him, yelled at him, and cajoled him. She'd have tied him up to prevent him from going on that trip. She had been too damn polite. If she ever felt that way about anything again, she would scream and fight. The whole memory was insanity. No matter how many times she went over it in her head, she could not change it. It was over, done. He had gone to Iraq. That was what had happened.

Rebecca regretted that she should have let her father walk her down the aisle when she'd had the chance. Why hadn't she? Because she was a strong, independent woman who didn't need anyone. Well, that was a myth. She needed everyone. Well, she had just needed one person, Mitch. Without him, there was no way to fill the void. But she hadn't died with him, and he wouldn't want her to act as if she had.

She wanted to show Emily that life might have punched her in the gut, but she had survived. Rebecca Stark Wilder was a survivor. But now she didn't want to just survive. She wanted to thrive.

Rebecca felt something she hadn't felt in a long time: hope. Hope for their future.

She readjusted the visor on the baby's stroller to make sure Emily wasn't touched by any of the rays of the sun. She might be wearing sunscreen, but Rebecca wasn't about to let her get exposed to the sun. A baby had such delicate skin. Emily's was absolutely perfect, but then Emily was a perfect baby. She was the most precious thing in Rebecca's world, and she would do anything to protect her. Mitch would have been so excited. Their baby was such a combination of them both. Now in a little pink outfit trimmed with little pink kittens, Emily looked up at Rebecca and smiled.

"Thanks, kid," she whispered, "I needed that. I love you with all my heart."

Emily did have her father's dimples. Every time Rebecca looked at her baby, she would see Mitch. It was a gift and a curse. Then she wondered if she could change the narrative. Maybe Mitch reminded her of her daughter, not the other way around.

What had her father said when he found out she was pregnant? He was Mr. Sensitive until her mother stopped him. Oh, yes. The reality of life. *It was highly likely she would get married again. And doesn't your baby deserve to have a father?*

And he really didn't get that it was too damn soon for her. The thought of dating, well, it made her feel a little sick. Could she make love with another person? She didn't think so. Besides, she was lactating, which led to leaking. What man wanted to get up next to that? Well, a father of a baby would understand, but a stranger wouldn't. And wasn't it just a moot point anyway? She didn't want to date. Her old boyfriend, Ken, had called from New York a few times when he heard about Mitch. How could she have ever dated him? By what he said, he was hinting at an invitation to visit her. That wasn't going to happen.

Alex had already volunteered to be there any time Emily needed a male perspective. *Uncle Alex.* She thought her brother was a goof most of the time, but he had stepped up. Uncle Alex was going to be a wonderful uncle. He already had bonded with Emily. They were going to be close. Spencer and their other cousin, Adam, a new father himself had also volunteered to help, although each of them had their own lives and lived far away. This baby would not be alone, but Rebecca was sad for her. Mitch was such a wonderful man. How would she ever be able to tell Emily about him?

Rebecca blinked, her face contorting with a sob she couldn't repress. So much for this new epiphany of strength!

Damn the breastfeeding. She could really use a glass of wine.

They had walked a long way on the beach, and finally, it was time to turn back. Tonight, she would be cooking a frozen lasagna her mother had made and left in the freezer when she'd been with Rebecca at Emily's birth.

It was amazing Rebecca could look at Italian food and not run as far away as possible. One thing she knew was that Mitch loved Italian food enough that he'd learned to make it, and there were promises of seduction with a certain pasta dish he had perfected. Well, she'd try not to think about that.

The beach was now full of people. There were families trying to decide if they could swim in the Pacific, which was not advisable because it would feel like ice and was rougher than anyone could imagine, even though it was summer. If they were lucky, they'd get in to about a knee and run the other way. Liquid ice had a way of taking away bravado. Others lay on the perfect sand, working on their suntans. Some looked for agates, but most of all, they enjoyed the sunny day.

The sun was high in the sky despite the late hour. She glanced at her watch; it was four-thirty, definitely time to head back. She tried not to think of the night ahead. The baby would distract her nicely, but then there would be lasagna and television. Finally, at midnight or one in the morning, she'd be exhausted enough to sleep for three hours before it was time for Emily's feeding, if Rebecca slept at all.

Maybe her brother or one of her cousins would call tonight. She was pretty sure they had a little rotation going on to help her in the evenings when she was at her loneliest. She could broach the subject of her plans to go back to Portland and get a job. Then they could talk it through.

It was easier to walk south toward home on the beach. The wind was blowing the other way. It was warm, but it had been a little annoying when she'd been walking north and facing into it.

Several groups were gathering driftwood for bonfires. There were dogs on the beach, happily running after sticks. It was shaping up to be a lovely sunset.

Maybe she should get a dog. Mitch had talked about that. He wanted a dog. She wondered what kind he'd want to get. Then she remembered the stuffed animal she'd found in his flat and decided she'd like to see what they might be able to get in the lab family.

As if on cue, a black lab ran up to her leg with a frisbee in its mouth, and she wondered if Mitch was trying to send her a message. Regardless, she tossed the frisbee for the dog and watched him chase after it. She tried to figure out who the dog belonged to, but to no avail.

A lone man walked her way, and something about him was familiar. He walked with a trekking pole, favoring his left leg. If she didn't know better, she'd swear he was making a beeline for her. Well, now she was just feeling paranoid.

The black lab was back, and she tossed the frisbee again.

Glancing up after she'd tossed the frisbee, she thought the man was definitely walking toward her. It didn't worry her because she still had her taekwondo training, and he looked like the wind would knock him over. What did he want with her? He must be a local. Her neighbors were friendly and quite curious about her. *The young widow with the little baby.*

She looked out at the surf and then started heading for the ramp that would take her and Emily off the beach, but now the man walking toward her had picked up his pace. He was headed right—

He looked more than a little familiar. He looked...like a ghost.

She stopped, not believing her eyes, and then he was close enough that she couldn't breathe. And then he smiled. The dimples were still there, but the face was so thin.

"M...M...Mitch?" she whispered as she stepped back and let go of the stroller.

CHAPTER TWENTY-FOUR

Rebecca

I t was his voice, but it couldn't be.

She was laying on something hard and cold, yet a warm hand was touching her cheek. It was very different than the wind that was blowing her hair. She realized she was still on the beach.

Opening her eyes, she saw the ghost of Mitch.

"Hi Bex," he said, and she wanted to scream, but no sound came out of her mouth. The man looked like Mitch, if Mitch had aged and lost a lot of weight. He held Emily in his arms and looked from her to Rebecca.

She was seeing a ghost. Maybe he was visiting her to see his daughter.

"Mitch...Mitch," she said as she managed to sit up. He dropped his trekking pole then and kneeled painfully on the sand. A moment later, he kissed her.

She kissed him back, her hand cupping his face. He was real. She kissed him again and felt the familiar tightening in her gut.

"I don't believe it," she managed.

He was looking at Emily, but now he met her eyes. "I escaped four, maybe five days ago. It is all kind of a blur. One minute, I'd escaped and was in this small village, and then a group of American soldiers, Marines, were rescuing me. It was crazy."

"You are dead," she said.

"No, Bex, I'm alive. Everyone else, everyone who was with me...they are dead. The other men from Donovan Security, I

225

was told they didn't survive. From what I can tell, I came pretty close to joining them on the other side. I was pulled out of the wreckage after the helicopter was shot down. My leg was broken, so I was in a tent until it healed. Then they put me in jail or some sort of cell. I thought I'd die. I think they were planning to kill me, so I escaped when I could. My leg got hurt... well, the other leg...but it will be okay, I'm okay."

"I...I must be dreaming," she said as her fingers dug into the damp sand. "I love you. I missed you so much. You're a ghost."

"I might look like one, but I'm not a ghost. I'm here. I love you and this little baby, our little baby," he said, looking at his daughter with a sweet look she had seen a few times before.

"*I* must have hit my head...Am I dead?" Rebecca asked and reached for Mitch again. He kissed her, her body trembling violently.

"You crumpled, hit the sand with your butt first, then fell backward. I didn't know if I should go for you or the stroller, but when the stroller started tipping, I grabbed it and then saw.... the baby..." his voice tapered off as he looked down at his daughter.

"Emily...I named her Emily...I...did I die?" she asked as she touched his arm, his shoulder, the side of his face. He felt solid under her touch, but she didn't believe it.

"No, Bex, I think you are in shock. Remember the night I left, you mentioned that your period was late, and then you took the pregnancy test?" he said as he looked down at Emily. "I think we conceived her...Emily... The afternoon we got married, when we spent the afternoon consummating our wedding in the bed with the red sheets."

"I...I tell me more," she said, still not believing the unbelievable. "I can't believe it is you."

"It is me," he whispered as tears streamed down his cheeks.

"Tell me something only you would know," she said as tears poured down her cheeks too.

He smiled kindly and kissed her. "I was the first man to make love to you. Remember, we drank some vodka and orange juice from the minibar at the Marriott because we were both nervous? But it was wonderful. We made love three times in that little hotel room with the view of Times Square, and each time was better than the time before. You had your first orgasm, and I felt so empowered because I'd been the one to give it to you. I was a bit in awe of you, how wonderful you were. You weren't in any pain. You had found your passion. We both had a little sheet burn, but it was nothing. Then we found any place we could be alone for the next two weeks before I left for London. It was the biggest mistake of my life leaving you then and leaving you for that last delivery to Iraq."

"Mitch, oh my God...Oh, Mitch." She reached for him then, and he carefully placed the baby back in her stroller and reached for Rebecca. She started sobbing then as she clung to him.

Mitch said, "Hey, everything is going to be fine. I love you. Thoughts of you made me keep fighting. And I had to know if we had a boy or girl."

"Emily is perfect. She looks like you."

Mitch glanced at the baby and smiled, Rebecca, noticing how thin his face was, as he said, "Emily...I love Emily. Maybe she has my dimples, but she is both of us. Our love."

Rebecca said, "I love her so much."

Mitch sat on the sand next to her and wiped away a few tears of his own. "She is beautiful."

"How...I don't understand. How did you get here?" she asked.

"Well, first, they flew me to Germany, to an American Military base, where I was put in the hospital. I don't clearly remember that first day or two...a blur. They had me on some drugs. There were a lot of conversations. Then they told me I could go home. I called Alex. He arranged it. He sent the plane to pick me up in Germany. I landed about four hours ago. Alex was waiting on the tarmac in Portland. He looked so shocked. It was so good to see him…to see you."

"He didn't tell me. Why wouldn't he tell me?"

"I think he was scared I wasn't real. He told me yesterday that you were at the beach, dealing with everything. He drove me here. We talked until I fell asleep in the car. I'm exhausted. I'm sorry I didn't call you first, but I tried, and I couldn't quite remember your number. I blame the concussion. I had his number memorized because it has been the same for ten years. I think I might have taken a few years off his life when he heard my voice. He was completely silent for a full minute. Then he came around. The shock wore off. He's coming back tomorrow with your Mom and Dad."

"He didn't stay?" she asked.

"He knew we needed a little time to ourselves. By being on the beach, you messed up him getting to see our big reunion."

"He didn't tell me. I cannot believe he didn't tell me," she said incredulously. "Is he going to tell them before they come here tomorrow?"

"I don't think so. What I did to him was a shock, and I have a feeling he doesn't want to do that to anyone else. I think he is worried about killing one of your parents. I know this is a shock, but it is me."

He leaned toward her, and they kissed. The way he kissed her was so familiar. She hadn't forgotten it.

"How did you find me on the beach?" She asked as she touched him, her hands running lightly over his body. He couldn't stop kissing her. He kissed her lips, her cheek and, finally, her neck before he answered.

"As we passed the bridge before turning down your drive, I saw you on the beach, so Alex let me off at the ramp. He was going to put my new luggage, purchased at the airport in Germany like I've done before with Heathrow, in your bedroom, and then he was going to leave, so I hope you want me to stay."

They heard a honk and looked up at the road. Alex was leaning out of his Porsche with binoculars up to his face and was waving. Even from that distance she could see his smile. They waved back, and then Alex drove away.

"Well, it looks like my ride has left. By the way, I have a new passport, courtesy of the U.S. government, but I've got to pay Alex back. He called ahead to a couple of stores that were waiting for me. I used his credit cards to pay for everything because I didn't have any cards. All my IDs, etc., they went down with the helicopter. So, really, I hope it is okay if I stay."

"I...I...Are you kidding? Even if you are a ghost, I'm not letting you go. You're my husband. I love you more than life itself. You're never leaving us again," she said as she put her arms around him and pulled him to her. "Do you understand?"

"Yes, I do," he said, wrapping his arms around her.

"Are you okay? You are so thin."

"I got checked out, even gave them blood at the hospital in Germany. Everything is normal. I need to gain forty or fifty pounds, but I'm okay. They gave me a haircut and a shave, probably deloused me. I don't want to know. They even cleaned my teeth. I also had a shower, several showers, which were heaven on Earth. I don't think you'd have recognized me a week ago."

Aside from the thin appearance, Mitch still had his smile. He looked so good to Rebecca that she still wasn't sure she wasn't seeing a figment of her imagination.

"I'd recognize you anywhere," she said.

"I hope so, Bex. And I never want to eat curry again."

"I don't know how to make curry," she said, her arms fitting loosely around him. "You're here. You're home. I'll feed you. You'll gain the weight."

"Just stay close. Having you in my arms is all the fuel I need," he said.

"What happened to your leg?" she asked.

"It is nothing. I'll be fine in a few weeks. I just hurt it escaping. Well, I got shot, but it is minor. It is what they call a nick because it didn't get the bone and was kind of on the edge, but they worried about infection because I was kind of dirty."

Rebecca took in his comment, stifled a cry, and helped him to stand. They walked slowly back to the house, leaning on each other for support, the stroller out before them. It took them a long time because they walked slowly with their arms around each other.

Back at the house, Mitch sunk into her plush couch, and Rebecca placed Emily in his arms. Tears slid down his cheeks, which he unabashedly wiped away. He asked questions about every detail of Rebecca's pregnancy and the birth of their baby.

"I just look at you, and my heart…You're so thin," she said as fresh tears started pooling in her eyes. "I'm worried about you."

"I'm fine, just very lean," he said as he smiled down at Emily. "I didn't work this hard to get back to you to not stay around. Heck, I did taekwondo every day to build strength."

"Forty pounds isn't enough, maybe fifty," she countered. "I think between me and my mother, we can make sure you're well-fed. Who were they, the people who kidnapped you?"

"From what the Marines told me and what I know, the people who kidnapped me were a local terrorist group that had apparently been taking over that little area. They had a tip-off that a big delivery was being made and shot us down. They wanted to loot the helicopters, but they thought they had lucked out when they found a rich British man still alive to kidnap. When they found out I was American, well, Christmas came early," he replied, glancing up to meet her gaze.

"I want to know everything," she said, sitting next to him, her hands reaching out to touch him, making sure that he was there. "Don't withhold anything from me, even if it's going to upset me. Do you understand?"

Stretching toward her as he cradled their baby, he quieted

Rebecca with a soft kiss that was meant to reassure her. "I'm back, and I'm never leaving again. But can we talk about what happened tomorrow? I just want to be with you tonight. Those people controlled my life for a year. I want tonight to just be about us. Okay?"

Mitch

Mitch and Rebecca talked from the afternoon into the evening, filling in the last eleven months of their lives. Rebecca cooked the lasagna, then picked at her dinner as the wind howled and the sun set just beyond the large picture windows to the west, turning the sky a pale pink. Mitch's stomach had shrunk enough he could barely get through his first serving of lasagna. He'd never felt more thankful, more grateful to be where he was.

He watched Rebecca move nervously around the cottage. At first, she'd looked at him like he had crawled his way out of a grave, but now she was starting to relax by slow, measured degrees, the initial shock beginning to wear off. Every few minutes, she would look at him blankly and then reach out and touch him, needing reassurance.

"You know that I'm not going anywhere," he said.

"You said that once before," she said.

"I'm sorry. I should have listened to you."

"I will never let you do anything like that again, understood?"

"Yes, understood," he said. "Now, come here and let me kiss you a bit more."

He never thought he'd see her again. Knowing she might never realize how much she meant to him was the single driving force pushing him to find a way to escape his captors. They might be married, but they hadn't been married long enough.

Never a patient man, he'd waited painstakingly for the

perfect opportunity to present itself with his captures. Then they opened his cell, and he was sure they had been given an order to end his life. They weren't prepared for him, and they lacked the training necessary to fight a man who was prepared to defend himself and hell-bent on survival.

Rebecca and Mitch kissed for a bit on the couch, but after a few minutes, the baby started to fuss, and Rebecca got up to comfort her. He could see that Rebecca was struggling, so he gave her a little space.

The fatigue of his ordeal was quickly catching up with him as he took in all that was familiar and new. Rebecca wouldn't allow him to help clear the dishes or do anything for that matter, except hold Emily. She treated him as if he were a guest. He knew she was barely keeping it together, but he could take no more of her overt politeness. It was time to recapture the happiness that had been stolen from both of them.

Once the baby was happy and content, Rebecca placed her in her bassinet and started cleaning up the kitchen. He walked quietly into the kitchen. He watched as Rebecca clumsily loaded the dishwasher. When he touched her arm, she dropped a plastic bowl, which clanked noisily to the floor, but she didn't notice. Without a word, she reached for him, and he kissed her the way he'd dreamed of for the last eleven months.

"It's going to be alright," he whispered minutes later.

"You know what terrifies me?" she asked, her eyes teary again.

"No, darling. Tell me."

"I'm worried I'll wake up, and you'll be gone. We'll be alone again. I'll have to think of raising Emily without her father. What if this is only a dream?" she asked, her tears dampening his shirt.

"I could pinch you, maybe poke you with something," he offered, adding a smile as he tried to lighten the mood.

She laughed softly. It was a timid sound, nothing like she'd once sounded when she laughed, but he felt her body relax just the same.

"If this is a dream, I don't want to wake up," she murmured and kissed his neck.

"Me neither," he said, then asked, "Could we stay like this for a few minutes?"

"Yes, at least until the baby needs me," she murmured, leaning against him.

"I've known you as a teenager, a woman, a lover, a wife, and now you're a mother," he said. "It is amazing."

"You made me a lot of those things, but I'm most proud of being a mother to our baby," she said as tears leaked out her eyes.

"And hopefully I'll do it again."

He held her for a long time, and they watched the waves crashing on the beach below.

"I hope so, too. But at the moment, you must be exhausted," she murmured.

"I've never been happier or more content in my life than I am at this moment with you," he said as she lifted her head from his shoulder and looked at him, her face so delicate, yet still he could read the worry in her expression.

"Not for a hint of a moment?" she asked, her lower lip trembling.

"No. Never."

"Me neither. You're in my heart. You're a part of me," she explained, placing her hand on his chest and rubbing it in small circles.

"Mrs. Wilder, would you mind if we continue this conversation in bed?"

"Are you in pain?" she asked, her brow wrinkling with concern.

"My heart suffered much more than my stupid leg. I'm tired,

but not that tired. I want to make love with my wife. That is, if you'd like to."

Her eyes widened, and then she smiled. Shyly, she said, "I'm the one who has dark circles under my eyes, and I look haggard. I'm not the same. I still have baby weight. I haven't had my hair styled in months. My body droops, my breasts aren't as perky—"

"You've never looked sexier," he said, pleased with the resulting blush. "I, on the other hand, am the Halloween skeleton."

"Not to me," she said sternly.

"Wait until I'm naked," he said, smiling. "Skeleton isn't sexy."

"Shut up," she whispered, wincing, "and let me be the judge of that."

"I'll take that as a 'yes' to my question," he said, and she kissed him.

"Yes, I've missed you so much," she said.

Sadness was overtaking her again. He had to get her to snap out of it. They had to find the playfulness that had always played a large role in the way they were with each other.

"When does the baby go down for the night?" he asked.

"You're kidding, right? Emily is awake every three hours for a feeding." As she spoke, the baby started to fuss in her bassinet. "And she is just about ready for her first three-hour nap of the night."

Over the next half hour, Mitch watched Rebecca bathe and feed Emily with complete fascination. This other side of Rebecca was as otherworldly as his life had been in Iraq. He knew she was kind and loving but hadn't seen this side of her. Of everything that happened that day, it touched him the most deeply. He felt the ever-present lump in his throat give a little squeeze. Rebecca was a mother to his child who fed hungrily at the breast he had kissed and held.

He bent and kissed the baby's head, then Rebecca's bare breast, and then her lips.

"Would you like to burp her?" Rebecca asked, interrupting his thoughts. He found he couldn't speak but merely nodded as he sat in a large, whitewashed rocking chair as Rebecca placed Emily in his arms and showed him what to do. When Emily finally shut her eyes and drifted off to sleep, Rebecca took her from him and gently placed her in her crib.

"Three hours starts now," Rebecca announced. "Our daughter is consistent. Three hours, almost to the minute."

Rubbing his knuckles along her cheek, he suggested, "Well then, let's take a shower and see where it leads."

After the briefest hesitation, she led him into the downstairs bathroom in Gary and Vic's master bedroom. She took her time adjusting the water to the correct temperature.

"I took this master on the main so I wouldn't have to walk the stairs with a baby."

"I'm glad," he said.

He pulled off his new navy cashmere sweater and the white t-shirt he wore underneath. By the time she'd turned around, he was naked from the waist up.

"I know you like to watch me shower. But this time, I'd like you to join me," he said. "I'd like to scrub your back, or your front and you can keep me from slipping."

For the first time in his life, he felt self-conscious about his body. He'd never been obsessed with his looks. Women seemed to like him the way he was, so it had never been an issue, but now, with Rebecca looking at his shrunken physique and battle scars, he was unsure. He'd been gone almost a year. She was an attractive, healthy woman. New fears came to mind.

"You're so thin," she cried as she ran her warm hands along his ribcage, bone protruding against the skin where there had once been muscle. Her fingers lingered over several of the fresh pink scars, which had once been open wounds, some inflicted by his captors, others from the helicopter crash itself.

"I'm sorry," he said, feeling stupid. "I don't look the same. I might have some good muscle tone, but it is really lean. I haven't been to the gym or jogged—"

"Shut up," she repeated a little more forcefully, kissing his lips to silence him, and then kissing a pathway down his body, paying careful attention to each of his scars. She lingered on his chest, sucking his nipples and scraping them with her teeth just the way he liked.

At her touch, his penis came to life and grew painfully hard. He was glad to see it still worked. It didn't matter that he'd been without her for almost a year; his body would always respond to her. She was his—for now, forever.

She unbuckled his belt, unbuttoned his fly, and pushed his jeans and boxers down to free his aching erection. When she bent and kissed the rosy tip, he had to grab the edge of the counter to keep his balance.

"Well, something is still the same," she said.

"Easy there, lioness," he hissed through clenched teeth. "When it comes to you, I have no control."

She smiled up at him and then continued her exploration, pushing his jeans down further, her fingers eventually reaching the two waterproof bandages on his thigh, which covered the bullet entry and exit wounds.

The color drained from her face, like a color photo turning instantly to black and white.

Bending, he grabbed her by the elbows to steady her and then gently raised her to a standing position. "They don't hurt, and I can get them wet, so don't look so scared."

"You said it was a nick. You have a bullet wound in your leg," she said. "You didn't mention it was a bullet hole. I can be scared if I want." There was an edge of feistiness to her voice. It had been a long time, and the realization made him smile.

"Enough about me. It's your turn," he said, reaching for the bottom edge of his old fleece pullover. "I cannot believe you kept this."

"It was yours," she said.

"You gave it to me."

Her body was rounder, softer. All the soft edges that he loved touching were lusher and sexier. Her breasts were swollen and larger. When he thought of how she had fed their baby, he had to grit his teeth to keep from losing it again.

"You're beautiful," he said and pulled her to him.

They stepped into the shower, a large, honey calcite tile structure her parents had updated when they updated all the bathrooms. Her father had once called it the fun shower. He could guess why.

Their bodies joined as warm water ran over them. Familiar textures brought back a flood of memories.

"Are you sure you are strong enough…that it's okay for us to—"

"Yes, I even asked the doctor, mentioned I'd be seeing my beautiful wife after a year without her," he said. "He told me I was a lucky bastard. Now, how about you? Are you healed after the baby?"

"Yes, I was cleared for all normal sexual activity almost three weeks ago," she said, smiling. "I can make love with my husband, if it is okay for him."

"Define normal."

"Well, don't ride me too hard in the beginning, but a little hard is fine."

"I've thought about making love with you every day for the last eleven months."

He nudged her legs apart as his hand slipped into her warm folds and began to stroke her intimately, using the movements he knew she liked. She placed her hands on his shoulders and threw her head back as she moaned in pleasure.

"Soon, I'll be well enough to make love to you standing up. Remember how you liked it when I pinned you to the wall?" he whispered in her ear as his hands continued to explore her.

"Oh yes," she managed.

"For now, let's take the fastest shower in history and find the nearest flat surface or, preferably, a soft bed. I want to be inside you."

Faster than he'd have thought possible, they were in her bedroom, a replica of the bedroom in her New York loft, complete with the red sheets.

She was there but having another moment.

"Rebecca, I'm here. This isn't a dream. I swear to you, I'm never leaving again. Would you like me to pinch you?" he asked as his hand rubbed over her naked bottom.

"You're never leaving my sight again," she murmured, burying her face against his chest. "Because this time, I won't let you go. No matter what you say. I'd tie you up to keep you from going to someplace like Iraq or even the corner grocery store. Understand?"

Her warm tears trickled down his chest. "I understand. I'm sorry. I know you didn't want me to go. I should have listened to you," he said, running his hand from her shoulder to hip, marveling at her curves as he tried to calm her.

Brushing his cheek with her fingertips, she whispered, "Help me to forget."

"Happy to," he said.

Moving down to the end of the bed, he started with her toes and kissed his way up her body, marveling at her smooth skin and how close he'd come to never seeing her again. Her calves were as muscular as he remembered, and her inner thighs were just as soft and welcoming as they had always been.

She smiled and spread her legs open in welcome. He wanted to taste her, but he was aching with need, so he addressed what needed the most attention first. He placed his hands under her butt and pulled her to him. Her hands reached for him and landed on his shoulders as she said, "Please, Mitch."

He felt the warmth of her skin as her legs wrapped around his waist. Then he guided himself into her, watching as her eyes fluttered, as her mouth opened and closed in surprise at the joining of their bodies. He felt her muscles contract around him, shut his eyes, and smiled. He was finally home.

"I didn't do that correctly," he managed, his voice surprisingly thick with emotion as they lay tangled together but hadn't started to move together.

"I know you were gone a long time, but that is the way you do it, and it feels good," Rebecca said, her first genuine chuckle cutting through the howling wind beyond the window. It was good to hear her laugh. For a few hours, he'd wondered if he'd ever hear the sound again.

"Not that," he said, his hand running the length of her back. "That, feeling your warmth, that is wonderful. And it is about to get better."

He kissed her then, and the emotions wrapped around him like tight silk cords. He'd come so close to losing everything. He couldn't get his mind around it. The only thing he could do was move forward and make it up to her and their child.

He started moving and saw her smile.

"I meant the proposal," he said as he paused, his hand still gently cupping her bare bottom as she snuggled against him, wanting to take him deeper.

"We are already married. Did you forget?" she asked, her head coming to rest on his shoulder as she pulled him to her. "I'm Mrs. Mitchell Wilder, your wife."

"I know that, but I want to do it again with your family there. My captors took my ring, so I want to do it with a new one." He took a deep breath and asked, "Rebecca Stark Wilder, my sweet Bex, will you do me the honor of marrying me again?"

"I'd marry you again tomorrow, or any day for that matter. If we can find an open justice of the peace, I'd do it now," she said as she looked into his eyes. "But if you don't start moving, I'm going to flip you over and take advantage of you."

"I'm sorry, but that was important. Next week is fine. We do have an anniversary coming up," he said as he gently started to move within her, watching her eyes grow cloudy as her voice hitched.

"I...haven't gotten you anything...yet," she managed.

"All I need," he said while he was still capable of speaking, "is you."

After they made love that first time, he held her softly, almost carefully. Her eyes never left his face as she looked at him, taking in each new line and change in his face. He hoped she wasn't disappointed with him. The last year had taken its toll on him. He might be only in his thirties, but he looked like he was in his sixties.

Their climaxes were a little muted, comfortable in the way they didn't elicit a scream but soft moans instead. And all too soon, it was over, and they were facing each other, side to side.

"I'm sorry that was so fast," he said.

"It was our first time in almost a year. It wasn't meant to be long. Next time or the time after..."

"I'll keep making love to you until we get it right. Here," he said, "Let me spoon you while we sleep. You must be exhausted."

"No," she murmured, her hand resting on his cheek. "I'm not letting you out of my sight."

"I'm right here," he protested, but she shook her head.

"I want you to hold me, but I want to be facing you," she said.

"You aren't going to sleep at all tonight, are you?" he asked.

"Maybe not," she admitted, and moved closer to him.

They made love several times that night. He was exhausted, his body demanding rest, but he wanted Rebecca more...to be with her, to hold her, and to be inside of her as he had dreamed of every night since his capture. Each time he woke up, he found her watching him. He'd kiss her, roll her onto her back, and another round of loving would begin. It wasn't their most adventurous lovemaking, but it was definitely the most intimate.

Several times in the night, the baby cried, and Rebecca had to get up to feed her. As she put her robe on, he could sense the pause after she tied her belt.

"Why don't I come with you?" he asked, reaching for his jeans and T-shirt.

"Please," she said. He didn't want to shut his eyes for fear he'd wake up back in the jail cell in Iraq, but he couldn't help it. She wasn't the only one who wondered if she'd died and gone to heaven.

They walked hand in hand across the hall to the nursery. Rebecca sat on a small loveseat and fed Emily, holding the baby to her full breast. After ten minutes or so, she would switch to the other breast. Mitch gently caressed the baby's soft head. His eyes met Rebecca's, and they smiled at each other.

"I was so worried I wouldn't find you again when I was in Germany, but that was stupid. I just needed to call Alex. Then I worried that you'd met someone while I was gone. That was a much different kind of Hell," he murmured.

"No one will ever compare to how I feel about you," Rebecca said.

"Good," he said, and kissed Rebecca.

Emily had finished nursing, so Rebecca handed her to him. He gently held Emily to his shoulder and patted her back the way Rebecca had shown him.

Rebecca smiled at him in a way that had him asking, "How am I doing?"

"You are doing great, Dad."

CHAPTER TWENTY-FIVE

Rebecca

Mitch had a nightmare right at dawn, when light was starting to stream in through the windows. He was thrashing, and it had awakened Rebecca from her tentative slumber. She was curled against him, but he fought with the sheets as if they were shackles.

Rebecca wasn't sure if she should wake him or let him ride it out. But when he sat bolt upright in bed, pushing her to the side, and cried, "Rebecca!" in the most tormented and painful voice she'd ever heard, she sat up and pulled him to her.

"I'm here. You're safe," she said, cradling his face in her hands, feeling the warm tears that had leaked down his cheeks as his body immediately started to relax. They were both nude, having tossed off their clothes after Emily's last feeding. If Rebecca had any say in the matter, they would always sleep in the buff. She couldn't get enough of the feel of Mitch's body warming her own.

Once Mitch realized where he was and that Rebecca was beside him, he pulled her to him and found her mouth. The kiss was ravenous and demanding as his hands traveled over her skin as if he'd never really touched her before. It fed his need and her own. Reaching between them, she grabbed his penis and squeezed it. And by how hard it grew so quickly, he wanted her too. They had made polite love to each other several times that night. Now, it was time to remember who they were and their passion. She wanted him to claim her.

Before long, he was inside her, having gotten there none too gently. Rebecca didn't mind. She was tired of being handled gently. She wanted her lover to take her. She panted with need and pulled him to her, wrapping her legs around him, and loved the way it felt to have him inside her. She had missed this man so much. This passion, this heat, was the kind of sex they had when they were in her little apartment with the red sheets in New York. Her actions caused a reaction in him. They rolled on the bed and got tangled in the sheets as pillows flew to the floor. They made the mattress squeak as he drove into her, and she raised her hips, encouraging every thrust he could deliver as their eyes met and held.

"Mitch... oh Mitch, harder," she said, crying his name over and over as he rode her. "Don't ever stop..."

"I love you, Bex," he managed as he paused to kiss her.

"I love you, too..." she said as one of the fiercest orgasms she'd ever had prevented her from speaking as she gave over to its power, her body jumping and thrashing underneath him as he pounded into her.

And just when she thought she might be coming back to Earth, coming back into her body, she felt his body contort with his own release that came with a scream he managed to contain. Her second orgasm came out of nowhere, a reaction to her lover's climax. They moved together to let the moment extend. When at last they had both finished, he lowered his body to hers, half-falling, half-collapsing onto her as he kissed any part of her flesh he could find.

Her body felt heavy and relaxed, so loose, she wasn't sure she could move. She was wrapped around Mitch, her ankles crossed behind his back as he feasted on her mouth and neck, whispering words of endearment as they cuddled after their frenzied coupling, their breath coming out in ragged exhalations.

"That is the way I like you to be with me," she said. "Not to say the first few rounds weren't nice."

"Nice was nice, but this was rocket fuel next to water," he said, "That reminded me of who we are." He looked at her, and she smiled. Then he moved down her body, kissing her neck, her breasts, and her nipples, which were particularly sensitive.

"Your breasts are larger," he said, pausing in the attention he was giving to her breasts.

"I just had your baby," she said as she threw back her head and enjoyed his touch.

"Isn't that something?" he asked with a smile.

"It amazes me each time I look at her," Rebecca said.

Mitch stayed where he was, Rebecca's arm and legs holding him to her when, eventually, the baby started to cry.

They sat up, Rebecca donning her robe, and Mitch slipping into the robe she had found in her father's closet.

Rebecca leaned against him as she nursed Emily. When she finished and Mitch had burped her, he asked, "Now what?"

"She has her morning nap."

"She sleeps a lot," he said.

"She's just a little baby," Rebecca said and kissed Mitch. "You have a lot to learn, and I can't wait to teach you."

Later, after the baby had gone down for her morning nap, they stepped into the shower. Mitch let the water gently spray his chest as he smiled with his eyes shut.

"You missed showers, didn't you?" she asked.

Eyes opening at the sound of her voice, he smiled and held out a hand to her. She didn't wait for him. She pulled his face to hers and kissed him.

"Yes," he said, "and having them with you makes them phenomenal."

After they'd finished their shower, they ended up back in bed and made love again, only this time, they were a little slower, smiling at each other as they gave and took pleasure from each other. And when at last they had both been sated, she said, "Go back to bed, darling. I've got to check on the baby, and I'll make breakfast."

"You're going to leave me alone?" he asked.

"I'm trying to believe it," she said.

"Believe it," he said and kissed her.

She wore Mitch's t-shirt, which almost hung to her thighs, her nursing bra, and panties. Mitch was asleep, as was the baby. She stood on the deck in the warm morning, her hair pulled up in a bun and her hands wrapped around a cup of coffee. What a wonderful day! There might have been a day when she was happier. She just didn't know when. The day she married was pretty great, but this was bliss.

The baby would want to be fed in another hour and a half. Maybe she should crawl back in bed with Mitch. Their hunger for each other was insatiable. It actually seemed stronger than it had been. The separation had made their hearts grow fonder. And when they were making love, it was as if the separation had never happened.

She thought of sliding between the sheets and kissing him awake, just enough for his body to recognize hers and take over.

It was then that she saw a black Mercedes with the license plate of STARK 7 pull into her driveway, followed by Alex's Porsche Panamera. Damn it, she had all but forgotten her family was coming today. She needed a few more weeks with Mitch before such an interruption would be welcome. Maybe what they needed was a honeymoon, a chance to get out all their feelings or at least try to get their needs a little more under control.

Well, she was glad she hadn't been in the middle of something with Mitch. She had just enough time to grab a floral robe and pull it on before her parents were softly knocking on her door.

She pulled it open and smiled. Quick hugs with each parent were exchanged.

"You look wonderful, darling," her mother exclaimed.

"Thanks. Hey, hi," she said softly. "Everyone is asleep."

Her brother, Alex, was leaning against his car door and smiling.

"Who is everyone?" her mother asked, confused.

"You really didn't tell them?" she asked Alex.

"Nope," he said.

"Rebecca, do you have a guest?" her father asked.

"Is it a man?" her mother asked, slightly horrified.

Rebecca smiled broadly and said, "It is a man."

"We should go," her father said.

Her mother didn't move and said, "Who is it?"

"Mitch," Rebecca said with a smile as a tear traveled down her cheek. Then she whispered, "He got out. They were holding him...He's here...He's really here. He didn't die."

"It's true. I don't know if I've ever been happier or more surprised," Alex said, stepping forward with a smile of his own. "I'm so happy for you and Emily, Becca. You'll have to fatten him up. He looks kind of thin. I'm just happy to have my best friend back."

Her father turned back toward her. Her mother put her hand to her face and gasped.

"Alex, what the hell is she talking about?" her father asked. "Is she okay?"

"Becca, honey, are you okay?" her mother asked, concerned.

Alex smiled and said, "Mitch called me from some military hospital in Germany a couple of days ago. I sent the plane over to get him and drove him down here yesterday."

"What? He's here?" Garrison asked. "And you didn't tell us?"

"Is he okay?" Victoria asked. "Where is he?"

Before Rebecca could answer, Alex did.

Alex nodded. "He is alive, but he is really thin. He's been in captivity for almost eleven months. He has a bullet wound in his leg from escaping, but it seems to be healing well. I've wanted to tell you since last night, but it was such a shock to me. I wanted to make sure that he was real. Lucien Donovan is an asshole."

"What did you say?" Rebecca asked. "I hadn't heard anything about Lucien Donovan. I don't think I understood what you said. What did you say?"

"Donovan is a piece of shit," Alex said. "He has known Mitch was alive for several months. He just refused to pay any ransom. Mitch told the Marines who rescued him. Donovan is looking at some serious charges."

"We could have paid," Rebecca said, frustration and anger coloring her words. "I could have had him back earlier. Oh, my god...I didn't know. That is why the State Department called me a few days ago and asked me about Lucien."

"Well, the State Department needs to handle it now, and it sounds like they are," Alex said.

"Bullshit. I'll kill him," Rebecca said menacingly. "Donovan's a dead man."

But another voice from behind her said, "Oh no, you won't. Bex, darling...Just because you can doesn't mean you should. Alex wasn't supposed to mention that."

Mitch, dressed in his borrowed robe, his hair rumpled, wrapped his arms around Rebecca's waist, and pulled her back so that she was leaning against him. Turning, she buried her face against his shoulder as her arms wrapped around him.

"Oh my god... Mitch...Mitch," Victoria said as she stepped forward and gave him a hug. "Oh, Mitch, sweet boy. I feel like I'm looking at a ghost."

Mitch leaned toward Victoria and kissed her on the cheek, never letting go of Rebecca.

"Holy shit, Mitch, holy crap. He really is here. He's alive," Garrison said and stepped forward to pull Mitch close for a hug.

Alex was the last to cross the threshold. He smiled at Mitch, pulled him close in more of a brother hug, and said, "I'm sorry. I thought you'd told her about Donovan. Nice dramatic entrance.

I forgot to mention this yesterday. Stay out of hostile countries. We can't lose you again. This family can't take it."

Mitch

He was glad to see the family, but he could see that Rebecca was upset with the latest revelation that Lucien Donovan hadn't paid his ransom. He had wanted to be alone with her for a few days, to make sure she was okay before he dropped that particular bomb on her.

A little before noon, Victoria volunteered to start making lunch as Rebecca sat next to Mitch, holding Emily and looking shell-shocked.

"It is okay," Mitch said in a soft tone as he cradled Rebecca and pulled her close.

"It is not okay," she whispered. "I'll kill him."

"No, you won't," he said.

"What is stopping me from jumping in my car, driving to Portland, and taking a plane to London?"

"Many things," he said. "First, you are breastfeeding our child. You can't leave her. Second, I need to rest, and that means staying here for a bit, and I don't want to be anywhere without you. Third, if you did kill him, which I have no doubt you could do, you would be arrested, and then we would be apart again. Fourth, I've had a lot of time to think of this and the State Department will handle part of it, I will handle the rest."

"How?" she asked.

"Legally, just wait a few more days. You need to trust me on this."

"Like I trusted you that this little helicopter delivery was no big deal?" she asked, then started crying again.

He looked pointedly at Alex, who quickly stood and said, "Let me hold my niece for a bit."

Mitch encircled Rebecca with his arms, and she sank against

him as she cried. Garrison stood and walked into the kitchen, where he hugged his wife and tried to act busy, helping her with lunch.

Over lunch at the large, whitewashed kitchen table, they ate several different casseroles and salads that Victoria brought with her from Portland. Garrison asked a few questions that thankfully had nothing to do with his kidnap.

"The security positions are still available for both you and Rebecca. I didn't have the heart to fill them, but mostly, I was hoping eventually Rebecca might have a change of heart. Would you two, after a little R&R, consider them?"

Mitch looked to Rebecca, then said, "I'd still be interested. Bex?"

She nodded and said, "As long as I can travel with him and be his partner. And I need to stress this: no danger."

"No danger ever again. You are my partner," he said. "Where should we R&R?"

"London," she said, smiling innocently.

CHAPTER TWENTY-SIX

Mitch

"Not London," Mitch said. "Trust me, I will handle it."

"Promise?" Rebecca asked.

"Yes," he said, grabbing her hand and squeezing it. Then he brought her hand to his lips and kissed it. "It makes me feel good that you want to kill him, but it is unnecessary. I need you to trust me. First the State Department needs to do what they need to do, then we step in."

She nodded and picked at her food. He didn't think she'd slept much last night. Well, he hadn't slept much himself.

"How about we go to a family hotel that offers private pools and beach access?" Mitch suggested.

"St. Barts," Garrison said. "We can get you a private bungalow."

"Didn't Adam and Melinda honeymoon there?" Victoria asked. Cousin Adam bore a striking resemblance to Alex. When younger, Adam did his undergrad at the University of Pennsylvania while Mitch and Alex were getting their masters at Wharton. Mitch would run into Adam on campus and mistake him for Alex. Adam and Melinda just had their first child, Adam Junior, or A.J. for short. He looked enough like Alex to be his son.

"I think they did," Rebecca said. "Melinda said it was magical."

"You never got a honeymoon," Victoria pointed out.

"Rebecca deserves a great honeymoon. I think she needs

one," Mitch said, looking at her. She smiled and looked at her plate. "I know I need one."

"How many babies can say they went on their parents' honeymoon?" Alex added.

"Is it possible to get a two-bedroom bungalow?" Mitch asked.

"There are a couple there. Let me make a few calls after lunch and see what we can do. The family plane can fly you to St. Barts, so you don't need to worry about commercial flight reservations," Garrison said.

"I like the idea of a private plane. I think I'm spoiled," Mitch said to Rebecca. He liked planes that came with bedrooms.

"I like that it brought you to me," she said.

They spent the afternoon talking as they sat in oversized furniture on the south deck in the late summer sun. Alex set up several umbrellas so that Emily would be out of the brightness of the sun. They watched the ocean as they contemplated the future. It was nice, but it was also too much for Mitch, who just wanted to be alone with his wife.

At the appropriate hour, Garrison made margaritas with a blender and ingredients Rebecca admitted she didn't know existed in her kitchen. Well, they hadn't until her parents showed up.

Rebecca had a virgin margarita, and Mitch made sure she never left his sight. If she was feeding the baby in the bedroom or putting her down for a nap, he was by her side. And in these alone moments, when their baby was contently sleeping in her crib, he'd pull Rebecca into his arms and kiss her. They still had that ever-present hunger for each other and, currently, not enough privacy to express it.

"There are too many damn people in this house," he whispered while his margarita waited on the deck.

"I know. Mom told me they are leaving tomorrow to give us some privacy."

"Good," he said, "because if they weren't here, I'd be showing you how much I missed you. I don't know if either of us would have gotten dressed today."

"A few hours until bedtime," she said. "And I'm not wearing my nightgown, but we will have to be quiet."

"Too many damn hours. I can be quiet, but you are the wild card," he whispered, then he kissed her again, and they tiptoed out of the baby's room.

Dinner involved steaks on the barbecue. Garrison oversaw the grill with Alex by his side, offering advice. Victoria assembled side dishes that she had known to be Mitch's favorites: scalloped potatoes and assorted roasted vegetables.

Mitch held Emily and marveled at how perfect she was.

Alex snapped a few photos of Mitch with Emily and then with Rebecca.

Mitch fought hard to get home to his wife and his baby. What if he hadn't made it? Mitch decided to stop thinking about it. He was home safe, and that was all that mattered.

After dinner, he saw the sadness return to Rebecca.

"What is it, darling?"

She wrapped her arms around him as she cried, "Two days ago, I thought you were dead. Now, you're here, and sometimes I can't believe it. I'm so tired."

"You can believe that I'm here," he said as he pulled her close.

"I do well for a bit, then it all hits me, you know?" Rebecca said as he dabbed at her tears.

"I know," he said, "I think we will all make some local therapist rich trying to deal with all we have been through."

"It is probably a good idea. I don't want to mess up Emily."

"You won't," Mitch said. "I've been watching you. You are an amazing mother to our little girl. It has just come so naturally to you."

"Well, I've read a lot of books. There wasn't much else to do when I was hanging out and waiting for her to be born."

"We are very proud of you, Becca," Victoria added. "You are a fabulous mother and a strong woman."

"Our little girl has been through a lot, but she kept it together," Garrison said, "She is a Stark, through and through."

Victoria waved her hand in the air, "She might be a Stark, but don't discount the Whitlow genes I gave her."

"You're right, darling. With us as her parents, how could she ever be anything but spectacular?"

"I love how they take credit for everything good in our lives," Alex said as he took a sip of his margarita.

Mitch pulled Rebecca onto his lap, making sure she avoided the injury to his leg. It was a little uncomfortable, but he wanted to hold her, to reassure her that everything would be all right.

CHAPTER TWENTY-SEVEN

Rebecca

Rebecca was tired. Every muscle in her body seemed slow and not willing to cooperate.

It was only 7:30 pm, and she had just put the baby down with Mitch's help. They had kissed over their sleeping baby, and she wanted to climb him like a tree, but the rest of her family waited in the living room.

Mitch whispered, "I want you so bad that I ache for you."

She kissed him and said, "I feel like I'm going to explode."

After a few more whispers of what they wanted to do to each other, they rejoined the family in the living room and sat together on one of the couches. As had become their new ritual today, she cuddled against Mitch and shut her eyes.

"Someone looks very tired," Victoria observed.

"Me or her?" Mitch asked as his hand gently rubbed Rebecca's back.

"Both of you, actually," Victoria said.

"I didn't sleep well last night. I was scared it was all just a dream," Rebecca whispered.

"And I dozed, but when I woke up, I'd touch her, making sure she was real," Mitch added.

"Why don't you two go to bed?" Victoria asked. "We don't need to be entertained."

"You both look like you're sleepwalking," Alex said.

"I think we are," Rebecca managed. "The adrenaline rush has ended."

Mitch stood with a little wobble, then extended his hand to Rebecca, who joined him.

They said goodnight to everyone, and went into their bedroom, and shut the door.

Mitch pulled her to him and kissed her. "Come on, I have an idea. Let's take a shower."

They slipped out of their clothing, and Mitch adjusted the water as Rebecca pinned up her hair, aware that he was watching her. She stretched her body, arching her back a little as his eyes traveled over her.

He ran a finger from hip to breast along her skin, which made her shiver.

"Come here," he whispered as he sat on a little stone bench that extended from the wall.

She smiled and joined him in the shower, whispering, "Why didn't we think of this last night?"

"By the time we got in the shower, my brain had shut off," he whispered as he placed his hands on her hips and slowly guided her onto his lap. She straddled him and then sunk onto his erection and gasped as her feet touched the floor.

"Oh Mitch, I'm...pinned..."

"Good, now start to rock," he said.

Leaning her forehead to his, she moaned a little and then slowly started to move. She rocked her hips as he lifted into her. When her gasps hitched, he slipped his hand between them and rubbed her with his deft thumb and forefinger until she threw her head back and stifled her climax.

Panting, she kissed him on the lips, on his face, and his neck, any place she could reach as her body quaked and trembled.

Their eyes met, and he smiled at her before lowering his head and kissing her right breast and then the left.

She rocked her body hard against him, lifting until she pulled away from his erection and then taking it in quickly. The fourth time she did this, she saw him grimace in erotic relief as his own climax took over his body.

After they finished showering, they climbed into bed and began kissing, their skin-to-skin contact all that they needed. Before long, they were making love again, both of them trying to be quiet as each thrust reminded them that they were together, the longing slowly fueling their passion.

And this time, when Rebecca climaxed, she screamed into her pillow as Mitch smiled and then had to grab his own pillow.

They both lay on their sides, facing each other and gently touching each other. Rebecca carefully examined each scar she could see.

"I thought they were scratches, but now I can see that you had stitches," she said, her voice hitching a little.

"I actually had four places with stitches, but they at least made sure my wounds all healed well," he said, pointing out a couple of the spots.

Rebecca kissed each spot and then met his eyes.

He could read her concern as if she'd voiced it. "I'm here. It is okay."

She nodded, and he kissed her.

"I've been thinking," Mitch said.

"Don't do too much of that," she said, reaching down to stroke him. She had missed this intimacy with him. "Unless it is with this."

He smiled and whispered, "I think you know, but in case you don't, I want to be inside of you at every chance I can. Making sweet love to you, screwing your brains out, or just having wild sex, I love that we do it all."

"When the parents leave, will you screw my brains out? I mean, we just made sweet love, and last night, that last time was kinda wild," she said. "I liked it."

"Your wish is my command, my love," he said and then kissed her. Then, he said, "Let's get married again on our anniversary. Then let's take Emily and go for a honeymoon on St. Barts. When we are ready, we come back to Portland, look into working for your family, and buy a house, maybe get a dog."

"I want the house to have a white picket fence, and I want a black lab."

Mitch nodded. "I will make that happen."

Mitch

He was elated to find himself in her arms when he woke the next morning. Mitch carefully pulled away from Rebecca, stepped into the bathroom, and took a shower. Once he dressed, he checked on Rebecca again and noticed she was sleeping deeply. She deserved it.

He quietly picked Emily out of her crib, changed her diaper, and headed into the living room. It was almost 9:30, and the rest of the family was up, sitting around the breakfast table and drinking coffee.

"There you are," Victoria greeted with a broad smile.

"Bex was up a few times with this one, so I let her sleep in," he said, sitting down at one of the empty chairs.

"My poor baby, all the stress of the last year is catching up with her," Victoria said as Mitch gently rubbed his baby's back and marveled at how perfect she was.

"I'm sorry for the pain I've caused," Mitch said as he held Emily and looked down at her.

"I think it showed you how much you are loved," Victoria said. "We are all very thankful."

"And so very lucky," he said, and added, "I didn't know how good babies smell."

"They do smell nice. And I made your favorite," Victoria said as she placed a plate of blueberry pancakes with a side of bacon in front of him.

"I can't believe you remembered, Vic," he said softly. "It smells wonderful."

"Of course, my sweet boy," she said as she set a cup of coffee before him and then kissed his cheek. "Give me my baby. I promise to give her back when you are done eating, maybe."

He handed her the baby, and then Alex punched his arm and said, "Sometimes, I think you are Mom's favorite."

"No doubt about it. Your mother has always loved Mitch," Garrison said, folding his newspaper and taking a sip of coffee.

Rebecca appeared in a floral silk robe, looking sleepy as she took the chair next to her husband.

"Good morning," she said to her family. Mitch leaned toward her for a kiss. She leaned into him, and he savored the feel of her. Rebecca was real and in his arms. Eventually, he let her go and sunk back into his chair.

"I'll have to get used to that. Seeing my best friend kiss my sister isn't easy," Alex said.

"We do a lot more than kissing," Rebecca said as her mother set a plate before her and then added, "Thanks, Mom. I'd better eat fast. I bet Emily wants breakfast."

Victoria showed Rebecca a bottle of milk Rebecca had pumped the day before. "Stop torturing your brother and enjoy your breakfast. I can take care of this feeding."

Mitch didn't think he'd tasted anything better in years. The pancakes were amazing, but his stomach wasn't used to anything but horrible curry. After a few bites, he pushed the plate away, looked at the bottle in Victoria's hand, and said, "May I?"

"Of course," Victoria said. Victoria handed Emily to Mitch, and she gave him the bottle with some instructions.

The baby sucked hungrily on the bottle as Mitch held her in his arms. His baby. His daughter. It was all he could do to hold it together. It must have shown because after a few minutes, Rebecca put her arm around him and rubbed his shoulder. Alex took photos, and Mitch was glad to have the moment with his wife and child. Rebecca kissed his cheek and returned to her pancakes.

"We made some decisions last night," Rebecca said between bites of her breakfast.

"I hope Portland made the cut," her father said.

Rebecca looked at Mitch, who said, "Yes, I think we are excited about Portland."

Victoria clapped her hands together and said, "All my babies in Portland. I get to be close to this little one." She looked lovingly at Emily.

"That is the plan. I was wondering if you could help us out with something else," Rebecca said to her mother.

"What do you need? I'd be more than happy to help decorate your house."

"We will take you up on that," Mitch said. "I loved Rebecca's apartment in New York, but we have something a bit more pressing. It is our first wedding anniversary next week, and we would like to get married again."

Then Rebecca completed his thought by adding, "And we were wondering if you wanted to plan it for us. That way, you can all be a part of it, and we know it will be done right."

"Then we will fly off with Emily for a two-week honeymoon to Saint Barts and for a little R&R," Mitch added.

"May I give away the bride this time?" Garrison asked.

"Yes, Dad," Rebecca said.

"Plan a wedding in a week?" Victoria asked.

"Well, we can get married at the hotel. Alex or someone else could officiate. I mean, we are already legally married. The catering staff can do the reception, but it will be just the family, more like a nice dinner, so I think you can do it," Rebecca said.

"Damn right, I can. Flowers, photographer, and, of course, you both need the proper attire," Victoria said.

"I actually need more than just one suit," Mitch said. "I only have a couple of things. I need everything."

"I donated most of his clothing," Rebecca said, looking at Mitch. "I'm sorry."

"You kept my favorite things, a few ties and an old fleece pullover," Mitch said.

"And you have the clothes from the luggage returned from Saudi Arabia," she said. "But most of those items are Donovan Securities logo attire, so they need to go."

"I agree, Bex."

"Oh, I'd be delighted to begin your new wardrobe," Victoria said with a glint in her eye.

"Not too much in the beginning. I'm planning on putting on some weight," he said.

"And anything you want us to take on the honeymoon. I think we both could use a few vacation duds," Rebecca said.

Victoria smiled and hugged her daughter as she said, "This is going to be such fun!"

"Keep track of what you spend, and we will pay you back," Mitch said.

"Come to think of it, we haven't given you a wedding present. This is *all* our treat," Victoria said.

Mitch looked at Garrison, who smiled at his wife and nodded in agreement.

Before everyone left that afternoon, Victoria made several pages of notes, including Mitch's sizes and Rebecca's measurements for a wedding dress.

When the last of the Stark vehicles had left their little beach house, and the baby had been fed and went down for a three-hour nap in her room, Mitch turned to Rebecca and asked, "Feel like a nap?"

She kissed him hard on the lips and playfully said, "Maybe later. First, I want you to make love to me... Are you up for it?"

"Yes, I think I can manage that," he said, taking her hand and leading her to the bedroom.

CHAPTER TWENTY-EIGHT

Rebecca

Six days later, they were back in Portland. Mitch had been given a guest bedroom in the Stark suite to change into his tuxedo. It was also an opportunity to see what Victoria had purchased for him.

Rebecca, who had visited a salon that morning for a trim, wore her hair in an updo. She wore a Stark hotel robe and was in another bedroom, looking through a rack of wedding dresses in her size from Trudel's Wedding Boutique. The salon also sent Trudel and two seamstresses to make sure they could personally fit her. They knew what to do and were fussing over the bride.

"I hope Mitch likes what I found for him. It was a lot of fun."

"Mom, thank you...seriously...more than I can say. I don't know how we can thank you."

Victoria hugged her daughter. "I loved every minute of it. Now, let's find you a dress worthy of that sweet husband of yours."

Rebecca was drawn to an off-the-shoulder satin gown that fit her like a glove, but in a good way. She was still self-conscious of her baby weight. She especially liked that there was a little flower detail at the bottom of the dress with delicate chiffon petals and that there was a veil to match that had the same flowers on the edge of it. After Trudel helped her into it, Rebecca asked her mother, "Okay, this is a contender. What do you think?"

"It is perfect. I love it," Victoria said and dabbed away a few tears. "It is the one I picked out for you earlier."

Rebecca smiled at her mother. "You know that when we return from Saint Barts, we are going to start house hunting."

Victoria looked like she could barely hold her excitement as she smiled and asked, "May I start looking for you?"

"Yes, please. And keep in mind, we are going to ask you to help us decorate it." Rebecca knew how much this pleased her mother. Over the last year, everyone had been there for her, but it was so wonderful to see how close they had become.

At 4 p.m. that afternoon, Rebecca was handed a bouquet of white dendrobium orchids. Then, both Rebecca's parents walked her down the makeshift aisle, which was lined with trees and twinkle lights, in one of the elegant hotel ballrooms to where Mitch and her cousin Spencer, a newly ordained officiant, waited. Adam and Melinda were in the audience with their baby A.J. from New York. Spencer's parents sat next to them, having flown in from Texas.

Mitch smiled when he saw her and then raised her veil to kiss her.

Alex sat in the first row, next to his parents, and held baby Emily.

When it came time to exchange rings, Rebecca slipped a new platinum band on Mitch's finger. It was an exact duplicate of what he had lost in Iraq, but she'd added one little detail: the date of their first meeting when they were younger, as well as the phrase, "It was love at first sight," to the inside of the ring. Rebecca hadn't been alone in adding a little something. Mitch had added the phrase, "To my Bex. I Will Love You Forever, Your Husband," to the inside band of her emerald engagement ring.

They dined on lobster tails and Beef Wellington, as well as drank sparkling cider for the bridal couple—in homage to their baby—before they were given a key to the honeymoon suite, which had been decked out with rose petals and a crib.

Two days later, they left for Saint Barts.

. . .

Mitch

They honeymooned in St. Barts and managed to have a lovely, relaxing time, making the most opportunity of Emily's frequent naps. Thanks to Garrison's assistance, they had a private beach and pool in their own little individual vacation bungalow, which they rarely left during their two weeks' stay.

The nightmares that plagued Mitch since his escape started to become a thing of the past. He was finally starting to believe that he was home and not living a nightmare.

Much of the clothing Victoria had purchased for them for their trip never left their suitcases. By the time they returned to Portland, almost a month after Mitch's escape, he had gained weight and looked tan but had no tan lines, and he was looking forward to the next phases of their life.

"Do you think we will ever curb our lust and stop making love at every opportunity?" Rebecca asked. It was the first night they slept in their new house, in their new bed, and had just christened the room by making love.

"First of all, there are twenty-one rooms in this house, and I thought we said we would christen each of them, which I'm looking forward to."

"I am, too," she said as her hand gave his butt a little squeeze. "Make no mistake. I have an addiction, and it is you."

"Good, and second," he said after giving her a few kisses that traveled down her body and touched every sensitive spot he knew she liked, "I think we are making up for all those years apart when I was in London, and then Iraq. Maybe by, like, our eighth anniversary or so, we will have tamed our mutual horn dog for each other."

"I really hope not," she said with a smile. "I think I love you more each day."

"Me too, Bex. I'm a lucky man to have been given the gift of you," he said, and his hand traveled over her skin and lingered where his lips had been earlier, which took her breath away.

Later, after they had made sure the room was not only christened but they had re-consummated their relationship for a second time that night, Rebecca's voice grew edgy.

"I have to say this because if I think about it, I don't know what to do with my anger. I haven't forgotten about Lucien Donovan," Rebecca said.

"Things are in play," Mitch said as he kissed her lips and tried to make her forget what they had been through. She kissed him back but then put a hand on the side of his face and made him look at her.

"I want to know what you mean by things are at play. We don't have secrets from each other, and that answer isn't cutting it for me," she said, and it didn't matter that they were naked, holding each other and that he was thinking of ways to distract her. She wasn't going to be distracted.

Mitch sighed, admitting defeat. "You're right. I don't mean to not tell you. You've just been through a lot yourself, so I'll tell you. I just don't want you to worry. And I certainly don't want you to kill him. Okay? I mean it."

"Okay," Rebecca said, but she sounded disappointed.

"The State Department is going after Lucien, and I've hired an attorney in London. He is looking over my original employment contract. You have one, too. Do you remember it?"

"What I remember is that it was a large contract," she said as her hand gently rubbed his back.

"There was a little clause buried deep inside it. It basically is written that if there was an abduction situation, the company, Donovan Security, would pay up to five million pounds in ransom if requested. They have insurance for just such an event. It is like hole-in-one insurance at a golf tournament. They insure against the possibility. You know, what are the odds? Get a hole-in-one, win a car, so the insurance pays off the amount of the car but only costs a few hundred dollars to buy a policy."

Rebecca scooted away from Mitch and turned on her side to face him. As was their practice, they hadn't turned off the lights when they made love, so just like he could see every nuance of pleasure on her face when he was bringing passion to her, he could see the anger there now. Stark anger was not to be under-estimated.

"Are you kidding me?" she asked. "Did he keep the money?"

"I don't know if he was ever paid on my kidnapping, but this is going to be a big deal. It might ruin the company. I know we don't need the money, but the fact I missed Emily's birth and caused you such pain, well, he has to pay for that."

"Damn. Straight. What if they had killed you when he refused to pay? My darling, my baby...the love of my life," she said and started to cry. He pulled her close and kissed her until she forgot everything but the feel of his body rubbing against hers.

Six months later, Lucien Donovan settled the lawsuit for twenty-seven million pounds. Mitch gave the money, less his legal fees and one million pounds, to the families of the men who had perished during the attack, where he had almost died. Rebecca actually paid back the life insurance on Mitch that she had placed in trust for Emily. On the same day Mitch added one million pounds to Emily's trust fund. The fallout, the way it played in the press, did not do Lucien any favors. His company declared bankruptcy the following year.

Rebecca's old boss, Bruce, picked up a lot of new clients when he started his own security company shortly after Donovan Security shut its doors.

8th Wedding Anniversary
Rebecca

Rebecca took a small sip of her soda, something that didn't go very well with the pasta her husband was making for their anniversary dinner she was watching him prepare in the sleek kitchen of their Portland home. Mitch was the head of security for all of the Stark Hotels. Rebecca worked with him but set her own schedule. She worked and traveled with him, but seven-year-old Emily, who was as bright as she was curious, was always their first concern.

Their dog, Windsor, a two-year-old black lab, waited for any fallout from the drainboard.

"Wouldn't you like some wine?" he asked. "I opened a nice Oregon Pinot from Forget-Me-Not."

"No, I am in the mood for ginger ale. My stomach is a little iffy." She had a little secret.

"Are you okay?" he asked, setting down his wooden spoon, crossing to where she stood, and cradling her in his arms.

"Yes, I'm wonderful. Really, I'm fine," she said and kissed him.

"You look wonderful, Bex. Was Emily excited to get a night off from her parents? To spend time with her favorite uncle?" Mitch asked.

"She was very excited to spend the night with Uncle Alex and Aunt Daisy now that they are back from Dubai. She loves their apartment and the view at the top of the hotel. She loves being close to her grandmother. And she loves playing with her cousins. They all spoil her. She did mention she would miss Windsor."

"She should have taken Windsor with her. They would have played nice in Alex's penthouse, all that beige interior with Windsor's constantly shedding black fur..."

"I couldn't do that to Daisy. Alex, yes. Daisy, no. She is a sweetheart. And when it is Alex and Daisy's wedding anniversary, we get their kids for the night."

"I can hear all the little girls screaming now," he said and returned to his pasta sauce. "I still cannot believe the change in Alex since he became a husband and father."

"Daisy is the one for him. He really adores her, and she knows how to keep him in line. I love seeing them so happy."

"I think we give them a run for their money on happiness," Mitch said, wooden spoon in hand, as he crossed to Rebecca and kissed her again. Unlike the other kisses they'd just shared, she let this one linger, and by mutual agreement, Mitch didn't seem to mind. He tossed his spoon on the counter to have both hands available to wrap around his wife and thoroughly kiss her. After almost twenty years since their very first meeting they never took for granted the ability to touch freely and did so often.

"Let's just say we set the bar pretty high," she said. "And I wouldn't change it."

"Neither would I," Mitch said as he squeezed her one last time and went back to his pasta.

They ate at the dining room table by candlelight, holding hands on top of the table as Diana Krall played in the background.

"How do you like it?" Mitch asked, glancing down at the pasta, which she had always proclaimed to be her favorite.

"You know how I like it," she said saucily.

"Well," he said in his aw-shucks way he'd had since he was twenty. It still made her stomach flutter.

"You make me this pasta when you want to get laid. Here's a

little secret: You don't need it. You are getting lucky tonight, any night you want, actually. I like making love with my sweet husband, but I like that pasta is our foreplay when you *really* want to make love."

"You know me too well," he said.

"Intimately," she said.

"I never take this, what we have—our love, our passion—for granted."

"Did you know that it is easier for me to count the number of nights we've been together and haven't made love than the nights we have?"

"I can't believe you counted, but I feel the challenge. Okay, in the seven years since I came back from Iraq, how many nights have we just gone to sleep and not made love, which already makes me feel sad?" he asked.

"One hundred and sixty-three out of about twenty-five hundred," she said.

"I'd better get on that," he said. "We can't let it get to one hundred and sixty-four."

"No way, darling," she said. "But you have to admit, that is a lot of sex."

"Is it too much?" he asked with a smile.

"No," she said and picked up her fork.

After they had finished dinner, Mitch said, "I want to give you your anniversary present."

He'd already given her something, which he didn't know yet, but she was excited to see what he'd picked out.

He placed a large and what appeared to be a heavy box on the table, which landed with a thunk. It was elegantly wrapped in gold paper with a large red ribbon.

"I went traditional for eighth anniversaries, something bronze, but you can expect jewelry at Christmas because I like seeing you wear something I picked out. There is something sensual about it."

She picked up his hand, kissed his wedding ring, and said, "I agree."

She smiled as she unwrapped the gift. He was so good to her. And she liked wearing his jewelry. She glanced again at the platinum band on his left hand. The sight of it did things to her, good things, because it meant that he belonged to her.

Looking inside the box, she looked up and met Mitch's eyes. He had surprised her again. It was a bronze sculpture of two people kissing. On further examination, she thought the lovers looked familiar.

"Remember when Alex took our picture at the beach the day after I returned from Iraq?"

"Yes, I love that picture...You had it commissioned? I love it!" She jumped up from her seat and ran around the table to kiss her husband. They held each other tightly and marveled at the sculpture.

"Living room?" he asked.

"Bedroom," she corrected. "Would you like to open your gift now?"

He reached for the first button on her blouse, which he unbuttoned, then slipped his hand between her breast and bra, giving the mound a playful squeeze. "And gift-wrapped too," he said.

She laughed, "No, I have something else."

"But I like this gift," he complained. She freed his hand, stepped away from him, returned to her chair, and pulled a small, wrapped package from where it had rested on one of the empty dining room chairs, where she had placed it earlier.

"Here," she said with a broad smile. "And before you open it, I have to say thank you."

Mitch smiled back at her questioningly with his dimples and then tore into the package. He looked down at the framed photo and then looked back at her. She had wrapped a photo from her ultrasound the day before.

"You're pregnant?" he whispered with a large smile.

They had tried to get pregnant since he'd returned from Iraq, but it hadn't been easy for Rebecca. She'd had two miscarriages, and there had been another ectopic scare that was unfounded, but Mitch hadn't been sure they should keep trying. They had Emily, and she was amazing.

"Two months, and everything looks good," she said and nodded. "The baby is where it is supposed to be. No ectopic worries."

This time, he stood and quickly was at her side. "I love you, Bex," he said and kissed her. They both knew the risks, but they always had hope. And like the other times she'd been pregnant, they didn't talk too much about it to get their hopes up, but this time felt different. Good.

They held each other for a long time until she said, "I have another little surprise for you."

"Twins?" he asked playfully.

"No, thank goodness," she said.

"As long as we end up naked, I'm happy with any surprise you have," he said. They were as in love as they had been when they had first laid eyes on each other almost twenty years earlier.

"We have a little game set up in the living room...a little strip Monopoly for old time's sake."

Mitch smiled. "Bex, you remembered."

He'd once mentioned that was always the way he wanted to play it, years ago, but knew her relatives would freak out. It was one of his dark little fantasies that involved owed rent on Boardwalk.

"Well, thankfully, this time, we don't have to play by anyone's rules but our own," she said.

They ended up on the living floor, sitting across from each other with the coffee table and the game set up between them. The dog was happily locked in the family room so they wouldn't have to worry about being goosed by a cold nose at an inopportune time.

They had been playing a speed game; the deeds to properties were already divvied up, so they each had the same number of monopolies. This cut to the chase of buying grand hotels, and large rents were to be paid in clothing only.

Rebecca handed Mitch a shoe, one of her red silk slingbacks that matched the all-red outfit she'd worn that day to their office at the Stark Hotel.

Mitch raised an eyebrow as he tossed her shoe across the room and pointed at her. "You landed on Boardwalk, baby."

"So?" Rebecca asked innocently.

"I have a hotel on Boardwalk, and this is strip Monopoly. One shoe isn't going to cut it. You owe me something more. I need to see some skin. Are you going to give it to me, or am I going to have to come over there and cop a feel?"

Rebecca saw the lust in his eyes. She had it, too, more of a pulsing in her more sensitive regions. Maybe she should chum for the shark. With any luck, he'd be inside her in a matter of seconds. The thought made her breath hitch, and he noticed a little hint of dimple showing on his cheek.

"Okay, you're right. I should give you a little more, but only if you know what to do with it." She unbuttoned her garnet silk blouse, exposing a black lace bra. She pulled the cool fabric away from her matching skirt, undid the cuffs, and then tossed the blouse to him. "Is that enough, or do you want more?"

"I want more. I want you," he said and crawled to the space next to her, their bodies close.

"That sounds like a win-win," she said and kissed him. He gently lowered her to the hardwood floor, which was covered with an elegant oriental rug.

His head was between her breasts, and he was exploring them with his tongue. He'd always loved her breasts, and she loved what he did to them, especially now that they were a bit tender.

A moment later, the bra was gone and flung across the room, and he was sucking on first her right nipple and then her left. He murmured, "Your breasts are larger. How did I not notice that earlier?"

"You know, when I'm pregnant, they get bigger, and I will require more attention be paid to them, as they are a bit sensitive."

"I can do that," he said. "I love you, baby."

"I love you too," she said, "Happy Anniversary."

"Happy Anniversary," he said as he continued his ministrations.

"Oh look," she managed. "You landed on one of my properties. You owe me."

"What do I owe you?" he asked, lifting his head with a smile on his face, as neither one of them had touched the dice.

"I want your boxers," she said.

He leaned close and whispered, "No, you don't; you want what is inside of them."

"You know me too well," she said, cupping his firmness and watching him grow.

"What Bex wants, my Bex gets," he said as he reached for the belt on his trousers.

Acknowledgments

A thank you to my BETA readers. You really make me shine. HUGS!!!

Mary Oldham is an award winning author, and three-time Golden Heart Finalist with the Romance Writers of America in the areas of Contemporary Romance and Romantic Suspense. Mary lives in Portland, Oregon when she is not sitting on her deck and looking at the Pacific in Yachats, Oregon, the Gem of the Oregon Coast.

Also by Mary Oldham

Don't miss any of Mary Oldham's other books, available in Print or Digital at Amazon or Barnes and Noble:

Stand Alone Titles

CRUSH, May 2022

The Poison Garden, 2023

The Silver Linings Series

The Silver Linings Wedding Dress Auction, October 2021

Sisters Before Misters, August 2023

Enchanted, 2024

The Hotel Baron's Series

A Paris Affair, November 2021

A Summer Affair, December 2021

A Roman Affair, April 2022

A London Affair, 2024

The Aphrodite Sisters Series

Sage's Redemption, Book 1, October 2022

Toni's Secret, Book 2, November 2022

Roxie's Circus, Book 3, December 2022

Kimberly 's Reckoning, Book 4, March 2023

Audiobooks

The Silver Linings Wedding Dress Auction Available April 2022

Narrated by Gildart Jackson

The Poison Garden

Available December 2023

Narrated by Robin McAlpine

Mary loves to hear from her readers! You can email her to sign up for her newsletter at www.maryoldham.com.

Printed in Dunstable, United Kingdom